The Siegel Dispositions

A Steve Stilwell Mystery

DAVID E. GROGAN

CAMEL
PRESS

Seattle, WA

CAMEL
PRESS

Camel Press
PO Box 70515
Seattle, WA 98127

For more information go to: www.camelpress.com
www.davidegrogan.com

Cover design by Sabrina Sun

The Siegel Dispositions
Copyright © 2014 by David E. Grogan

ISBN: 978-1-60381-981-7 (Trade Paper)
ISBN: 978-1-60381-982-4 (eBook)

Library of Congress Control Number: 2014943163

Printed in the United States of America

To my father and late mother,
Mike and Norma Grogan

Acknowledgments

———∾∾———

THE CLASS IN human rights at The George Washington University Law School looked interesting to me primarily because it helped fill out my schedule. It met during the day, so I wouldn't have to return to downtown Washington, D.C., for yet another night class. The course had the added benefit of being taught by Professor Thomas Buergenthal, a world-renowned expert on human rights. As an Auschwitz survivor, he spoke with authority. That was enough for me and I signed up.

To be honest, I didn't expect to get much out of the course. After all, who is not in favor of human rights? Plus, as a military attorney, I was very familiar with the Geneva Conventions and the Law of War, so I expected the class to simply reinforce what I already knew. Instead of being a review, the course opened my eyes to the fundamental importance and need for continued vigilance in protecting human rights worldwide. The varied perspectives of the international graduate students were particularly interesting, and I was fascinated by what a German graduate student and an Eritrean army commander had to say.

Intrigued by human rights and by Professor Buergenthal's soft-spoken command of the subject matter, I surfed the Internet at home to learn more about my mentor and his field. One night, late, I stumbled across a website that gave me the idea for *The Siegel Dispositions*. Inspired by Professor Buergenthal and his class, I saw writing the book as an opportunity to make a difference in a small but meaningful way by promoting human rights awareness and discussion. I also hoped the book would be entertaining—I will let you be the judge of that.

Lots of people encouraged and supported me along the way, but there are a few to whom I am particularly indebted. Retired Navy Captain Eric Geiser worked with me early on and helped me transform the manuscript from a legal treatise into a story someone might be interested in reading. Dr. Ellen Oppenheim was the first objective person to read the manuscript and her enthusiasm and words of encouragement provided the spark I needed to push the project forward. Joanne Sherman's editor's eye gave me the specific direction I needed to refine the prose so that it was ready for a critical read by an agent. Finally my daughter, Chelsea, proofed the manuscript and provided the last round of comments to give it polish and make it inspection ready.

That would have been the end of it, had it not been for my agent, Steve Hutson, at WordWise Media Services. After he and his wife read the manuscript, Steve sent me an email stating, "My wife has a complaint. She started reading your story and couldn't bear to put it down until it was over. Forced her to miss out on her TV soaps and court shows." Steve then agreed to represent me and marketed the manuscript until Camel Press picked it up.

The team at Camel Press has been nothing short of superb. Jennifer McCord and Catherine Treadgold's insight and experience helped me take the manuscript to the next level. Together, we closed gaps, corrected weaknesses, and tightened prose. *The Siegel Dispositions* is a direct result of their dedication and passion for the art of writing.

Last but not least, I need to thank my family—Sharon, Erin, Chelsea and Ethan—for putting up with me while I wrote the book. Already dealing with long absences due to military assignments and even longer hours at the Pentagon, they had to listen to my incessant updates on the latest chapter or critique my thoughts on the way ahead. I think they realize now they were part of something special to me.

—David E. Grogan

1

Tuesday, September 30, 1997
Düsseldorf, Germany

EMIL WEISENTROPE CLUTCHED the brown paper package with both hands as he shuffled past the shuttered shops on Malpelstrasse. He had to get to a mailbox. Twisting old bones no longer able to move without pain, he looked over both shoulders, certain he was being followed. All he saw were the preoccupied faces of early-morning commuters hustling anonymously off to work. Still, something told him death lurked nearby.

He couldn't report his suspicions. The authorities would hear nothing but the ramblings of a crazy old man. They might even put him in a home. But he knew. He'd witnessed death from every angle. In Auschwitz, though, there had always been others—some with names, some without—who held his hand whenever death drew near. Now he faced its foul presence alone.

He quickened his pace toward a mailbox up ahead. As he focused on his goal, a figure slammed into him, nearly causing him to drop his precious cargo. Gasping, he pulled the package close to his heart to shield it with his body.

"Watch out!" a young man yelled without bothering to look back or slow his stride. A commuter late for work couldn't be bothered to make way for an ambling old man taking up more than his share of the sidewalk.

Emil exhaled in relief and trudged the last fifty steps to the mailbox. Yanking the flap to the drop shoot open, he paused. Could he be wrong? Once gone, his package could never be retrieved. It was so final, like death itself. Tears moistened weathered cheeks and his frail five-foot, eight-inch frame trembled to its core. He had no choice. Felix Siegel would take care of it. There was no one else he trusted more.

Gnarled fingers relaxed and the package slipped away into darkness. Feeling both profound despair and inner peace, he wiped away his tears with the gray wool sleeves of his overcoat and took a deep breath. It was time to go home.

2

DETECTIVE GÜNTHER BELMAR took the call at 9:47 a.m. on his way to the office. He made a quick U-turn and headed for the scene. A dead body in an alley, and it wasn't even noon; what a way to start a day that was already blustery, threatening rain, and colder than usual for early autumn. Belmar turned onto Malpelstrasse, cruising barely faster than the pedestrians on the sidewalks. Just up ahead, the piercing shriek of a whistle and a policeman gesticulating with his arms moved a group of onlookers away from an alley cordoned off with yellow tape. A mobile news crew pressed forward, despite the officer's protests.

"How do they always get there before me?" Belmar wondered as he eased his car toward the crowd. "Leeches, nothing but leeches." He rolled down his window.

"Get out of here," the policeman yelled, stepping toward Belmar's vehicle while keeping a close watch on the crowd. "Can't you see this alley is closed?"

"I'm Detective Günther Belmar," Belmar shouted and held up his *Polizei* credentials.

"Sorry, Detective Belmar. I didn't know it was you." The

policeman pulled aside the yellow perimeter tape and herded the onlookers out of the way so Belmar could pass.

Belmar slowly headed his car toward the alley and a knot of crime scene personnel and possible witnesses, stopping close to the policeman tugging on the tape. "What do we have?" he asked. The onlookers quieted. The reporter, with her cameraman in tow, worked at getting closer to finagle an interview or capture a sound bite.

"Pierdahl's up there. An ambulance, too." The policeman cast his eyes toward the reporter. "You better let Pierdahl fill you in."

Belmar looked past the policeman down an alley darkened by the soot-stained backs of yellow brick three-story buildings on both sides. About twenty-five meters ahead in the shadows, he could see the ambulance. Neither its siren nor its lights were on—bad signs. He maneuvered his car past stacks of broken-down cardboard boxes and a puke green shell of a sofa with the stuffing popping out, stopping about ten meters behind the ambulance. He called his dispatcher to let her know he had arrived at the scene. It was 10:02 a.m.

He got out of his car and walked toward the ambulance. Beyond it was a trash dumpster, just in front and off to the left. Veering around the vehicle's right side where there was more room to walk, he could see Officer Rolfe Pierdahl in his inspection-ready green *Polizei* uniform talking to a short, stocky man taking puff after puff of a cigarette. Of course anyone would look short next to the tall, gangly officer, only a few centimeters taller than Belmar himself. He looked down at his own rumpled clothing and smoothed the few remaining strands of light brown hair atop his otherwise barren forehead. Pierdahl's locks, he noted, were still full and black, though neatly cropped. It reminded Belmar that he needed to get what little hair he had left trimmed, once he could find the time. He watched a couple of paramedics stringing yellow perimeter tape across the alley well in front of their vehicle. A dozen or so people on the other side of the tape watched as Belmar approached.

The body lay just beyond the ambulance's cab. The victim was on his back with a dark red liquid halo radiating from his head. One arm was pinned beneath his lower back, the other folded across his stomach. As Belmar drew closer, he could see the entrance wound on top of the bloody, gray-haired head. It was a sickening sight, even for a veteran detective. He needed a distraction or he'd see oozing brains and splintered skull for days.

"Hey, Pierdahl," Belmar called, "give me a minute, will you?"

Pierdahl made his excuses to the man he was talking to and sauntered over, wearing a grin incongruous with the scene. "It's damn good to see you again, Günther," Pierdahl said, shaking Belmar's hand with a vice-like grip. "How long's it been? A couple years at least."

Belmar and Pierdahl were old friends. They'd started on the force together eleven years ago, but in their mid-thirties, their careers had taken different paths. The brass gave Belmar a detective's badge after he snagged a high profile murder suspect and made the front page. Pierdahl's ship had yet to come in.

"Too long, Rolfe, too long. How've you been?"

Pierdahl shrugged. "You know how it goes. Same shit, different day."

Belmar laughed, slapping his friend on the back just as he'd done years before. "You always did have a way with words. So, how's the family?"

Pierdahl shifted his weight away from Belmar and drew his smile back into his lips with a hiss. "Not so good, Günther. Marta left me six months ago and moved to Berlin. Took the kids and my damned dog with her. Guess she got tired of spending my big paychecks."

Belmar wished he hadn't asked. He didn't know whether to grab onto Pierdahl's halfhearted attempt at humor or show some sympathy. He decided to play it safe.

"Sorry to hear that. I didn't know."

"Shocked the hell out of me, too. Can't blame her much, though. Buy me a beer and I'll fill you in when we've got some time. Anyway, look what some asshole did to this old man."

Getting back to business was a relief to Belmar. Murders he could deal with; relationships were a different story. "Do you know what happened?"

"Not much more than the obvious," Pierdahl said, consulting his pocket notebook. "The man I was talking to, Peter Miller, knows the victim. Says it's Emil Weisentrope—an old man who lived in an apartment building just up the street. Said the old man walked by his newsstand this morning at around seven carrying a package. That's the back door there." Pierdahl pointed to a reinforced metal door next to the brown dumpster. "He didn't see the victim again until he found the body. Said he was coming out to throw away some trash when he saw him lying there. That was about 9:15."

"Did he see who did it?"

"Didn't see a damn thing. Just came out and found the body. He ran over to try and help, but when he saw the victim's head, he knew there was nothing he could do. He called the old man's name a couple a times, but the guy didn't move. So he went back in and called us. He's pretty shaken up. Said the old man was a regular customer of his and had been in the neighborhood a long time."

Belmar's eyes swept the area around the body, not finding what they were looking for. "What about the package? Did you find the package Miller saw him with?"

"No, and neither did Miller. He said it wasn't out here when he found the body."

"So what do you think, a robbery?"

"Could be. But the old man could have ditched the package before he got shot. Who knows?"

"You got anything else?"

Pierdahl shook his head then changed his mind. "The

paramedics got here right after me and checked the victim out. You might want to see if they got something."

"Thanks. We'll also need to do a pass up the alley to see if anybody saw anything. Can you have the uniforms take care of that? And be sure they interview the gawkers behind the tape."

"Yes, sir!" Pierdahl replied, tossing Belmar a mock salute.

Belmar shooed Pierdahl away. It was time to refocus his attention back on the crime scene. He stared at the cold, lifeless figure lying contorted on the pavement. Although it didn't make sense, he felt responsible every time he saw a murdered corpse. Children and elderly victims were the worst. They seemed so innocent, so helpless, so defenseless. It was as if he'd failed to protect them by not preventing their murders, even though there was nothing he could have done. He tried to make up for his failing by tracking down their killers until they paid, and paid big. It was never enough, though, because in the end, the victims were still dead. But it was the best he could do. He vowed to do what he could for the old man.

"Günther, get your ass over here for a second," shouted Pierdahl, this time peering into the dumpster just down from the door to the newsstand. "Look what I found." Belmar hurried over to the dumpster and looked inside. His head recoiled from the stench of rotting God-only-knows-what.

"What is it?"

"Down in the corner. Looks like a wallet."

"Good eyes," Belmar said, giving Pierdahl another slap on the back. "How are we going to get it out of there?"

"What's this *we* bullshit?" Pierdahl quipped. "You know damn well I'm the one who's gonna have to climb in there and get it. You detectives can't get your pansy-ass suits dirty."

"It's about time you realized that," Belmar joked, but before he could say anything else, Pierdahl grabbed the top edge of the dumpster and started to climb inside.

"The least you can do is give me a boost."

Belmar grasped his hands together and Pierdahl used

them as a step to get into the dumpster. Belmar lifted a bit too enthusiastically and Pierdahl sailed over the top and in, landing on some garbage bags on the bottom.

"Pffffew. Does it ever smell like shit in here!" Pierdahl wheezed. He hooked the wallet using a pen from his shirt pocket and stood up, gasping for fresh air. Belmar couldn't help but chuckle.

"Let's do that again!" Belmar laughed a little louder, enjoying the sight of his friend standing in a pile of trash, gingerly balancing a wallet on a pen. Pierdahl looked like a contestant in some outlandish game-show stunt.

"Shut up, you fool, and get me something to put this wallet in. Do you want my uniform smelling like rotting trash for the rest of the shift?"

Smiling, Belmar reached inside his pocket for a plastic evidence bag. "I'll have to think about that." He held the bag open so that Pierdahl could drop the wallet inside. "Is there anything else in there?"

"No package, if that's what you mean. Now, get the hell out of my way so I can get out of this thing." Pierdahl stepped on some trash bags stacked in a corner of the dumpster and jumped out. It was about a five-foot drop, but the fresh air was worth it. "I'll have the evidence team go through it more thoroughly in case I missed something."

"Thanks. That was a good find. I'll be sure your name is highlighted in my report." With the dumpster in good hands, Belmar returned his attention to the victim. Four or five department specialists now combed the area, sifting for clues. A police photographer snapped away, lighting up the shadow-filled alley with his camera flash while the forensic technician stood by his side, giving directions.

"Anja, what does it look like to you?" Belmar asked as he walked toward the young platinum blonde forensic technician. He circled around the body to avoid disturbing anything Anja might need to see.

Anja's fresh young face broke into a smile, revealing dimples and giving her blue cat eyes a more dramatic tilt. "Hello, Detective Belmar. It's good to see you," she said. "I'm afraid I can't tell you much, though. Looks like it happened within the last hour, hour and a half; the blood hasn't completely dried yet. There's also a hat over there next to the dumpster. And he's got a large bruise on his head where it looks like he was struck. My guess is just before he was shot."

Belmar liked Anja. She was sharp and dedicated. He'd had trouble on a couple of occasions getting forensic people out to his crime scenes in the middle of the night. They took their time, knowing everything had to wait for them. Not Anja. When he needed solid, dependable work, he could count on her. What she lacked in experience, she made up for in attitude. If she kept it up, he'd be working for her someday. She didn't act that way, though. She was all about helping detectives solve crimes. Belmar walked over to the hat lying alongside the dumpster and kneeled to look at it more closely. "Did you notice that one side's pushed in?"

"Has to be the old man's," Anja answered. "I don't see any holes or blood on it, so it probably got knocked off his head before the gun was fired. We'll see if we can get a match with any hair residue."

"You got anything else?"

"Looks like it was a nine millimeter. We found a shell casing in there." Anja pointed to a large crack running through the pavement near the center of the alley, about six feet from the body's head. "We'll take it in and check it for prints. These guys may be careful with everything else, but they always forget to wipe the shells clean before they load their guns."

"Do you think they were trying to be careful?"

"Can't tell yet. What I can tell is, judging from the bullet hole in the top of his head, he was on his knees when they shot him. And then they rolled him over, probably to get the wallet you found in the dumpster."

"What makes you think that?"

"Look at his arms. One's behind his back and the other's on his stomach. He wouldn't have fallen that way, especially if he was on his knees. I'd say it's a robbery. Just seems a little violent for this neighborhood."

"Got to agree with you on that. Matter of fact, I can only think of one other murder occurring around here in the last few years. As I recall, it was a domestic dispute. Some woman got tired of her husband beating on her and she paid him back one night. But nothing like this, out in public and in broad daylight."

"Maybe some punk thought he'd find easy pickings here."

"Looks like he was right. How much more you got to do?" Belmar was ready to move on. He still needed to speak to the paramedics, but he'd follow them to the medical examiner's office and interview them there. He'd also review the witness interviews when they came in. Maybe he'd get lucky and somebody saw or heard something.

"Not much. I'll watch 'em load the body and we'll finish mapping the scene. Then it'll just be a matter of waiting for the autopsy and lab results. Anything else you need from me?"

"Only your report." Belmar knew she'd have it on his desk as soon as possible. He didn't worry about Anja.

"I'll call you if anything comes up."

Belmar gave her the thumbs-up. The forensic part of the case was in good hands. Anja smiled and turned toward the two paramedics waiting at the back of their ambulance.

"Go ahead and take him in," she told them. She always watched the paramedics closely in case something fell from the body that she hadn't noticed while it was lying on the ground. The two men pulled a collapsible gurney out of the back of the ambulance and rolled it near the old man. One of them also retrieved a black body bag from inside the ambulance. The body bag wasn't something they liked the public to know they carried, as it would have a decidedly negative impact on a passenger's confidence if he or she knew such a conveyance was so close at hand. The paramedic looked around to see who was watching before he started unfolding the bag. Satisfied the area was clear, he laid out the bag next to the body and unfolded it so it paralleled the old man. Unzipping it, he pulled the flaps back as far as they would go.

The paramedics had performed the task all too often. They worked silently, one lifting the feet while the other held the bag open. Once the feet were in position, each man grabbed one of the body's shoulders and worked the corpse inside. They pulled the bag's flaps back over the body and began to zip it up from the end closest to the feet. As the bag zipped closed, the last bit of daylight disappeared forever from Emil Weisentrope's face.

3

~~

Williamsburg, Virginia

STEVE STILWELL'S MORNING began to unravel as soon as he arrived at his new law office. He knew his boss wouldn't be in until 9:00 a.m., but he'd been told the firm's secretary/paralegal, Marjorie Weldman, always arrived promptly at 7:45 to get the office ready for the day. Well, maybe Marjorie came in at 7:45 every other day, but she certainly had not done so today. Steve, the forty-eight-year-old retired naval officer, said he would be there at 8:00 a.m. on September 30, and, by God, at 7:55, he was waiting by the locked front door. There were no signs of life in the building, but he knocked anyway, hoping Marjorie was somewhere inside. No such luck. Already fuming to himself about how Marjorie would never make it in the military, he grabbed a seat on a nearby bench with his boxes of books and wall hangings and began to wonder whether leaving the Navy had been such a great idea after all.

Last year, retiring seemed like the way to go. He envisioned opening a small town law office somewhere and settling down to a life of leisure. Even better, he expected the big bucks of a civilian law practice to roll in right away. The money was there, he'd been told. All he had to do was go for it.

He was excited about the idea until he realized he didn't know how to be a civilian attorney. After twenty-two years as a lawyer in the Navy Judge Advocate General's "JAG" Corps, he was well versed in the Law of War and in negotiating with foreign governments on the fate of wayward sailors. But he didn't have a clue how to file a simple lawsuit after a car accident or write a complex will for a client worth a few million dollars.

The solution surfaced in the person of William P. Smythe of the venerable Williamsburg law firm Smythe & Botts. Mr. Smythe opened the firm with his partner, Alford W. Botts III, in 1956. Although Williamsburg was then little more than a sleepy Virginia college town—albeit with tourists flocking to see Colonial Williamsburg and The College of William & Mary—the firm became widely regarded for its expertise in trusts and estates. Then, in 1994, Mr. Botts died of a heart attack, leaving Mr. Smythe to run the practice on his own. By the summer of 1996, the increased workload had taken its toll. He gave himself a year to shed his clients and ease out of the practice, and then he would retire.

After hearing that history at a continuing legal education seminar in Norfolk, Steve saw the break he had been hoping for. He approached Mr. Smythe about buying into his firm and the two struck a deal. Mr. Smythe committed to teaching Steve what he needed to know so he, too, could become an expert in trusts and estates. In return, once Steve established himself in the practice, Mr. Smythe could transition gently into retirement.

The faint sound of a telephone ringing over and over from somewhere inside the locked office building interrupted Steve's reverie. "Maybe Marjorie's calling to tell herself she'll be late," he mumbled a little too loudly. A moment later the phone stopped ringing. "I wonder what important call that was?"

"Oh, hello, Mr. Stilwell," a pleasant voice called from

somewhere just behind where Steve was sitting. He turned to see an attractive fortyish woman with slightly plump, pleasant curves. She wore glasses and styled her tinted blonde hair in a neat, chin-length bob. You wouldn't necessarily notice her on the street, but if you stopped to talk to her, you might appreciate her wholesome Midwestern looks. "Hi, I'm Marjorie Weldman," she said, her blue eyes twinkling beneath her glasses. She shook his hand with a surprisingly firm grip. "As soon as I saw that military haircut I knew it was you. I hope you haven't been waiting long. I stopped to buy some bagels for your first day, but the shop didn't open until eight. I'm sorry if I kept you waiting."

"No, not at all," Steve lied, praying she hadn't heard his grumbling. He felt his face and ears turn red hot with embarrassment. "It gave me a chance to relax before a busy first day." Now he felt bad for thinking ill of Marjorie, when she was just trying to show some kindness. Maybe things would go better once he got started in the office.

They didn't. Marjorie showed Steve his "new" office, the one previously occupied by Mr. Botts. "How do you like it?" she asked, smiling with the pride of someone who had played a significant role in choosing the décor.

Steve heard himself saying, "It's great. I can't wait to get started." In truth, he was thinking of the three "D" words that best described the room: dreary, drab, and dead. Dim, recessed lighting illuminated dark paneled walls and musty oxblood leather upholstery. Row after row of state and federal case reporters lined bookshelves behind glass doors on ancient oak bookcases. It looked just like what Steve expected a small town southern law office to look like … in 1935. He didn't want his estate-planning clients to think he selected the décor to speed their dying process. He could tolerate the gloom for a few months, a year if he had to—he didn't want to appear too eager to discard old ways—but the office would have to change. Until then, all he could do was hope the surroundings would become less noticeable and try to concentrate on learning his new job.

"Just so you know, Mr. Stilwell, Mr. Smythe had to make a court appearance in Surry this morning and won't be in today." She paused for a second and took a deep breath before continuing in her most efficient-sounding office voice, "By the way, the bagels and coffee are in the kitchen; please help yourself. Oh, and let me tell you about the telephones. Your extension is three-five. You need to dial a nine to call out, and our office number is right on your phone. Let me know if you need anything else."

A little winded after rattling off so much information, Marjorie smiled politely and waited to see if Steve had anything to say. When he didn't, she withdrew to her desk in the lobby and started to get her already orderly desk even more orderly.

"That's just great," Steve muttered. "Now what am I supposed to do?" He couldn't allow the entire day to be wasted. He decided to start with a bagel and a cup of coffee. He could always press Marjorie for a more thorough office orientation. He'd hang up his University of Virginia Law Degree and College of William & Mary undergraduate diploma and start making the office his own. Tomorrow he'd see Mr. Smythe and get started with whatever it was he was supposed to be doing. At least he had a plan.

Toward the end of the day, and after Steve had dusted, unpacked, and reorganized everything he could, Marjorie took a telephone call from a prospective client. She elicited some preliminary information, placed the caller on hold, and spoke to Steve over the intercom.

"Mr. Stilwell, I have a Mr. Felix Siegel on the line. He wants to come in and see you tomorrow at two for a will, but Mr. Smythe has that time blocked off to go over the practice with you. What should I tell him?"

"Ask him if we can make it Thursday instead."

Marjorie was back on the intercom a moment later. "Mr.

Stilwell, he says the only time he can make it is tomorrow at two. He says it's important."

Steve had no idea who Felix Siegel was or how he knew Steve had joined the firm, especially since Mr. Smythe hadn't publicly announced it yet. Steve racked his brain trying to place the name but just couldn't. He was also concerned about taking a will client without any orientation from Mr. Smythe. But because Mr. Smythe would be there to consult when Steve prepared the will, he told Marjorie to go ahead and schedule the appointment.

Steve slumped back into his chair, wondering whether he had done the right thing. He had expected to hit the ground running, but not quite this fast. He rationalized it was better to jump right in rather than be bored waiting for work to trickle his way. Plus, with a little luck, this might turn out to be a relatively simple will, like the kind he drafted in the Navy all the time. Then again, maybe it wouldn't. In any case, a lot depended on the office's will drafting software, which he suddenly realized he hadn't looked at yet.

"Marjorie," Steve called from his chair, ignoring the intercom. "Would you make sure I've got the most up-to-date software on my computer? I'd like to take a look at the will drafting materials before Mr. Siegel comes in. By the way, do you know who he is?"

Marjorie replied over the intercom. "Never heard of him, Mr. Stilwell. And I can install the software for you, but you'll have to get off your computer. Better yet, why don't you go home now and I'll have it ready for you by the time you get in tomorrow? Oh, and that reminds me," she said as she opened the middle drawer of her desk. "I need to give you an office key."

Steve grinned as Marjorie walked into his office. "You're not just trying to get me out of your hair, are you?"

"Oh, but I am." Marjorie wore just enough of a smile so that Steve couldn't tell if she was kidding or telling the truth.

"All right, I can take a hint." He gathered up some papers, stuck them in his daily planner, and headed for the door. "Thanks for your help today, Marjorie. I think this is going to be lots of fun."

"Me too, Mr. Stilwell. You have a good night and I'll see you tomorrow morning."

* * *

AFTER STEVE WENT out the door, Marjorie turned and looked into his office. The space had seemed so empty the day before. Now the room looked different—it looked alive. Maybe that was because Steve was such a vital person. She supposed that years in the military produced that sort of disciplined appearance—the strong, slender build, the tapered hair that showed off the contours of his face and complemented his deep-set brown eyes, thin lips, and long, straight nose. She guessed his age at somewhere around 50—he was mostly gray—although people did turn gray as early as their thirties. His face was lined but not fleshy; he could certainly pass for someone in his early forties. That's what physical fitness did for you.

For the first time in a long time, Marjorie was excited about coming to work. She could tell the office was in for a change.

4

⌁

Washington, D.C.

"NEXT PLEASE," CALLED a female customs inspector standing behind a dull, scratched stainless steel inspection table. Wilhelm Strauss walked up and set his computer and garment bag on the table. Before the inspector had a chance to ask for it, he handed her his German passport. She opened it to the signature page and thumbed to the entry stamp. "Mr. Strauss, do you have your customs declaration with you?"

Strauss hesitated. Customs inspectors never used names. It was supposed to be a scripted, anonymous exchange of information.

"Mr. Strauss, do you speak English?"

"Yes, I'm sorry. Here it is." He handed her the form he had hastily completed just after taking off from Germany. The inspector scoured both sides before continuing.

"Is this everything you have to declare?" She stared at the form as she spoke, signaling disinterest and a return to the bureaucratic script. Strauss missed the signal.

"Of course it is," he snapped. The inspector glared from behind the form, letting him know he'd just made a serious mistake.

"Okay, then, Mr. Strauss. What's in your bags?"

"This one is my laptop and the garment bag just has my clothes." He propped both bags up on the table.

"Have you brought any food with you today?"

"No."

"Do you have currency valued in excess of ten thousand U.S. dollars with you?"

"I wish I did, but I don't," Strauss said, pretending to be personable, hoping a more pleasant disposition would repair earlier damage and discourage further inquiry. He was almost certain he was carrying less than ten thousand dollars, but knew it would be close. In any case, his smile was lost on the inspector.

"Mr. Strauss, please take your computer out of its case and turn it on. There's an outlet on the side of the counter if you need one."

Strauss' palms began to sweat. This type of inspection would make anyone nervous, let alone someone who had just killed a man. Had the German authorities called ahead to tell the Americans to look for him? Is that why the inspector called him by name? There was nothing he could do even if they had, but that gave him little comfort. He had no choice but to comply. He took his laptop out of its case, turned the screen toward the inspector, and switched it on. There was a whir as the hard drive engaged and the computer booted up. Within seconds the familiar multicolor window appeared on the screen.

"That's all I needed to see—you can put it away now. When you're done, though, please empty your garment bag out on the counter."

"Have I done something wrong, Inspector?" His steady voice belied his growing concern.

"Standard procedure, Mr. Strauss." The inspector let a

perceptible smile escape her lips. Strauss took it as a positive sign. At this point, he would have seized upon even the most minor sign of encouragement.

Strauss opened his garment bag and placed the contents on the counter. Shirts, socks, underwear, pants—the usual, until he reached into one of the zippered compartments and pulled out a fistful of condoms. He'd seen male officials all day, but when it came time for the condoms, he got a female inspector old enough to be his mother. Her face, however, reflected the same expressionless stare as with every other item he stacked on the counter.

"That's everything," he said, thumping his toiletry bag on the table.

"You need to empty that, too."

Strauss did as instructed, relieved, at least, that there was nothing else to inspect.

"Mr. Strauss, I need you to wait here for a minute, but you can go ahead and put your bags back together. I'll be right back." The inspector walked about ten feet away on the uncontrolled side of the customs floor to a uniformed man Strauss hadn't noticed before. She began to confer with the man, glancing back toward Strauss every now and then. Strauss strained to hear, but couldn't make out what she was saying. After a minute or so, she started back with a stern look on her face.

All Strauss could think was, "Oh, shit." Now he was certain they were onto him. Where had he gone wrong? As she approached, he grabbed his bags with a false air of confidence and prepared to leave.

"Mr. Strauss, please bring your bags and come with me." The inspector maintained her poker face, giving Strauss nothing to read. Fear set in. He contemplated making a run for it, but without a weapon or an escape route staked out, he'd never get away. Better to just play along for a while longer.

"Is there a problem, Inspector?"

"No. You're just one of the lucky ones we've selected for a

more detailed inquiry. It should only take a minute."

"You know, this is not the best welcome I've had to Washington, D.C.," Strauss responded, indignation returning. Even though he didn't know what the inspector had on him, he wanted her to think he believed he was being wrongly accused of whatever it was.

Ignoring his comment, the inspector led him past a row of inspection tables and through a door at the end of the inspection area. It opened into a large, whitewashed room with several desks and a few customs agents milling around. It was a typical government office—plain white walls, no artwork or windows, and the pictures of President Clinton and Vice President Gore prominently posted. The inspector called to a sturdy African-American agent in his late twenties combing through some paperwork at one of the desks.

"Rafe, can you give me a hand for a minute?"

Rafe looked up from his work to see who was calling. When he saw it was Marta Ruiz, he set his paperwork aside and headed her way. "Whatcha need?"

"Inventory and pat-down." Ruiz said it so matter-of-factly that it didn't sound like a big deal. But Strauss knew what was coming and it was a big deal. Now he wished he had taken the time to count his cash. He tried in vain to remember how much he had left after paying for his airline ticket in Düsseldorf. If it was more than $10,000, he was screwed. He'd have no choice but to plead ignorance and beg for mercy. The whole thing had the potential to get ugly fast.

"Mr. Strauss," Ruiz continued as they walked into a cubicle at the rear of the room. "I need you to empty your pockets and place everything you've got on the table." Rafe walked into the cubicle too, blocking the only exit.

"Would someone tell me what is going on here?" Strauss asked, throwing his wallet on the table.

"Routine procedure," Ruiz replied. "I'm sorry for the inconvenience, but we'll be done real soon."

"This isn't routine," Strauss protested. "I've come to America many times before and I've never been treated like this." He was getting worked up, but reined himself back in because he wasn't sure how much money he had. The inspectors ignored him.

After the wallet, Strauss tossed a wad of currency from one of his front pants pockets onto the table. A two Deutschmark coin fell out of the bundle, bounced a couple of times, and rolled off the edge and onto the tile floor. No one tried to stop it or pick it up. Instead, all eyes were on Strauss as he drew a second wad of currency from his jacket pocket. When the second stash of bills hit the table, the inspectors made eye contact with each other; their facial expressions remained neutral.

"That's everything," Strauss announced.

"Are you sure?" Ruiz asked.

Strauss checked his pockets one last time. The last thing he wanted was to give them an excuse to arrest him. "I'm sure." His voice reflected displeasure just short of disrespect.

"You need to empty your wallet, too, Mr. Strauss. You've got a lot of cash and we're going to have to count it."

Once again, Strauss complied. It took him only a minute to display his wallet's contents because he liked to keep it devoid of clutter. It contained more cash, an international driver's license, a prepaid telephone card and a folded piece of paper with "JINENIGHEILEN" handwritten on it. He looked up at Ruiz to see what was next.

"Okay, Mr. Strauss. We're going to count your money now. You should watch us carefully." Ruiz picked up Strauss' currency and sorted it into two piles, Deutschmarks and dollars. She counted the Deutschmarks first and announced that he had 7,845. Then she counted the dollars.

"Looks like you've got exactly five thousand U.S. dollars, Mr. Strauss. Rafe, you know what the exchange rate is for Marks?"

"Around two. I'd say he's got about nine thousand bucks total."

"That sure is a lot of cash, Mr. Strauss. We don't see many

people come in with this kind of cash, do we, Rafe?"

"Sure don't. Most people'd be afraid to carry that much money on 'em. Whaddya plan on doing with all that cash, Mr. Strauss?"

Now, knowing he was below the ten thousand dollar declaration threshold, Strauss dropped his restraint. "Look, I like cash, all right? Everybody accepts it and I never go hungry. So how about letting me get out of here?"

Ruiz was ready for him. "Fair enough, Mr. Strauss. But first Inspector Rafe here needs to pat you down to make sure we inventoried everything. Just put your hands on the table and spread your legs and this will be over before you know it." Ruiz stepped back from the table while Rafe walked behind Strauss. Rafe began under Strauss' armpits and continued down his body.

"I have never been so humiliated!" Strauss exclaimed as Rafe ran his hands along his legs. "My embassy shall hear about this. I will not accept being treated like a criminal." Undeterred, Rafe slid his hands over Strauss' front and back pants pockets one last time, then walked back around the table to stand with Ruiz.

"Sorry about the inconvenience, Mr. Strauss. All we have left to do is give you a receipt to show you received everything back from us and then you can go." Ruiz pulled an inventory sheet out of a drawer beneath the table, filled out the identifying information on the top using Strauss' passport, and cataloged the items one by one. When she got to the folded piece of paper, she studied it for a second and then wrote down, "piece of paper with 'JINENIGHEILEN' written on it."

Strauss wasn't paying attention to what Ruiz was writing. He was busy putting his belongings back into his pockets after Ruiz recorded each item. When Ruiz returned the piece of paper to him, he slipped it into his wallet and put his wallet away. After all the items were inventoried and returned, Strauss signed the receipt and stuffed his copy into his laptop bag. "I take it I'm free to go now?" he asked, disgusted.

"Oh, there is one more thing," Ruiz answered. "We need to take your picture to close out our file."

"I thought you said the receipt was the last thing you had to do," Strauss objected.

Ruiz smiled. "I forgot."

"Let's just get this over with. I've got your names. Tomorrow my embassy will hear how German businessmen are welcomed to America." Strauss hoped his last statement might get the inspectors to change their minds about the picture. He didn't want to cause too big of a scene—after all, they just might be on to him for something. But the fact that they wanted his picture told him they didn't have enough to hold him right now.

Ruiz retrieved the 35-millimeter camera she used to take pictures of contraband. She asked Strauss to stand against the wall and took two pictures in quick succession. "We're finished," she reported. "Inspector Rafe will show you out of the office. Thanks for your cooperation, Mr. Strauss, and once again, I apologize for the inconvenience."

Not waiting for Rafe, Strauss grabbed his bags and stormed out in one last act of defiance. He hated having kowtowed to the customs agents. *He* was supposed to be the one in control, not some middle-aged, overweight, female border buffoon. At least, though, she'd let him pass. He eased the stranglehold on his bags. Now what he needed was a good, stiff belt of American whiskey, a bed, and someone to lie down with. And eventually, sleep … precious sleep.

BACK IN THE cubicle, Rafe looked at Ruiz and laughed. "Take a picture so we can close out the file? Where the hell did that come from?"

Ruiz just smiled. "Hey, it worked, didn't it?"

Rafe laughed harder. "What was that all about, anyway?"

"What's it always about? We had a tip some thirty-year-old, tall blue-eyed blond male would be coming through on a German passport tonight with heroin."

"What good's that? There'll be fifty guys like that in the next hour alone."

"Trust me, they won't all look as good as this one did. Did you see his arms? He had to be a weightlifter. There's nothing like a man who keeps himself in shape."

"I'm serious, Marta. You're wastin' your time."

"What do you want me to do, Rafe, let 'em all go 'cause it's too damn hard? Besides, this was our man. You saw the cash. He just got lucky and cashed out before we got him."

"Yeah, right. Good luck provin' anything. I think you got nuthin.'"

But Ruiz figured she had her drug smuggler and she wanted to be able to find him again. She took the camera and set out to track down her supervisor. She needed permission to get the pictures developed right away. She knew she was onto something ... she felt it in her bones. She just didn't know what it was.

5

———∿∿∿———

Wednesday, October 1
Williamsburg

DAY TWO STARTED with an unexpected twist. Although the key Marjorie gave Steve got him into his office without a hitch, a ringing phone soon delivered a frenzied call from Mr. Smythe. During the night Mr. Smythe's nonagenarian mother had suffered a stroke, and he was going to whisk off to California as soon as Marjorie could arrange the tickets for him, taking with him all the secrets of private practice he had yet to divulge. One day in the office, and Steve was already on his own.

Steve tried to convince himself he was ready for Felix Siegel's two o'clock appointment. He'd read portions of the estate planning guide and worked through several problems on the will drafting software, but he still wasn't sure he could discuss a complex estate plan with a new client. He knew the key was to ask the right questions, and he had a standardized questionnaire for that. He could work on a draft of the will and get everything approved by Mr. Smythe after his return. It sounded simple enough.

Steve looked at his watch. It was 1:30 and he hadn't eaten lunch yet. He was so busy reading and working on the computer that he'd forgotten to get hungry. Now all he had left was half an hour. He printed out a fresh questionnaire and annotated it. Then he straightened the chairs on the other side of his desk and tidied up his office. There was nothing more to do but wait.

"Mr. Stilwell, I'm sorry to interrupt you," Marjorie began, walking into Steve's office with yellow legal notepad in hand, "but I've finally finished making Mr. Smythe's flight arrangements. He needs me to pick up his tickets and bring them by his house because he's still trying to get everything ready to go." Marjorie spoke uncharacteristically fast and her face was flushed. "I've got to go right away because his flight leaves out of Richmond at 4:55. I know you have Mr. Siegel coming in, and I can stay if you need me to, but I'm afraid that might be cutting it too close."

"Go ahead, Marjorie," Steve said, forcing a smile. "I can certainly handle one client a day by myself. But promise me you'll get back as soon as you can."

"I will, Mr. Stilwell. Oh, and let me give you one more thing before I go. Here's the fee agreement Mr. Smythe uses. It's generic for Smythe & Botts, so you can use it too. I should have given it to you earlier, but with all this going on, I forgot."

"Don't worry about it, Marjorie. Just get going so Mr. Smythe doesn't miss his plane. And tell him to let us know if there's anything we can do for him." Steve was so involved in trying to prepare for the appointment that he had overlooked the fee issue entirely. Now he was really worried. What else had he overlooked? Plus, he had only ten minutes to read and digest the fee agreement so he could explain it to Mr. Siegel. Maybe Mr. Siegel would be late.

"I'll see you in about an hour, Mr. Stilwell," Marjorie shouted from the lobby as she prepared to leave. "Good luck."

Steve didn't hear her. He was already poring over the second page of the fee agreement. "Why do lawyers write this much just to say how much it's going to cost to prepare a will?" he murmured. At least, though, the agreement was not that complex. The basic fee was based on the value of the estate, although the exact amount depended on the complexity of the estate and the estate planning options the client chose. Its simplicity buoyed his confidence.

Steve heard the outer door open and glanced at his watch. It was 2:05. He got up to intercept the visitors entering the lobby before they concluded the place was deserted. As he walked through the office, he felt the butterflies of a third-year law student preparing to take the bar exam for the first time. He arrived in the lobby just in time to see an older gentleman holding open the door, apparently waiting for someone coming in from the parking lot.

"You must be Mr. Siegel," Steve said as he extended his hand to greet his first official client.

"That I am," Mr. Siegel said with a distinct foreign accent. "I'll shake your hand as soon as my daughter gets in. She's almost here."

Five seconds later, the most beautiful woman Steve had ever seen walked into the lobby. He stared for a second; he couldn't help it. Her long, wavy hair, her alluringly bronzed skin, and her curve-accentuating red business suit with its tight skirt and plunging neckline all combined to command his attention to the point that he forgot where he was. Only after he noticed Mr. Siegel accepting his offer to shake hands did he snap back to reality. He grasped Mr. Siegel's hand firmly and hoped his client hadn't noticed him gawking at his daughter.

"It's a pleasure to meet you, Mr. Siegel," Steve said, shaking the man's hand. Steve took a chance on the introduction, gambling that they had never met.

"The pleasure is mine. Please let me introduce my daughter,

Michelle." Michelle shook Steve's hand, although she made no effort to grasp his hand or participate in the customary greeting. Her hand was cool and limp.

"I'm pleased to meet you, Michelle," Steve said. Michelle cut the handshake short without a smile or reply, clearly communicating she was unhappy about being there.

"Please, come into my office," Steve said in search of words, caught off guard by Michelle's attitude. "May I get either of you a cup of—"

"I'd like a glass of Perrier, *if you have it*," Michelle interjected, "and I prefer it with a twist of *fresh* lime."

What Steve thought and what he said were two different things. He thought Michelle had already established herself as a condescending, egotistical woman who knew she was beautiful and could demand and get what she wanted. But what came out in response to her request was a pleasant, "I'll have to see what we've got." He completed his offer of coffee to Mr. Siegel.

"A cup of coffee would be grand," Mr. Siegel replied, evoking the opposite impression from that of his daughter. "If you don't mind, I prefer it black."

"That I know I can do." Steve was grateful that at least Mr. Siegel was tolerable. He wondered, though, why Mr. Siegel had brought Michelle along and whether he was actually there to draw up a will or if that was just a pretense for getting into the office to discuss something else—something that affected his daughter, perhaps. Or was she really his daughter?

Steve escorted the pair into his office and got them situated in the two large oxblood leather chairs sitting in front of his desk. Before getting down to business, he wanted to produce a disclaimer so his new client wouldn't think he was a one-man show hanging onto solvency by the skin of his teeth. "You must excuse me," he began. "My partner's mother had a stroke last night, so he had to leave the office unexpectedly this morning. Our paralegal prepared his travel arrangements and

she's taking the tickets to him now. Until she gets back, I'm it."
Michelle rolled her eyes and huffed, affirming Steve's fear.

"Please, take your time," Mr. Siegel remarked, attempting to
compensate for his daughter's reaction. "We're in no hurry."

"Thank you, Mr. Siegel. Now, if you'll excuse me, I'll be
right back with your drinks." As Steve started for the door, he
decided to prepare Michelle for the shock that there might be
no Perrier. "Michelle, if we're out of Perrier, would you like a
soft drink instead?"

"No," she retorted.

Taken aback by Michelle's curt reply, Steve waited for a
moment, thinking she might add something. When she didn't,
he shrugged it off and headed for the kitchen to see what was
available. On his way, a sickening thought came over him. With
Marjorie gone, what if there was no coffee? As he walked into
the kitchen, though, he could see a full pot of coffee steaming
on the coffee maker. It smelled fresh, but at this point that
didn't matter. It was coffee and it was black—it would do. All
he needed now was a cup.

He was looking at a cupboard above the coffee machine
when a tray on the counter off to the left caught his eye. The
tray had two clean china cups and saucers on it, together with
spoons and sugar cubes. Marjorie had come through again.
Between the coffee fixings and the fee agreement, she had
already saved him from embarrassment twice. He was sure
there must be cream in the refrigerator, as well. Although Mr.
Siegel had asked for his coffee black, it would be a nice touch
to present cream on the tray in case he changed his mind. He
opened the refrigerator to see.

As expected, there was a silver creamer sitting in the front
of the refrigerator, positioned so that even he would notice
it. Also loaded were cans of various types of soft drinks, and
unbelievably, four or five bottles of Perrier. He took one and
put it on the tray together with a glass he scrounged from one
of the cabinets. He tossed in a couple of ice cubes and hurried

back to his office. It was time to find out what Mr. Siegel really wanted.

When he returned, he saw Mr. Siegel surveying the room, taking in all of its details. Michelle, in contrast, sat in her chair with her legs crossed and her hands folded on her lap. Her back was rigid and she was looking out the window behind Steve's desk. Everything about her body language conveyed she had more important things to do.

"Here's your coffee, Mr. Siegel," Steve announced, "and here is your Perrier, Michelle—although I'm sorry we don't have any limes." Steve's announcement tended toward the melodramatic, but he stopped short of outright sarcasm. For once he heeded his wife's oft-given advice, *Don't be obnoxious*.

Mr. Siegel slowly lifted his coffee from the tray. "Thank you," he said dutifully. He took a sip and then set the cup and saucer on the table between him and his daughter.

Michelle took her Perrier next. Although there was initially a look of surprise in her eyes, it quickly transformed to disgust. She didn't say thank you or take a sip. Instead, she set the drink on the table between her and her father, shunning the cork coaster Steve set out for her. Although the depth of Michelle's rudeness amazed Steve, he didn't waste much time thinking about it because he was ready to get down to business. He returned to his chair, and rocking back slightly, asked the question he'd been dying to ask ever since Mr. Siegel scheduled the appointment the day before.

"So Mr. Siegel, if you don't mind my asking, how did you get my name?"

Mr. Siegel smiled. "A neighbor of mine in New York, Admiral Frank Bancroft, told me to look you up. He said you were the only lawyer he'd ever trusted and he'd trust you with just about anything. That was good enough for me."

Steve couldn't help but grin and let a ray or two of pride escape. "I guess I owe Admiral Bancroft a thank you. I'm sure he must have told you I worked for him aboard the U.S.S.

Saratoga. We cruised the Mediterranean together back in the late eighties. It was an interesting time. But I know you didn't come to talk about that, so how about we get down to business? I understand you're here for some estate planning. Is that correct?"

"More or less. What I really want is to update my will. I updated it after my wife passed away, but I moved to Tappahannock about two months ago from Long Island, and I'd like my will to reflect that I no longer own any real estate in New York. I also purchased a home in Tappahannock, and I'd like my will to reflect that as well. You can keep everything else the same." While her father spoke, Michelle stared out the window, showing no interest in what he was saying.

"That sounds like something I can do. By chance do you have a copy of your current will?"

Mr. Siegel pulled a yellow business envelope from inside his suit coat and handed it to Steve. Steve opened it and found Mr. Siegel's current New York will, executed on January 14, 1995. He breezed through the boilerplate language and focused on the substantive provisions. They made it clear Mr. Siegel was not an ordinary man of ordinary means.

"Well, Mr. Siegel, I don't anticipate this being any problem at all. But I'm going to need to get a bit more information so we can structure this in the manner most beneficial to your estate now that you're under Virginia law. We can do this in one of two ways. I have a questionnaire you can take home to complete and bring back to me when you're finished. Or I can go over it with you now and fill it in as we go. It's up to you."

"Let's get it over with now. I'm leaving for Israel soon and I need to have this finished before I go."

"All right, then. Let's get started." Steve dreaded what he had to say next. Based on what he had seen so far, he expected sparks to fly. But he felt ethically obligated to at least raise the issue. He knew he had to choose his words carefully so that they would not be misconstrued, even though he knew they most probably would be.

"There is one preliminary matter I need to address with you, Mr. Siegel."

"What's that?" Mr. Siegel asked.

"Since we're going to be going over your assets and prospective beneficiaries, I strongly recommend we discuss this in private. Of course, you'll be free to share everything with Michelle after we speak, but I find conversing in private makes it easier to discuss these difficult issues."

"That's absurd!" Michelle declared, acknowledging for the first time that she was paying attention. She accentuated her protest by banging her hand on the table, nearly knocking over her bottle of Perrier.

Steve braced himself. Only fifteen minutes into his first appointment and he'd already alienated his client's daughter. He wished it had been possible not to raise the issue, but knew he'd had no choice. He had no way of knowing what the real dynamics of the relationship were. They could be friendly or strained, close or distant. He couldn't afford to guess incorrectly.

"My father has nothing to hide from me," Michelle pronounced, leaving no room for doubt. "I'll stay, thank you."

Mr. Siegel spoke in a conciliatory tone. "Michelle, if Mr. Stilwell prefers to do business this way, perhaps we should humor him." It was not the response Steve expected, and it gave Steve the luxury of remaining a spectator to the feud he'd fueled. He'd already said everything that needed to be said, anyway.

Michelle crossed her arms and shifted back in her chair, staking the claim to her territory. "Father, you can't be serious." She gave Steve the evil eye.

"Michelle, I need you to comply with Mr. Stilwell's request," Mr. Siegel stated firmly. "This is difficult for me and you're not making it any easier."

Michelle grabbed her purse and stood up, still glaring at Steve. "I'll wait for you in the lobby, Father." Then she turned and left the office, slamming the door behind her.

Steve spoke first to diffuse the tension. "I'm sorry to have made this so unpleasant. But I really do find things work better this way."

"No need to apologize, Mr. Stilwell. Michelle just isn't herself anymore. She moved back in with me after a very painful divorce. I just haven't been able to reconnect with her. It's like her divorce put a wall up between us and it's getting worse. With all that going on, I just can't burden her with the details of my will. Those are for me to worry about. Now tell me, what is it you need to know?"

"For starters, I need to get a better picture of you and your estate. Can you tell me a little bit about yourself and your assets?"

"Well, I'm seventy years old and widowed. My wife, God rest her soul, died three years ago of breast cancer. That's really why I left New York. I tried to stay there after she was gone, but I needed a new start." Mr. Siegel paused briefly as the discussion resurrected a hidden sadness. "Anyway, I retired from teaching at Columbia University in 1996 and here I am."

"Can you give me an idea of the types of assets you have?"

"Mostly Treasury bills. I've got about two million in Treasury bills and about three-quarters of a million in bonds. I've also got my house in Tappahannock; its value is about six hundred thousand. Oh, and there's my pension from Columbia."

"Is that everything you can think of?"

"Aside from a modest checking and savings account, that's about it. In fact, if you look at the last page of the will I gave you, I included a list of my assets. That should be everything."

"So you don't have any insurance policies or annuities?"

"None."

"What about liabilities?"

"I don't owe any money," Professor Siegel said softly. "I don't believe in being indebted to any man."

Professor Siegel had a quiet air of dignity about him that Steve had never sensed to such a high degree. He didn't know how to describe it, but the man exuded peacefulness. Steve needed to probe further. He felt as if he was in the presence of someone extraordinary, but couldn't pinpoint the source of that impression. "Are you an American citizen?" he asked. His pen was poised to take more notes.

Professor Siegel sat up in his chair as if coming to attention. "Yes I am." Steve guessed he was a naturalized citizen, but since the Professor didn't offer the information, he didn't pursue it. The fact wasn't relevant, anyway, although it did cause Steve to respect his client even more.

"All right then, let's look at the proposed disposition of your property. I see you're giving two hundred fifty thousand dollars to a synagogue in New York and five hundred thousand apiece to three individuals. Is that still your desire?"

"Yes, it is."

"And are their names correct in your current will?"

"Of course."

"Can you tell me what your relationship is with these men? I like to spell out the relationships of any beneficiaries in the will. It eliminates questions down the road and makes contesting the will more difficult, if it ever comes to that."

Professor Siegel's facial expression suddenly became sullen. "I can't imagine that happening, but if you need to know, they are friends—good friends. In fact, they're like brothers to me. I met them during the war and I owe them my life. Aside from Michelle, they are all I have. I don't want any of that to change, Mr. Stilwell. I just want my will updated now that I live in Virginia."

Steve could tell the Professor wanted to get through this section quickly. It seemed difficult for him. Not so much that he disliked talking about his own demise, but that the discussion somehow tarnished his friendship with these men.

Steve pressed ahead cautiously. "I understand, but I've still got a few more questions I have to ask. For example, I see here that you've named your daughter as executrix. Do you still want her to be the one who manages your estate through probate?"

"I'm glad you asked that. No, as a matter of fact, I don't. I want you to do that."

"Are you sure? I'll have to charge your estate a fee. Are you sure that's what you want?" Of course Steve wanted to do it, but he needed to make sure Professor Siegel understood what he was committing to.

"Absolutely. After my discussions with Admiral Bancroft, I trust you. I want you to be my executor."

"Okay, then. Just a few more questions. I know you said you wanted the dispositions to be the same under your new will as under your current will, but I need to be able to say I discussed every bequest with you. That way if a question ever arises I'll be able to verify your specific intentions."

"Please, do what you have to do, Mr. Stilwell. That's why I came to you."

Steve nodded. He was just getting ready to confirm that Professor Siegel's entire residual estate was to flow to Michelle when he glanced at the telephone on his desk. The intercom light was on! Someone was on the phone in Mr. Smythe's office or at Marjorie's desk listening to everything he and Professor Siegel said. It had to be Michelle. He hadn't heard Marjorie come back, and why would Marjorie do such a thing? She'd see the will anyway.

Steve nonchalantly reached over and pushed the telephone's "Do not Disturb" button, disabling the intercom. What in the world was Michelle doing eavesdropping on the conversation? Steve decided not to tell the Professor. It would only upset him, and after all, he couldn't prove Michelle had actually done anything—although he was certain she had. He tried to pick up where he had left off.

"Let's see here. It looks like the entire remainder of your

estate goes to your only child, Michelle. Is that correct?"

"Yes, that's correct."

Now Steve had the opportunity to get some information about Michelle and he had no intention of passing it up. "Is Michelle your natural daughter?"

"She's adopted, Mr. Stilwell. My wife and I couldn't have children, so we adopted Michelle in 1964 right after she was born. She was a gift to us from God."

"You mentioned Michelle is divorced. Was she married just that one time?"

"Yes, that's correct," Professor Siegel replied. "She was divorced about three years ago and never remarried. I never approved of the marriage in the first place. Her husband was a minor league baseball player. He was not a good man; I could see that from the moment I met him. I can read people, Mr. Stilwell, and he was no good. Michelle won't talk to me about it, but I know he hurt her deeply. As far as she is concerned, it's as if the marriage never happened."

"Are you certain her divorce is final?"

"Quite. At the final hearing, she changed her name back to Siegel. I don't think she's seen or heard from him since the day they were divorced."

"I take it she has no children."

"No, thank God. But maybe when she meets the right man."

"And how old did you say she was?" Steve asked more out of curiosity than out of any real need to know.

"I didn't say, but she's thirty-three."

The response embarrassed Steve. Obviously, the professor was keeping close track of the conversation. He decided to bring the questioning to a close. "Well, that should do it." Steve glanced back at the telephone to make sure the intercom light was still off. It was. "You mentioned you were planning on traveling soon. What's your schedule?"

"I'm leaving for Israel on Saturday." Professor Siegel reached into his pocket and produced a tattered pocket calendar, flipping it open to October, 1997. "Yes, that's correct. I'll be leaving Saturday afternoon from Washington, D.C."

"How long will you be gone?"

"I'm not really sure. It could be a couple of weeks; it could be a month. That's the beauty of being retired."

"I take it you'd like to have your new will done before you leave?" Steve hoped Professor Siegel forgot what he'd said earlier. He didn't know if he could get the will done before Saturday. Of course, if Mr. Smythe were here, it wouldn't be a problem. But with Mr. Smythe's mother on her deathbed, Steve didn't want to ask for help unless it was absolutely necessary.

"I'd like to sign it Friday, at the latest. You can never tell about Israel. I want to make sure my affairs are in order before I go." Then he laughed and added, "Signing it will be my best insurance against anything happening. Now, if I don't sign, something will happen for sure."

"Friday it is then. How about 2:30?" Steve had no idea how he would get the will finished by then. There was no way he was going to do a multi-million dollar estate without his boss' supervision. There was also no way he was going to let his first client slip away without helping him. He would just have to find a way.

"That'll work just fine," the professor said. "Now, what about the money? I suppose this isn't free."

"I always save the bad news for last." Steve shuffled some papers on his desk, looking for the fee agreement Marjorie gave him. As he picked it up and prepared to hand it to Professor Siegel, Michelle opened the office door.

"Will you be much longer, Father?" Michelle glared at Steve as she spoke. Steve glared back and went on the offensive by addressing her question.

"We're just about finished here. I'd guess no more than five minutes."

Michelle didn't retreat into the lobby; instead, she stood by the door, holding it open with her arm.

"Mr. Stilwell, I have no objection to my daughter joining us now."

"That's fine," Steve said, breaking off his staring contest with Michelle. "Please, Michelle, come over and sit down with us." Michelle did just that and immediately resumed her gaze out the window. After the eavesdropping incident on the intercom, though, Steve knew her disinterest was only a ruse. He wondered how a woman that beautiful could be so socially bankrupt, but managed to return his focus to his discussion with Professor Siegel before his opinion of Michelle became too much of a distraction.

"I'm sorry, Professor, we were going over my fees, weren't we? Normally my fee for preparing your will would be based in part on the amount of your estate. Given the nature of your will, though, I'll limit it to one thousand dollars. If I serve as executor, I'll charge your estate a full three percent. That, of course, isn't payable now, but I want to make sure you understand that if I'm the executor, your estate will be billed for my services." When Steve mentioned that he might serve as executor, he saw Michelle briefly shift her eyes toward her father. She said nothing, though, and soon returned to gazing out the window.

"I understand," Professor Siegel acknowledged. "It sounds reasonable."

Michelle broke her silence. "It sounds outrageous."

"Michelle!" Professor Siegel chastised.

This time, Steve waded in to try and calm the situation. "I'm sorry you feel that way, Ms. Siegel, but I can assure you my fees *are* reasonable."

"I'm sure they are," she said, completely unfettered by the etiquette that usually applied during a meeting of this sort. Steve knew having her leave the room earlier destroyed any chance of a civil working relationship; still, he had to try.

"Professor Siegel, I'm sorry to have to go through this in so much detail, but it's important we both understand my fee. It precludes misunderstandings down the road." Steve wrote the $1,000 fee limitation into the fee agreement and handed it to the Professor.

Professor Siegel took a few minutes to read over the agreement. Michelle rose from her chair and started to walk toward the door. Professor Siegel briefly looked up to see where she was going, but quickly returned to reading the two-page document.

"This looks fine," the professor concluded. "May I use your pen?"

"Certainly." Steve handed the professor a pen from his desk. Professor Siegel placed the fee agreement on a corner of Steve's desk, signed it, and handed both the agreement and the pen back to Steve.

"There's just one more thing," Steve added. "May I have your telephone number in case I need to call you for additional information? I'd also like to get your address for our files."

"Of course," the professor replied. Steve handed him a client card, which he filled out.

"That's it," Steve said as he took the card back from the Professor. "We're set to go on Friday at 2:30."

"I'll see you then," the professor said as he got up from his chair. Steve stood as well and maneuvered around his desk to shake his new client's hand.

"I enjoyed meeting you, Professor Siegel, and I look forward to working with you." The two men shook hands and headed for the door; Michelle was already well ahead of them. Just as she reached the far side of the lobby, the front door popped open and Marjorie came in.

"Hello," Marjorie said to Michelle as Michelle walked past. Michelle didn't answer and continued on her way to her car.

"Is something wrong?"

"No, it's okay, Marjorie. Come in, come in. Professor Siegel, let me introduce our office manager, Marjorie Weldman."

"It's a pleasure to meet you." Professor Siegel bowed slightly in Marjorie's direction.

"I'm pleased to meet you, too," Marjorie said, working her way behind her desk.

"Professor Siegel will be coming in on Friday at 2:30 to execute his will. Would you please make the necessary arrangements?"

"Certainly, Mr. Stilwell."

"I've got to be going," Professor Siegel said. "I can tell it's going to be a long ride home." With that, Professor Siegel left the office and Steve's first appointment was history.

"How did it go, Mr. Stilwell?"

"It went fine with Professor Siegel. But that daughter of his is a real piece of work."

"So I noticed. What did you do to her?"

"You got me." Steve conveniently forgot to mention that he had asked Michelle to leave the room before he spoke to her father. "But I've got a will to write and it has to be done by Friday. Let's hope Mr. Smythe calls in so I can run it past him."

"Don't worry, Mr. Stilwell. If Mr. Smythe said he'll call, he'll call."

Steve didn't hear Marjorie's assurance. He was already formulating the professor's will in his mind. Two days was all the time he had to learn how to properly draft and execute a multi-million dollar estate plan under Virginia law. He had his work cut out for him.

* * *

Tappahannock, Virginia

MICHELLE SAT AT her computer and pecked at each key as if she were sounding out the words as she typed. It was past midnight and she was tired, but she had to get some information on the Web right away before it was too late. She stopped for a minute to compose her thoughts but instead her mind wandered. God, that attorney made her angry. He actually asked her to leave the room. *What nerve!*

Just thinking about the loss of control made Michelle feel dizzy, and the memory of her rape came pounding back. She could sense her ex-husband's drunken hands pinning her to the bed, tearing at her clothes, and groping her body. She'd tried to resist, but he was too strong. He would have his way this one last time. He leaned forward to kiss her and she spit in his face, earning his backhand in return. The throbbing pain on her cheek helped draw her focus away from the rape that followed, but the pain from the backhand eventually faded away. The pain from the rape never did. It was always there, grabbing her and holding her down, screaming to her that she'd never be more than a pawn to be moved around on someone else's chessboard.

Even her doting father's love made it hard for her to breathe. She knew he was only trying to protect her, but that didn't make him any less controlling. Having to move back in with her parents after her divorce made matters worse. Her mother saw her being smothered and buffered the effect, but when her mother died, Michelle felt the full force of her father's fierce determination to keep her from getting hurt again. He wanted her with him all the time, mostly so he could stand watch over her and keep her safe, but partly because he was getting older and craved her companionship. She couldn't say anything to him; he was her father and he'd been through so much himself. So she kept her emotional distance from him, and from everyone for that matter, looking for opportunities where she could be the one moving the pawns. Heartless manipulation was the only way she could drive the prisoner—the memory of her husband's abuse—back into the cell.

Michelle looked back at the computer screen to see if she needed to add any more information. No, it looked good. Then she heard footsteps coming down the stairs. It was her father. "What is *he* doing up?" she mumbled. She hurriedly closed the Web browser and returned to the desktop menu, pretending to be deep in thought.

"Michelle, what are you doing up? It's almost one o'clock in the morning and you're not even dressed for bed."

Michelle turned and saw her father standing at the foot of the stairs. He was wearing blue and white pinstriped pajamas, with his wiry gray hair all in a tussle. He looked like a frazzled Albert Einstein without the mustache. She said nothing to him.

"Are you still not talking to me?" After a further period of silence he added, "You are so much like your mother."

"I take that as a compliment," Michelle replied defiantly.

"Michelle, you know the attorney was just doing his job. He has procedures he needs to follow. You shouldn't take things so personally."

"Of course you're right, Father," Michelle said condescendingly. "By the way, what are you doing up this late?"

"I was having trouble sleeping. Actually, it was a nightmare. I thought I'd get a cup of tea and a couple cookies and try to go back to sleep again."

"Well, I shall go to bed then, too." Michelle reached around the side of the computer and turned it off. Then she switched off the desk lamp and got up to leave the room, acting as if she were the only one there. She was still angry with her father, so she didn't say goodnight. Her silence didn't deter him, though. He always said goodnight.

"Goodnight, Michelle. I'll see you in the morning."

Michelle was already halfway up the stairs. She heard him, of course, but she continued on her way without guilt or remorse for leaving him behind in the darkened study—the one man who loved her more than anything else on earth.

"Someday she'll understand," he whispered to himself. He walked slowly into the kitchen and sat down at the table alone.

6

⁓

Thursday, October 2
Düsseldorf

TWO DAYS HAD passed since Belmar began his investigation, and only now was he receiving detailed reports on the homicide. He set a stack of about fifty witness interviews on his desk and rolled back his chair so that he had full access to his desk drawer. He imagined that when the desk was new, the original government servant could open it with one hand while still writing with the other. But now the twenty-year-old gray metal desk fought every effort to divulge its contents. Belmar braced his left leg on the desk's inside corner and gave a sharp tug on the file drawer with both hands. With a loud pop, the file drawer opened and exposed his sack lunch. It was a lot of work for a cheese sandwich and an apple.

Belmar began to eat the sandwich as he read through the statements for the first time. Most were short and of no value. *How can an old man get shot in the head in broad daylight and no one see or hear anything?* They would just have to try harder; something had to turn up. He took another bite of his sandwich and was about to turn to the next statement when a knock on the door interrupted him.

"Detective Belmar, may I come in?"

"Of course, Anja. My favorite forensic technician is always welcome. Please, come in and take a seat." Belmar set his sandwich on its wax paper wrapper and took a quick sip of tepid black coffee.

"I'm sorry to ruin your lunch," Anja said, taking the gray metal chair with the green vinyl seat cushion directly in front of Belmar's desk.

"You can't ruin a lunch like this," Belmar chuckled. "Besides, it's two forty-five in the afternoon and lunchtime is over. So, what brings you here?"

"I've got the preliminary autopsy report on the old man in the alley." Anja handed Belmar a manila envelope and sat back in her chair while Belmar opened it. He pulled out the report and thumbed through it until he came to the cause of death.

"Evidence of blunt trauma to the head and gunshot wound to the head," he read out loud. "Cause of death: gunshot wound to the head. Victim died instantly." He continued down the report. "Estimated time of death: between seven and eight a.m. What else can they tell us that we already know?" Belmar's voice rang with frustration. "An old man brutally murdered and this is all I have to go on. How am I supposed to solve the case?" He tossed the report back toward Anja and the pages flew apart in Belmar's man-made breeze. Two or three of the pages landed on the floor next to Anja. She picked them up and put them on top of the ones that landed on the desk, aligning the corners and setting the reassembled report atop the doodle-filled blotter on Belmar's desk.

"Did you notice that the man was Jewish?" Anja asked as if Belmar's tossing of the report had never happened.

"No, I haven't seen a family history yet. We've identified him as Emil Weisentrope and that's about it."

"Look at page six—the tattoo," Anja said, proud that she

had found something Belmar had not yet noticed. "He was a prisoner at a concentration camp. His prisoner number's tattooed on his left forearm." She rearranged the report from her seat until page six was on top and then pointed to the picture of the tattoo so Belmar could see for himself.

"So what do you think, skinheads? They've been more active lately, but never in this neighborhood. Do you think they could have done it?"

"If they did, it'll be hard for 'em to keep it quiet. It's worth following up."

"You could be right," Belmar said, swayed by Anja's theory. "If the press finds out, though, it'll be front page news. Then they'll know we're onto them and will lay low. We can't afford that, Anja. I don't want this released. Can you seal the report?"

"I can keep it close-hold for a couple of weeks. After that, it will take a letter from the Prosecutor's Office, and they rarely agree to that. They say it makes it look as if they're hiding something."

"Well, at least that gives us fourteen days." Belmar rocked back in his chair with his hands locked behind his head. "That is, if they *are* skinheads. I'll put some feelers out right away." Belmar smiled. "And by the way, good catch."

The corners of Anja's mouth curled up with pride. "Let me know if you need anything else."

"You know I will." Belmar began to scour the report as Anja left. There was nothing else remarkable. A nine-millimeter slug in the victim's head. Seventy-one years old. Otherwise healthy. Aside from the tattoo, that was all it said.

Belmar set the report aside and contemplated the skinhead theory. Something didn't add up. The bullet hole in the top of the head suggested an execution. The wallet in the dumpster indicated a robbery. Although it was certainly possible skinheads had both robbed and killed the man, the job seemed too clean for that. What was he missing?

Belmar refocused his attention on the witness statements.

He started going over them again from the beginning. The statements were all the same: short, nondescript, and concluding with "I don't remember seeing anything unusual."

When Belmar got about three-quarters of the way through the stack, he came to a statement that was noteworthy if for nothing else other than its length. He read it out loud to himself:

> At about eight a.m., I was walking on Tabelstrasse on my way to work at Hilduff's Women's Apparel. It's a small shop on Malpelstrasse. I turned down Malpelstrasse and got to the shop a few minutes after eight; the shop opens at nine. As I looked in my purse for my keys, I saw something—a movement—out of the corner of my eye and turned to see what it was. I noticed a tall blond-haired man walking down Malpelstrasse just beyond the last shop before you get to the alley. I remember thinking that was odd, because the man wasn't on the street when I was walking down Malpelstrasse. When he saw me looking at him, he stared right at me. He had an angry look on his face, like he was mad I saw him. It kind of scared me, so I started digging for my keys and I went into the shop as quickly as I could. I never saw him again.

Belmar grabbed the statement and hurried into the detectives' pit outside his office. "Hans, who brought in these statements regarding the Weisentrope case?" Hans Schueller was one of the junior detectives in the office and the unfortunate soul who happened to be sitting closest to Belmar's door. The only other detective in the room was on the telephone.

"I don't know, Detective Belmar. Would you like me to find out?"

"I can't believe this, Hans," Belmar vented, ignoring Hans' offer. "I get a stack of fifty statements on my desk from witnesses in the Weisentrope case. No explanation, no heads up—just a stack of statements. Almost at the bottom is a statement from somebody who might actually have seen the killer. What idiot buried that statement at the bottom of the stack? And why wasn't I told as soon as this statement was taken?"

"I'm sorry, Detective Belmar, but I haven't worked that case. I didn't even know there was a witness to the murder."

"There is, dammit." Then Belmar clarified, "Well, maybe she didn't actually see the murder, but it looks like she saw the killer just moments after it happened. She puts him at the alley between eight and eight-fifteen. This has to be the guy." Belmar started walking back into his office, still shaking his head. "Hans, come in here."

Hans followed and plopped down in the chair in front of Belmar's desk. "What do you need me to do, Detective Belmar?"

"I need you to pull in the woman who made the statement. I want to talk to her personally." Belmar thought for a moment. "Arrange for a sketch artist too. I want a picture while he's still fresh in her memory."

The younger man nodded and pushed his wispy brown hair out of his rather bland face. "I'll get to work on it right away."

"Good, Hans. We're on to something—I can feel it. Now we're gonna catch this bastard." Belmar looked at the statement one last time just to make sure he hadn't missed anything. Then he looked back at Hans, who was waiting to be dismissed. "Go, Hans, get this set up. I want you to work the interview with me. Can you make it tonight if the woman can come in?"

"I'll be there," Hans said, grinning. "Thank you, sir."

"Get going, Hans," Belmar added. It was good to see such youthful enthusiasm.

Belmar walked around his desk and sat back down. He threw what was left of his cheese sandwich into the garbage and took a drink of his now-cold coffee. It was time to go through the rest of the statements. Even though there were only four or five left, maybe one would corroborate some aspect of what the woman saw. Then he would give the statements to Hans to go through. A fresh set of eyes never hurt. At least now he had something to work with.

7

Berlin, Germany

Hermann Borne personified Germany's rise from the ashes of World War II. Born on December 11, 1940, he was only four years old when the war ended. Like many in Germany, the war cost his family almost everything worth living for. His six-year-old brother died in a nighttime bombing raid in 1944. The family's Berlin home was destroyed during the Allied assault on the city. And when the war finally ended, his family had nothing—not even food.

Hermann's mother refused to fall victim to circumstances. She was determined to give her two remaining children, Hermann and his two-year-old sister, some semblance of a normal life in spite of what the war had done. So she worked long hours to put their lives back together, starting out as a schoolteacher for second graders. She pushed getting the neighborhood's schools open again, even before the debris was cleared. "The children," she said, "cannot wait."

At night, after spending time with Hermann and his sister and putting them to bed, she earned extra money by making children's clothing. A small shop opened at the end of her street as soon as the people started returning to what remained of their homes, and the owner allowed her to sell the clothes she made on consignment. Because so many people had nothing, the clothes sold well, although they didn't bring in a lot of money; the people didn't have much to spend. But it was a beginning.

More than the importance of education and keeping the family fed, Hermann's mother instilled in her children a sense of patriotism for Germany. She was a proud woman, and Germany's crushing defeat and wartime atrocities did little to dissuade her from her loyalty. In fact, she taught her children to work hard at school and excel in athletics, for it would be up to them to make Germany strong once again.

At four years old, Hermann had a long way to go before he understood his mother's values. As he grew, though, his mother's effort bore fruit. Hermann worked hard to succeed at everything he tried, and succeed he did. He was a natural at mathematics and graduated first in his class from secondary school. His academic prowess led to his acceptance into the University of Bonn, where he studied mathematics and the emerging field of electronic engineering. He saw a future in electronics and wanted to be ready to seize the opportunity when the time came.

But Hermann's school years weren't easy. His working class background meant he had to toil full-time to pay for the expenses not covered by his scholarship. Plus, he sent any extra money he had home to his mother and sister, who were still living off the income from his mother's full-time teaching and part-time sewing. Until then it had never occurred to Hermann that his family didn't have money and others did. It made him wonder why other families had come through the war so much better than his. Where was the justice? What had his family done that others had not? The seeds of bitterness were sown.

During his first year at the university, Hermann met a core group of four friends. They remained his closest and only true friends for the rest of his life. After discovering they had much in common, they rented a large flat and lived together until graduation. All five young men were brilliant; they thrived on academic challenge and were driven to succeed. Three of the four had backgrounds similar to Hermann's—families devastated by the war. Only Werner Klecken was different. His father was an army general who survived the war. Although loyal to the Reich until the end, General Klecken believed Germany lost the war on the day it invaded the Soviet Union, so he put a significant portion of his family's wealth in Swiss banks. He'd wanted to be ready when the end came, and his foresight paid off.

The five friends challenged one another over everything—whether it be grades, girls, athletics, or money. Yet politics and the war, not sex and football, dominated the majority of their late night discussions. Otto Felder and Martin Horst's fathers were both killed on the Russian Front. Neither son remembered his father, but each was proud of his father's service. Albert Henschel's father survived the war. He fought in France and was captured shortly after D-Day. He served out the rest of the war in a prisoner of war camp and returned to Germany in 1945. He worked construction, and with no shortage of buildings to rebuild, provided a comfortable middle-class living for his family. Then, of course, there was Werner. He never ran out of General Klecken stories. The general actually served on Erwin Rommel's staff and was looked at as a hero not only for his North African exploits, but also for simply surviving to the end of the war.

Conspicuously missing from the discussions was any mention of Hermann's father. All noticed Hermann spoke only of his mother. On one occasion, after an afternoon soccer game and some late night beer drinking, Werner asked Hermann if his father survived the war. Hermann's expression grew sullen and at once intense, clearly communicating an inviolate line had been crossed. "Yes, he survived the war," Hermann told them, "but my father never came back to our family. My mother brought our family out of the war." Hermann offered nothing more and no one pursued the issue. It would be thirty-five years before Hermann discussed his father again.

Three months prior to graduation, the roommates got together on a Thursday night for one of their weekly academic and political discussions. After a couple of hours and a number of beers, the discussion reached a level of introspection and honesty uncommon among young men. But these five were different and they knew it. They pledged their support to one another forever, no matter what the cost. They also vowed to work to make Germany great again so that their families might not have suffered in vain. None advocated a return to the days of the Reich or to the international aggression that had cost Germany so dearly twice in the preceding fifty years, yet they saw a greatness in their country in those days they could not help but admire. They were products of their parents and the rule of Adolf Hitler, once removed from the atrocities themselves but still susceptible to the overt prejudices that permeated German society for twelve long years. They would bring wealth, not war back to Germany—to the real German people.

Deep into the next morning, the roommates were still awake and still drinking. Werner Klecken called for a toast, a toast that would change the course of their lives. At 3:45 a.m., they raised their schnapps above their heads and clinked their glasses together.

"To the fatherland," Werner shouted, suddenly standing straight and sounding eerily like his father had eighteen years before.

"To the fatherland," they responded in unison as they lowered their glasses to drink. But before their first sip, Hermann added one more phrase. "To the Five." In a moment, the schnapps was gone and the night was over, but the conversation, the pledge, and the label lived on.

The Five graduated from the University of Bonn in 1963, all in the top three percent of their class. With the German economy making a strong comeback and the labor shortage still controlling the marketplace, they all took jobs that would eventually place them well in German industry and government. They felt destined for greatness.

Werner Klecken used his father's connections to secure a position in the West German Foreign Service. His diplomatic experience would take him around the world over the next thirty years, weaving a web of contacts the Five exploited for business and personal gain. Albert Henschel made his fortune as an investment banker by combining an uncanny knack for putting together successful business deals with an almost messianic ability to get people to accede to his will. Albert's money left him well connected with the ruling political elite, whoever that happened to be at any point in time. Otto Felder signed with West German Air and was one of the principal architects of the airline's strategy to capture a leading share of the European market dominated by Britain after the war. Finally, Martin Horst became an officer in the German Army, eventually rising to the level of Brigadier General and commanding an elite brigade of German Special Operations Forces.

Hermann took the road less traveled. Instead of accepting a position with the government or an established industry, he opted for a position with Spanz Electronics Ltd., a three-year-old West Berlin based technology company exploring banking and defense applications for the large mainframe computers then available on the market. When he joined the firm in 1963, he was one of ten employees. He agreed to work for what amounted to a subsistence salary, but only if he were given thousands of seemingly worthless stock options. "Bet on me," he told Spanz's president, "and I will make us both rich."

Spanz assigned Hermann to the four-man banking group, and within a year he was project team lead. Toward the end of 1964, the breakthrough occurred: the group developed a computer program to fully automate bank account maintenance, something banks had done by hand for centuries. Within two months, a large Bonn bank decided to try the program together with a large mainframe computer purchase. Hermann's work was an instant success. Overnight, Spanz's reputation spread to Switzerland and London and the demand for its product became insatiable. However, Spanz couldn't hire salesmen and technicians fast enough to keep up with the demand, so it merged with its mainframe strategic partner and marketed the program and the mainframe together as a banking system. Both Spanz's president and Hermann became millionaires, each receiving cash and stock in the deal and leading the new Spanz Division in the acquiring mainframe computer giant.

Hermann was set for life, yet he continued to work hard just as his mother had taught him, never forgetting his roots. Those same roots also caused him to shun society's limelight and continually reflect on what the war did to his family, robbing him of his father. It haunted him like a dirge running constantly through his head. His only relief was to resolve to one day do something about the war, although he had no idea just what that might be.

At thirty-seven, Hermann married twenty-eight-year-old Sonja Wolfsen from Munich. Sonja came from a broken family. Like Hermann, her mother raised her. Her father served in the Wehrmacht during the war and drank heavily after it ended. The situation at home grew so bad that when Sonja was ten, her mother took her and her brother from their West Berlin apartment and moved to Munich. Bright and personable, Sonja returned to West Berlin to attend college and remained there after graduating. She met Hermann through a mutual acquaintance and they began to date. Although Hermann had wealth beyond Sonja's wildest dreams, money was not a major factor to her. Instead, she sought stability, rationality and protection—all of the things her own family lacked and Hermann willingly offered. Hermann fell in love with Sonja and they married a year later.

The couple had two children—both strong, healthy boys. Hermann and Sonja spared nothing on them. They attended the finest school in West Berlin and were accomplished in sports and music. Moreover, Hermann took care to instill in them the same pride in Germany his mother taught him, including the prejudices of a past generation. Not overtly, as before, but quietly. Subtly.

Hermann's visionary success with Spanz continued until 1990. Now one of the wealthiest men in Germany, he decided to retire at age fifty and simply manage his investments. He also wanted *his* sons to spend time with a loving father, something he was deprived of as a child. So he took an active role in their lives. The boys worshipped their father and they did much together as a family, especially traveling throughout Europe and the reunited Germany. Hermann wanted his sons so see all of Germany and learn its history. They would not be products of the shame he felt growing up.

His satisfying family life made Hermann forget his deep-seated desire to rectify past wrongs. The fire of youth dimmed with every passing year and Hermann focused more on what was good for his boys and Sonja. He had everything a man could want—a wonderful family, his health, and unimaginable wealth. Then, in 1996, two things occurred to change Hermann Borne's destiny.

The first event took place late on a Saturday night in February. Hermann was at home in his flat in Berlin with Sonja and sixteen-year-old Peter, while eighteen-year-old Erwin was away on a ski trip in the Swiss Alps with a group of friends from school. Hermann sat comfortably in his chair in the living room, reading a book. He had his feet propped up on a footstool and a light next to him shining brightly onto the text of each page. Sonja sat across from him reading a newspaper while Peter was in bed.

As midnight approached, Hermann closed his book and stretched his arms over his head, groaning as he did. "I'm going to bed," he announced as he started to get up out of the chair. Just as he shifted his weight onto his feet, the telephone next to his chair rang, startling both of them.

"I can't believe someone is calling at this late hour," protested Sonja, folding the newspaper across her lap and waiting to see who it could be.

"Perhaps it's Erwin asking for more money," mused Hermann. He let the phone ring three times before picking it up, just in case it was a wrong number.

"Hello, this is the Borne residence."

As soon as he heard the caller's voice, Hermann sensed this was one of those telephone calls a parent hopes never to receive. He felt himself weakening, even before the caller completed his first sentence.

"Hello, may I speak with Mr. Hermann Borne, please?"

"This is he," Hermann said. "How may I help you?"

Hermann could see Sonja's lips moving as if she was talking. She was asking him who it was, but things were starting to move in slow motion and she seemed distant and detached from the reality on the telephone. The only sound he could hear was the voice on the other end of the line.

"Mr. Borne," the voice said, "I am detective Frosch with the Swiss Police in Bern. I am afraid there has been an accident." The caller paused briefly. Hermann tried to speak but couldn't. The detective went on. "I am very sorry to have to tell you that your son, Erwin, was killed tonight in a skiing accident. He did nothing wrong; another skier collided with him and your son struck his head when he fell. He died instantly. I am so sorry, Mr. Borne."

Hermann felt dizzy and he couldn't manage a response. His

face turned ashen white. Sonja could tell something was very, very wrong.

"Who is it, Hermann?" she said more emphatically. But Hermann didn't hear her. All he heard was the voice on the other end of the line.

"Mr. Borne, are you all right?" the man inquired.

"Yes, of course," Hermann responded. He had to muster enough strength to get through the call. "Please allow me to get a piece of paper to take down some information."

"Hermann, who is it, and what's going on?" Tears formed in Sonja's eyes. Her imagination caused her to fear the worst, but her heart told her to hope it was not so serious. Hermann vaguely heard her this time, but ignored her. He had to tell her this without the distraction of the telephone. If he could just get through the telephone call.

"Please, Detective, give me your name and telephone number and tell me where you are located," Hermann said as he prepared to write with a pen on a piece of paper he pulled from a drawer on the telephone stand. He didn't look over at Sonja but could hear her beginning to sob quietly.

"My name is Detective Frosch," the detective responded. "I am located at the headquarters of the Bern Cantonal Police. Your son's body will be taken to the morgue in Bern. I suggest you arrive here tomorrow, if possible, and make any necessary arrangements. Of course, my department will assist you in any way we can, Mr. Borne. I am so sorry to have to relay such news."

"Thank you for your kindness, Detective," Hermann responded, staring at something across the room. "I'll contact your office as soon as we arrive in Bern tomorrow."

Hermann hung up the phone and looked at Sonja sitting on the couch with tear-filled eyes imploring him for a word of reassurance.

"Sonja," Hermann said, walking over to her and finding strength in his desire to comfort her. He sat down next to her and took one of her hands. "Erwin was in an accident. He hit his head skiing and he is gone." Sonja buried her head in Hermann's shoulder and began to cry. For a moment Hermann was strong. Then he too, began to cry.

In the aftermath of World War II, grief was commonplace in Germany. Hermann saw his mother's friends collapse or cry hysterically when they learned their husbands or lovers would never return. He watched mothers and fathers at the train station grip each other's arms when a disfigured or legless soldier who used to be their handsome son struggled to get off the train. But Hermann also saw that once the initial shock wore off and the challenges of everyday life reappeared, most learned to deal with the tragedy, put it behind them, and move on with their lives.

Hermann wasn't one of the "lucky ones." He couldn't move on. He couldn't get past the grief and he reacted with bitterness. After Erwin's death, instead of looking to the future, he looked to the past. Deeply hidden emotions bubbled to the surface, emotions that may not have even been real. Now Hermann felt pain not only for the loss of his son, but also for the loss of his brother during the bombing raid in 1944. Perhaps there was no way for Hermann to remember that. His mother never spoke of his brother around him, but the pain was real nonetheless and Hermann looked for someone to blame. If he could point his finger at someone and tell them "*You* must pay for the deaths of my son and my brother," then, he thought, things would be right again. But someone had to pay.

These thoughts were dangerous not just because they were bad; Hermann had the means to follow through with them. Given his vast wealth and connections in the business community, he could financially ruin any ordinary man, and if he put his mind to it, he could do much worse. He wasn't at that point yet, but he was getting there fast. Because his days were mostly occupied with managing his investments, he had nothing to distract him from the loss of his son. Everything he saw reminded him that his life was ruined. Sonja became distant, talking less and less and desiring not to leave their flat in Berlin. Peter accepted his brother's death and tried to get on with his life, but his recovery actually caused Hermann to resent him. Hermann felt that Peter hadn't shown sufficient grief after Erwin's death and he held it against him in subtle ways, like being too busy to help with homework or to go to a soccer match with him. By mid-October 1996, Hermann didn't even like spending time with Peter because it reminded him he couldn't spend time with Erwin. Erwin's death was destroying the Borne family.

The consequences of Erwin's death went far beyond Hermann's relationship with his family. His search for someone to blame rekindled his hatred toward Jews. When he found out the other boy involved in the collision was a Jewish boy from Denmark, Hermann was beside himself. Worse yet, the other boy was only shaken up and walked away from the accident. Why couldn't the other boy have died? Why did it have to be Erwin? Now he understood what his mother meant when she told him about the Jews—how they were the reason for Germany's defeat and for the Borne family's poverty. He recalled as a young boy overhearing his mother tell her friend that her oldest son would still be alive if it hadn't been for the Jewish "problem" in Germany. Such were the teachings Hermann grew up with.

So Hermann learned to hate the Jews. He didn't know any Jewish people; he hadn't associated with any Jewish people, yet he didn't like the Jewish people. Now that a Jew had "killed" his son, he had nothing but utter contempt for them. At least he limited his reaction to contempt. That is, until the second major event of 1996 occurred in mid-December: Hermann's father was released from prison.

8

Friday, October 3
Williamsburg

IT WAS FRIDAY morning and Steve had worked the better part of two days reading about trusts and estates and preparing Professor Siegel's will. In fact, he'd worked nonstop from the moment the professor and Michelle left his office on Tuesday afternoon. He'd even interrupted Mr. Smythe's family visit long enough to get him to approve a fax copy of the draft document. He was finally confident the will was ready to be signed.

At 9:10 a.m., Marjorie put a call through from Professor Siegel. His flight to Israel departed earlier on Saturday than he previously thought. In order to avoid driving to Washington, D.C., early that morning to catch his flight, he wanted to leave Friday afternoon and stay at a hotel near the airport on Friday night. He couldn't do that, though, if he had to drive to Williamsburg to sign his will. Instead, he wanted to sign the will at his house and leave for Washington from there. This would save him over three hours of driving, but it meant Steve had to drive to Tappahannock. They decided to meet at 2:30.

Steve's drive was uneventful. He didn't bother turning on the radio; instead, he ran through the will execution procedure over and over again to make sure he had it down. He also couldn't help but think about Professor Siegel's three friends. Each one stood to inherit half a million dollars, as long as they survived the professor. Why would the professor do that at the expense of his only daughter? He wished he'd asked when he had the chance, as it was too late for those kinds of questions now.

After passing through Tappahannock proper, Steve continued on Route 17, searching for a white mailbox the Professor had described. He spotted it and slowed. The driveway cut through dense woods; the mailbox was the only indication a house was hidden somewhere behind the trees. The only other driveway within a quarter mile in either direction was about twenty-five yards down on the opposite side of the road. There were no woods on that side—only soybean fields and an older but well-kept whitewashed farmhouse set far back from the road. The area seemed like a wonderful place to retire.

Steve turned and drove through the wooded area into a clearing dominated by a large two-story brick Williamsburg colonial on a rise no more than seventy-five yards from the Rappahannock River. The view, even from the driveway, was magnificent, and the breeze felt comfortably cool as it swirled through Steve's car. Three or four large oak trees shaded much of the yard with their swaying green canopies.

Steve parked under one of the trees. Three other cars were already there; he presumed they belonged to the witnesses and the notary public he'd arranged at the last minute. He checked his watch. It was only 2:15, so he was actually a little early. He took his time walking to the front door, enjoying the breeze and the view of the mile-wide Rappahannock River. When he finally made it to the front door, Michelle was there waiting. Although dressed much more casually than when she visited his office with her father, she was no less stunning.

"All the people you wanted are here and waiting," Michelle quipped without bothering to say hello.

"They're early, then," Steve responded, glad that he'd checked his watch. "Perhaps your father will be able to get on his way a little earlier as well."

Michelle held the screen door open only long enough for Steve to grab it and then turned and walked to where her father had assembled the will execution party. Steve followed close on her heels until Michelle entered a room at the end of the hall.

Steve walked in and saw four people, including Professor Siegel, chatting at the far end of the room around a circular conference table. The table sat in front of a giant bay window with a panoramic view of the river. Professor Siegel's desk captured the same view. Large portraits of Michelle and an older woman Steve presumed was Professor Siegel's late wife dominated the wall opposite the bay window. Smaller photographs of both women in various frames adorned the professor's desk. None of the pictures included Professor Siegel.

"Thanks for coming all the way out here, Steve," Professor Siegel said, offering him his hand. "Did you have any trouble finding the place?"

"None at all. In fact, it was a very relaxing drive."

"Good. I hope you don't mind if we get right down to business. I'd like to leave as soon as we're finished."

"Fine with me. This won't take long since you've already seen a fax copy of the will. Do you have any questions about it?"

"None. It's exactly what I want."

"Great. Let's get started then." After the notary public and the witnesses were introduced, Steve produced Professor Siegel's new original will and a step-by-step will execution checklist. He wanted to run the execution ceremony as formally as possible because he feared Michelle would contest the will, given the professor's sizeable bequests to his friends. Having Michelle present made things even dicier. She rarely took her eyes off him, making him feel as if she was trying to cause him to make a mistake. He was glad he'd brought the execution checklist. After carefully going through the preliminary formalities, it came time for the final act.

"Professor Siegel, have you read your will in its entirety?" Steve asked, reading from the checklist.

"I have."

"Does it accurately express your desires as to the disposition of your property upon your death?"

"It does."

"Very well, then. Please sign your will in the presence of the witnesses." All the parties sitting around the conference table had their eyes glued on Professor Siegel's slow-moving hand. He signed his name on the signature line using broad, sweeping strokes befitting his colonial surroundings. The witnesses followed suit and the notary public made the document official.

"I hope you all realize I don't plan on needing this document anytime in the near future," laughed Professor Siegel. "And by the way," he added, his accent a little more pronounced than usual, "I truly appreciate all of you coming here on such short notice."

"Well, that's all then," Steve added. "I appreciate your assistance as well." With that, the group began heading for the door.

"Won't you stay for tea?" Professor Siegel offered. Although they thanked the Professor for his thoughtfulness, none accepted. After a few short goodbyes, only Professor Siegel, Michelle, and Steve remained.

"Steve, you must have a cup of tea and some cheese and crackers before you leave," Professor Siegel insisted.

"That does sound good."

"Be sure he doesn't bill you for the time, Father."

"Michelle! I will not allow you to be rude to our guest." Professor Siegel's voice was firm and in control. Michelle held her ground and didn't offer an apology. Instead, she started toward the parlor, where the tea was waiting along with an assortment of cheese and crackers.

Professor Siegel shook his head. "I'm sorry, Steve," he said, shrugging his shoulders and motioning for him to follow.

"Don't worry about it," Steve said graciously. The two men walked to the parlor behind Michelle, but Professor Siegel stopped at the parlor's entrance.

"Please, make yourself at home, Steve. Unfortunately, though, I've already loaded my car and I've got to be going. Thanks again for driving all the way out here to help me. I must say, Admiral Bancroft was right."

"It was my pleasure. Please have a safe trip to Israel."

"It's not Israel I'm worried about—it's Washington D.C." With that, Professor Siegel turned, kissed Michelle goodbye, and walked out the front door for Washington.

"I trust you'll help yourself to some tea," Michelle said, her invitation devoid of hospitality.

"Thanks," Steve replied, intent on not giving Michelle even a hint that her manner disconcerted him. He started pouring a cup of tea. "May I pour you some?"

"No, thank you."

Steve surmised Michelle's response was more out of habit than sincerity, but it was the first time she had shown any civility toward him. Thinking he had an opening, he tried to leverage it into an explanation for her attitude.

"May I ask you a personal question, Michelle?" Steve placed several pieces of cheese and a couple of wheat crackers onto a small china plate and braced for Michelle's reply. He tried not to look overly eager for her response.

"If you must, but in all honesty, there's little chance I'll answer it."

"I can accept that. How about you let me ask you the question and then you can decide. You obviously weren't pleased with your father visiting my office. May I ask why?"

"Actually, I don't mind answering that question," Michelle said enthusiastically, her voice softening somewhat from its more directive tone of just a moment before. "I hate lawyers. I don't like what you do, I don't like your attitude, and I don't like how you treat the people you are supposed to be helping. You don't know the first thing about my father and me and yet you charge him a thousand dollars to retype a will that was perfectly good before we came to your office. Is that enough, or shall I go on?"

Steve saw humor as his only escape. "No, I think I understand," he replied, as stony-faced as Michelle. "You're not very fond of attorneys."

When Michelle didn't answer, Steve felt the need to say something more to at least feign civility until he could finish his tea and leave. Before he could think of just the right words, the doorbell rang. *Thank God*, he thought to himself. *A way out.*

9

———❧———

STEVE MUNCHED ON a cracker and chased it with a swish of hot tea. Although this was the perfect opportunity to make a gracious exit, he was so hungry he couldn't pass up a quick snack before the two-hour drive back to Williamsburg. When he heard footsteps coming back down the hallway, he took one more sip and set his cup and saucer down on an antique table with a marble top. Michelle reappeared, but not alone.

"Wilhelm, this is my father's attorney, Steve Stilwell."

Wilhelm Strauss entered the parlor as if on cue. He looked fresh from the cover a ski magazine. Tall and muscular, blond hair and blue eyes; even Steve thought he was handsome. No doubt he and Michelle would have gorgeous children.

The two men shook hands and exchanged greetings. Steve shifted back a step while Strauss looked to Michelle for the next move.

"Wilhelm wants to ask me a few questions about our neighborhood. He's German and was referred to my father by the man who built our house. He wanted to talk to my father, but since my father's already gone, I've offered to help."

"That's very nice of you," Steve commented, doubting

Michelle could ever be motivated by kindness alone.

"Would you like a cup of tea and some cheese and crackers, Wilhelm?" Michelle asked.

"I should like that very much. May I help myself?"

"Of course. When you get what you need, we can talk."

After allowing Strauss a short time to stock his plate and pour some tea, Steve reinitiated the conversation. "So, Wilhelm, how long have you been in the United States?"

"Actually, just a few days," Strauss said as he sat down, carefully balancing his cup of steaming tea in one hand and a plate of cheese and crackers in the other. He eased back in the chair and continued, "I have an American business associate who knows I'm looking for a house within a few hours of Washington. He recommended I look in Ta-na … I'm sorry, I can't pronounce the name."

"Tappahannock," Michelle corrected gently. "What is it you're looking for?"

"Well, to tell you the truth," Strauss began after swallowing a bite of cheese-topped cracker, "I really haven't decided yet. I need a house in America where I can stay during my longer business trips. I'd like to be near Washington, though, and I prefer to live by the water. That's why my friend recommended this place."

Strauss leaned forward and looked directly into Michelle's eyes. When she returned his gaze without embarrassment, he smiled approvingly.

"I'm sorry I missed your father. I was looking forward to speaking to a fellow German. Will he be back soon?"

"I'm afraid not. He left just a few minutes before you came by. He's on his way to Israel."

"Will he be back soon, or shall I have to wait until my next visit to meet him?"

"Well, that depends on how long you plan to be here."

"I can only stay a few more days. I take it your father will be gone longer than that?"

"Actually, he'll be gone for at least a month, maybe two. He's visiting family. In fact, I'm joining him in Haifa on Monday."

Steve was amazed at how much information Michelle freely shared with a perfect stranger. But the way she made eye contact with Strauss was not lost on Steve, and he could see he was swiftly becoming a squeaky third wheel. Worse yet, he saw no easy way to extricate himself. All he could do was watch the chemistry between the two grow and hope it did not become too embarrassing.

"Oh, that's too bad," Strauss continued. "I'm afraid I'll have to head back to Washington without seeing him then. I must say that I am very disappointed."

"I don't want you to be disappointed, Wilhelm. Why don't we go out and have dinner and I'll try to answer your questions for you? I'm not my father, but maybe I can help." Michelle closed with a look so seductive that no man on earth could refuse. Steve's eyes widened.

"I'm sure my drive to Washington can wait a few hours," Strauss said coolly, smiling just enough to make Steve think he'd expected the offer. Strauss' subtle arrogance matched Michelle's.

Michelle turned to Steve and pretended to care about him. "Mr. Stilwell, would you like to join us?"

Knowing when an invitation to dinner was really an invitation to leave, Steve couldn't help but play a little.

"I'd love to," he said, pausing just long enough for contempt to register on Michelle's face and disappointment on Strauss', "but I have to be on my way back to Williamsburg. Perhaps some other time." As the color returned to Michelle's cheeks, Steve was delighted to have finally scored a direct hit. "In fact, I need to be heading on my way right now."

"I'm sorry you aren't able to stay," Michelle lied. Then, in the same breath and with a degree of insincere politeness Steve found nauseating, she added, "At least let me show you to the door."

As Steve prepared to leave, he walked over to Strauss and extended his hand. "I hope you enjoy your dinner in Tappahannock, Mr. Strauss."

"Thank you, I'm sure I will."

After the two men shook hands, Steve followed Michelle to the door, leaving Strauss in the parlor. "Goodbye, Mr. Stilwell," Michelle said shallowly, holding the door open for Steve in an all-too-obvious effort to speed his departure.

"Goodbye, Michelle. And be careful."

Steve wasn't sure why he said "be careful." He thought about the comment as he walked to his car. He didn't have any daughters, so it wasn't a hidden paternalistic instinct finding its way to the surface. What it boiled down to was he just didn't like how quickly Michelle had warmed to Strauss. He reached out and opened the door of his faded blue car and slowly climbed inside. "I'm the one who needs to be careful driving this old piece of junk," he mused, as if to resolve the matter once and for all. He tossed his briefcase into the passenger seat and let out a sigh of relief. His first will client was finally behind him.

10

![ornamental divider]

Tuesday, October 14
Düsseldorf

Belmar's investigation into the Weisentrope murder had turned up nothing, and Anja Fordahl's skinhead theory had hit a brick wall. If the skinheads did the killing, they weren't talking about it and that just wasn't their style. Anja wasn't giving up, though. She was young and determined. As far as she was concerned, the skinheads' failure to claim responsibility didn't mean they weren't involved; it only meant she had to dig deeper. But Belmar knew she wouldn't find anything. Her theory looked promising at first because it was all they had. The problem was it just didn't fit the crime scene. Belmar's experience told him this was a professional hit—an execution. All he needed now was the evidence to prove it.

What made the case unnerving was his unusually vivid mental image of what took place. When he closed his eyes, it was almost as if he were there watching the murder go down. He could see the victim walking down the alley until the killer suddenly pistol-whipped him to his knees. Then, while the stunned old man crouched on all fours and tried to recover, the killer shot him in the head from point blank range. It all fit—the bruise on the left side of the forehead and the bullet wound on the top of the skull. Plus, hair samples from the hat found near the body matched the old man's hair.

But his vision didn't stop there. He could picture the killer reaching down and turning over the lifeless body to grab its wallet. Belmar knew that part had to be a ploy. The only fingerprints the lab found on the wallet were the victim's. The common street thugs he usually dealt with weren't that careful or that smart. This was too clean to be a botched robbery. Someone was trying to paint a picture.

Belmar had no idea who that someone could be. As detailed as his vision was, it stopped short of actually identifying the killer. The killer appeared only as a faceless form drifting onto Malpelstrasse and fading off into the city. The harder Belmar focused on the killer's face, the more blurred the image became. If Belmar wanted to put a face on the killer, he'd have to find another way.

Belmar thought he had done just that after reading Frau Hinkle's statement. She was in the right place at the right time and had actually seen the killer. All she had to do was describe the killer's face. But, damn it, she couldn't do it! Her description of a tall blond-haired man fit seven out of ten men in Düsseldorf. The angry look the man gave her made her sure she could identify his face if she saw it again, but she couldn't describe it sufficiently now to get even a rough artist's rendition because his anger was the dominant feature in her memory. Belmar even had Detective Schueller sit with her in the office for three hours looking through photographs, but still she saw nothing. "Don't worry," she said, sounding more like a mother reassuring her child than a crucial witness to a murder. "I'll recognize him when I see him again."

That was where Belmar's case stopped. No matter how hard he and Detective Schueller tried, they couldn't get Frau Hinkle to *see* him again. Belmar stared at the coat rack on the other side of the room. The shrill ring of his telephone made him flinch. He grabbed the receiver and gave a curt "Detective Belmar here."

"Detective Belmar? This is Kommissar Isabel Rotter in Public Relations. There are several reporters here asking for a statement on the murder of Herr Emil Weisentrope. Would you be free now to come down and brief First Chief Inspector Meyer about the case?"

Belmar knew it didn't matter whether he was free or not; First Chief Inspector Meyer was a heavy-hitter. He was always on the firing line with the media and the force was expected to support him by doing whatever he asked. But Belmar was from the old school. He didn't like the press meddling in a case until he had it solved. Reporters rarely made an investigation go any smoother and often their involvement produced just the opposite result.

"I can be there in an hour," Belmar answered. He could hear muffled conversation.

"First Chief Inspector Meyer asked if right away wouldn't be more convenient for you."

"I understand, Kommissar," Belmar said, cursing under his breath. "It'll take me a minute to gather my notes."

"Thank you, Detective Belmar. I'll tell First Chief Inspector Meyer you're on your way."

Belmar knew he was in trouble—he just didn't know how much. He had intentionally kept the case quiet because he thought it would help him catch the killer. Maybe a little too quiet. Although he had passed the details of the murder along to his superiors, he conveniently forgot to mention the victim was a concentration camp survivor. He feared leaking that information to the press would wreak havoc with the investigation. But as he gathered his notes to talk to First Chief Inspector Meyer, he could see another vision taking shape. In this vision, the victim had a face, and the face was *his*. He desperately hoped some reporter hadn't blindsided Meyer about the concentration camp connection. If someone had and Meyer was publicly embarrassed, Belmar knew he was dead.

With notes and notepad in hand, Belmar walked through the detectives' pit and into the outer hallway. Distracted by the verbal thrashing he knew was coming his way, he nearly collided with a mail cart barreling to its next destination. The mail clerk swerved at the last possible second, causing five or six pieces of mail to slide off the cart and land on the floor behind Belmar.

The clerk gave Belmar's retreating form a foul look and picked up the mail. One of the wayward pieces was a manila interoffice envelope from the District Polizei Headquarters. As he picked it up, its flap came open and three color photographs flew out onto the floor. He chased them down and slid them back into the envelope, this time making sure the tie string was fastened securely around the envelope's grommet.

With the exception of the photographs, the mail that fell was addressed to Belmar's detective unit. The mail clerk was just about to stop his cart outside the unit's door when the near-collision occurred. The clerk gathered up the mail, now including the manila envelope with the photographs, and tossed it irreverently into the inbox on the desk just inside the detective unit's door. Then he continued down the hallway to make the rest of his deliveries.

No one was sitting at the duty desk when the mail clerk tossed the mail into the detective unit's inbox. The duty detective, Peter Borman, had stepped out for a smoke, only to return to find the inbox full and the office empty. He grabbed the stack of mail to distribute it to his fellow detectives, but before he could sort even the first piece, the telephone rang.

"Detective Borman."

"Borman, it's Belmar. I'm in PR waiting to see First Chief Inspector Meyer. I need you to go to my office and pull the autopsy from the Weisentrope file and bring it to me right away."

"Where's the file?"

"Should be on my desk. If it's not, it's in the large gray filing cabinet in the active section. Now hurry up. I need that report before I go in to see First Chief Inspector Meyer." Belmar hung up without a thanks or a goodbye.

Borman started toward Belmar's office with the stack of mail from the inbox still in hand. Rather than wasting time walking back to the duty desk, he tossed the mail into Detective Hans Schueller's inbox. He figured Schueller wouldn't mind going through it for him—Schueller owed him anyway. He continued into Belmar's office and found the Weisentrope file sitting on the desk right where Belmar said it would be. Instead of fiddling with the file to try and get the autopsy report out, he grabbed the entire file and hastily left the office in search of Belmar.

Borman was gone for over an hour. He stayed in First Chief Inspector Meyer's office to hear about Belmar's predicament and lend him moral support. They both agreed Meyer must be furious, because although he had ordered Belmar to drop everything and report to his office, he was now making Belmar sweat in the waiting room in anticipation of the meeting. Borman forgot about the mail he tossed in Detective Schueller's inbox. He also forgot about Detective Schueller's field interviews, which would keep Detective Schueller out of the office for the next few days.

11

HAIFA SAT UNDER a cloudless sky. The port city near Israel's northern border with Lebanon glistened in the late morning sun, a stiff breeze delivering the scent of the Mediterranean to thousands of open windows throughout the city. These were the mornings Felix Siegel lived for.

The Professor walked out onto the balcony and stretched his arms above his head. He'd already taken an hour-long walk along the beach and enjoyed several hours of early morning study. He'd devoted his adult life to academia and the incessant pressure to publish brilliant insights into the secret world of nuclear physics. Now, he studied because it set him free.

Yet there was more to his exhilaration than the pure pursuit of knowledge. Just being in Israel thrilled him. He admired Israel's David-like ability to stand alone against seemingly insurmountable odds. Each time its people would rise to the occasion and vanquish yet another would-be oppressor. Israel offered hope when all else seemed lost.

He thought every now and then about immigrating to Israel, but he could not forsake the United States. America opened her doors to him when he was a stateless refugee after the end of World War II. He arrived penniless in New York at the age of nineteen. His mother and father and two younger brothers were dead—victims of the Holocaust. He had survived Auschwitz, he was convinced, only thanks to the outstretched hand of God. That same hand found a Jewish foster family for him in New York City—a wealthy couple in their fifties with no children of their own. They made him their son, tutored him in the ways of America, and sent him to Brown University. Now, thanks to his adoptive parents and the welcome he received in America fifty years ago, he was a world-renowned physicist and retired college professor.

Personal success wasn't the real reason he'd stayed in America; Margaret, his late wife, was. She wasn't like him, ripped from his ancestral home and family by the cruel grip of senseless hate. She had a loving family and childhood friends she would have had to say goodbye to. Of course, she would have gone if he had asked. In fact, she never would have said a word about it because she loved him so. But he knew what it would have done to her, and so he never asked. Even now, three years after her death, he couldn't leave her behind. Yes, America was *their* home.

Professor Siegel caught himself staring out over the Mediterranean and checked his watch. It was nearing 11:00 and he had plans to take Michelle to a local tavern for lunch. They were supposed to meet the tavern's owner, Mr. Leo Berevsky, at 11:30, so he went in from the balcony to call Michelle. As he reached for the telephone, he heard a knock at his door.

"Who is it?"

"It's me."

Professor Siegel unlocked the door and opened it. There stood Michelle, ready to go, wearing a bright yellow, red and white floral designer dress perfectly suited for a warm Mediterranean fall afternoon.

"You look very pretty," Professor Siegel said, forgetting his daughter was no longer a schoolgirl. He leaned forward to kiss her on the cheek. Michelle accepted his greeting, more out of courtesy than affection.

"I'm very excited about you meeting Mr. Berevsky," the Professor said as he pulled the door closed behind him, tugging it once to make sure the latch had caught. "Leo is a good man—a man of character. There aren't many around like him."

Michelle's lips tightened into something short of a smile.

"Not everyone is like your ex-husband, you know."

"Father, do you have to start that again?"

"I just want you to open up again, Michelle. Like you used to before that *man* hurt you. Some of us really do love you, you know."

"I know you do and I'm over him, so let's just change the subject. Okay?"

"You've got to talk about it sometime, Michelle. How can I help you if you won't open up to me?"

"Then why is it you never opened up to me about your past?"

"That's different. I kept things to myself to protect you from pain."

"Well, maybe I'm doing the same thing."

As they walked past Michelle's room on their way to the elevator, Michelle heard the telephone in her room ringing. She seized the opportunity to change the subject.

"It's my phone," Michelle said, digging into her purse. "I promise I'll only be a minute." She pulled her room key from her purse and opened the door. The phone was still ringing, so she hurried around the bed to answer it. Professor Siegel didn't enter the room, but propped the door open to hold Michelle to her word about the brevity of the call.

"Hello," Michelle said. "Yes, this is she …. Yes …. Yes …. I understand. Goodbye." She hung up and walked back to where her father waited.

"Who was that?"

"It was nothing, Father. Just some information on the dry

cleaning service," Michelle replied, avoiding her father's eyes. The two walked to the elevator and rode to the lobby in stranger-like silence, neither one wanting to pick up the discussion where it had left off.

"So, are you at all looking forward to lunch with Mr. Berevsky? You know he fought with the Soviet Army in World War II and for Israel's independence in 1948. He will bring Israel's history to life for you." Professor Siegel hoped Berevsky's exploits would extract some emotion or response from his daughter. She seemed melancholy, even more so than usual. When they reached the parking garage entrance, he held the glass door open for her and they headed in the general direction of his rental car.

"I know he will," Michelle said, unconvinced. "But I'm not sure I'll have anything to say to him."

"You needn't say anything, Michelle. Just listen. He's such a colorful conversationalist; you'll soon be chatting away like old friends."

Professor Siegel reached into his pocket and pulled out his keys. He raised his right hand and pointed to a yellow Mercedes parked in the far corner of the garage. "There's the car over there."

As they started walking toward it, Michelle began rooting through her purse. "Oh dear, Father. I've forgotten my passport and my traveler's checks. You must let me run back to get them. I want to do some shopping after lunch."

"I'll loan you the money. If you go back now, we'll be late." The force of his voice made it clear he was displeased.

"You go ahead and get the car and meet me in front of the main entrance. I'll be there by the time you get there. Besides, what else does Mr. Berevsky have to do?" Michelle gave him a diminutive smile. She knew he would give in; he always did.

"Hurry up, then. We'll not be rude to our host."

Michelle's smile widened as she turned and trotted toward the lobby. Professor Siegel watched until she disappeared through the glass door and then made his way to the car. He shook his head, wondering if he was making any progress with her. Unlocking the door, he climbed into the driver's seat, fastened his seatbelt, and checked his watch. It was 11:16 a.m. There was no way they would make it to Leo Berevsky's on time, and he didn't even have a telephone to call and tell him they would be late. He hated making friends wait. He put the key into the ignition and turned.

The explosion shattered the glass door leading to the hotel lobby and caused passersby within a block of the hotel to run for cover. The fireball originating from under Professor Siegel's seat consumed what was left of the Mercedes in seconds. Professor Siegel died instantly.

Inside the hotel, Michelle was hurrying to the elevator when the explosion rocked the lobby. She stood perfectly still, wondering what had just happened. She could hear a child crying and a woman screaming for help near the door to the garage. *THE GARAGE!* The thought sucked the air from her lungs, and she gasped. She ran back through the lobby toward the garage entrance. Through what used to be the glass door, she could see flames shooting out of the area where her father's car was parked. She rushed to the door and tried to open it, but the doorframe was bent and the glass so thick on the floor that she couldn't get it open. Suddenly a man restrained her from behind.

"I'm sorry, Miss, but you can't go out there," he said with a British accent as he rather roughly moved her out of the immediate vicinity of the door.

"But my father's out there."

"I'm sorry, Miss, but I'm sure he's all right." After hearing about her father, the man's movements became gentler but nonetheless direct.

Michelle looked over her shoulder as she moved away from the door. When she finally lost sight of the flames at the back of the garage, she dropped to her knees and cried.

* * *

STRAUSS HEARD THE explosion a full three blocks away in a small café just down the street from the garage. The café's outdoor seating, umbrellas for protection from the intense Mediterranean sun, and unobstructed view of ground zero made it the ideal place to watch the events unfold. Strauss camped under one of the café's blue and white umbrellas around 9:00 a.m. with a newspaper and an occasional cup of bold Israeli coffee. Siegel used his car every day around lunchtime, so Strauss had not expected to wait any longer than noon. The loud blast at 11:15 confirmed he'd done his homework well.

As others scurried to take cover or get a better look at the source of the explosion, Strauss slowly finished his last cup of coffee and left a generous tip for the waiter. He folded his paper under his arm and walked down the street away from the garage and the black smoke billowing from its side. Already there were sirens and fire trucks converging on the scene and he didn't want to be caught in the melee that was sure to follow. When he reached a pay phone on Ben Gurion Avenue, he inserted a prepaid phone card and dialed a number from memory. He let the phone ring once and hung up. After repeating the process, he returned the card to his wallet and continued toward his hotel.

* * *

HERMANN BORNE SAT alone in his study. Through a glass partition, from his chair in front of his computer, he could see his father sitting silently in his wheelchair, staring out the window overlooking Berlin. His father sat there, day after day, motionless, speechless, seemingly lifeless. He had not spoken a word since his arrival last December, yet his presence was deafening. It resonated throughout the apartment. It shook Hermann to his very inner being. It drove Sonja to take Peter and leave her husband in May. She didn't ask for a divorce, but she said she could no longer handle the constant, piercing, silent gaze of Hermann's father in the aftermath of Erwin's death. She took refuge at the family's summer estate on the southern coast of France. Even there she could ever so faintly hear the presence of Hermann's father, but it was sufficiently muted to allow her life to go on.

Hermann couldn't run away. He had done that for far too long. It began when he stopped visiting his father in prison. His mother didn't force him to go because she thought the phase would pass, but it never did. In fact, the more visits Hermann missed, the easier it became to keep on missing them. His father wrote him and asked him why he never came anymore, but Hermann didn't respond. His motives were too complex for his teenage mind to sort out. The obvious reason was Hermann's anger at his father for not being available to do things with him or to teach him what he needed to know to be a man. But lots of boys had that same problem; the war had decimated Germany's adult male population. Like most of the other boys, Hermann could have dealt with his father's death, but his father didn't die.

It really came down to shame. Hermann was deeply ashamed his father was in prison. Why he was there didn't matter; as a teenager, just acknowledging his father was in prison invited embarrassment and condemnation from his peers. So Hermann cut his father out of his life, expunging the word "father" from his vocabulary and changing the subject whenever a discussion headed in that direction. Hermann convinced himself he didn't love, need, or want his father, never thinking or caring that his father might love, need, or want him.

The first chink in Hermann's armor appeared when his mother died. Her death forced Hermann to think of his father, alone and in prison, with his final meaningful connection to the outside world now gone forever. But the chasm Hermann welcomed as a teen now served as a curse, preventing rapprochement. He considered visiting his father, but couldn't figure out how to bridge the years of neglect and separation. So he didn't visit him. It was easier that way.

As Hermann's sons grew, the chink in his armor widened. His boys enriched every aspect of his life. He worked harder because they benefitted from the fruits of his labor. He loved his wife more because doing so gave the boys a more stable family. They simply made life worth living. Over time, Hermann came to realize he had deprived his father of that same sense of parental fulfillment by severing their relationship. The realization transformed Hermann's shame into guilt, a guilt Erwin's death and the disintegration of Hermann's family distorted in intensity beyond the man's ability to deal with it.

As the time of his father's release from prison drew near, Hermann saw the event as the bridge he had been searching for, finally allowing him to reconnect with his father and put Erwin's death behind him. Against Sonja's better judgment, Hermann brought his father home to live with his family. He told Sonja his father had nowhere else to go, so what choice did he have? What Hermann didn't anticipate, though, was his father's inability to reciprocate emotionally after so many years of incarceration and neglect. Instead of healing, Hermann's father brought misery and pain, his presence a constant reminder of Hermann's failings as a son and father. He had failed to protect Erwin and he could not prevent Sonja and Peter's departure. Reeling mentally and emotionally, Hermann rationalized that if he could restore his relationship with his father, all would return to normal. All he had to do, he reasoned, was prove to his father he was worthy of admiration. Then his father would have no choice but to respond.

Hermann looked away from his father and turned his attention to his computer screen. Nowadays he spent hours on end waiting for progress reports. Here it was October 14, and he hadn't heard anything. He was beginning to think something had gone wrong and was about to pull up the Reuters newswires when the telephone rang. He waited for a second ring, but none came. The caller had obviously hung up. Then a minute or so later, the telephone rang once more. Again Hermann waited for a second ring. None came. It was finished. Hermann rocked back in his chair and smiled. For a brief moment, he forgot about Sonja and Peter in France. He sensed the scales finally returning to balance.

Hermann clasped his hands behind his head and began to pivot slowly until he could once again see his father staring out the window. His visions of balance evaporated. The sight of his father, sitting rock-like and silent, rekindled his anger. No, retribution was not complete; perhaps it never would be. But Hermann had to make those who had done this to him and his family pay. He turned back toward his computer screen. It was time to log on to the Web. There was yet one more assignment to complete.

12

Thursday, October 16
Williamsburg

"MR. STILWELL," MARJORIE announced over the office intercom.

"Yes, Marjorie," Steve answered as he looked up from the will he was proofing for a client coming in later in the day.

"There's a Mrs. ... excuse me, a *Ms*. Michelle Siegel here to see you. I tried to get her to schedule an appointment, but she insists it's an emergency. Are you able to see her?"

Steve could tell by Marjorie's voice that she had done all she could, but he knew she was no match for Michelle. Michelle would insist on having her way. She was the type who believed appointments were for *other* people. Besides, he was tired of reviewing the will and could afford to take a short break. And he was curious to see what she wanted.

"Go ahead and send her in."

"Very well, Mr. Stilwell."

When Michelle walked in, Steve stepped around his desk to greet her. He was prepared to give her a speech telling her he was her father's attorney and he had to be careful about conflicts of interest, but as he drew closer Michelle's face told him something was wrong. She didn't have the same fight in her eyes he'd seen before. She seemed subdued.

"Hello, Ms. Siegel," Steve said, saving the lecture for later. "What brings you back to Williamsburg so soon?"

"My father's dead, Mr. Stilwell, and I need to know if his will contains any special instructions that I have to act on right away." Michelle spoke dispassionately, as if negotiating a real estate deal.

"My God, Ms. Siegel, I'm so sorry. May I ask what happened?"

"Do you mind if I sit down first?"

"Of course not; please sit down. I'm sorry for inquiring so quickly, but I'm so shocked. Can I get you a Perrier?"

"I'd like that very much," Michelle said with just a hint of graciousness as she sat down. Steve picked up the telephone and pressed the intercom button. "Marjorie, would you please bring a Perrier for Ms. Siegel, with a twist of lime." Steve hung up the telephone and returned his attention to Michelle. "After your last visit we stocked up on limes," Steve remarked clumsily. Michelle was unimpressed. She pulled her hair back off her shoulders and gripped the arms of her chair. She looked tired, very tired.

Marjorie entered Steve's office and set a tray with a bottle of Perrier, a frosted glass, and a slice of lime on the table next to Michelle. "May I pour it for you, Ms. Siegel?"

"Oh, no thank you. This will be fine."

"Thanks, Marjorie," Steve said when Marjorie looked at him to see if there were any additional instructions. Receiving none, she left Steve's office, closing the door behind her.

"My father was killed two days ago by a car bomb." Michelle took a deep breath. "I buried him in Israel yesterday, and I'm back to arrange a memorial. I need to know if his will contains any special instructions."

"Please forgive me, but you'll have to give me a minute,"

Steve said, unable to get any other words to come out. "I'm still so shocked. Do they know who did it?"

"A Palestinian group claimed responsibility. Now, please, Mr. Stilwell, can we get to the will? I've got a lot to do and not much time to do it."

"Of course. But I hope you'll understand that before I can disclose the contents of your father's will, I'll have to have some proof of his death. Do you have a death certificate or something else issued by the Israeli government?" Recalling the fireworks at their first meeting, Steve braced himself for Michelle's response.

Michelle opened her purse and pulled out a folded newspaper clipping. "I knew you'd need something like that. Israel wanted to send the death certificate through diplomatic channels, so I may not have it for a few days. Please tell me this article gives you what you need."

Steve leaned over his desk and took the article from Michelle's outstretched hand. It was from the front page of the *Jerusalem Times* for Wednesday, October 15. The headlines read, "American College Professor Killed in Haifa Car Bombing." Steve read the first paragraph of the article as Michelle sat back in her chair.

"Yesterday, world renowned physicist Felix Siegel was killed when a bomb exploded in his car as he prepared to leave his Haifa hotel for a luncheon engagement." Next to the article was a picture of the professor smiling broadly as he did when Steve first met him less than a month ago. Steve couldn't believe his first will client was already dead.

"This will do." Steve set the article down and again pressed the intercom button. "Marjorie, would you bring Mr. Siegel's will into my office?"

"Yes, Mr. Stilwell."

Steve didn't know Michelle, so he didn't know whether she wanted to talk about what happened or whether she just wanted to get her business done and leave. He decided to err on the side of conversation, as he personally didn't like extended periods of silence, especially during times of sadness. He made an effort to keep the dialogue going as he waited for Marjorie to bring in the will.

"Did this Palestinian group give any reason for targeting your father?"

"I have no idea," Michelle replied, not bothering to make eye contact, "and frankly, why they did it doesn't matter. All I know is my father is dead."

Steve got the message loud and clear. If Michelle desired to talk about what happened, it was either the wrong time or he was the wrong person. Fortunately, before any silence had a chance to make the situation even more uncomfortable, Marjorie arrived with Professor Siegel's will.

"Thanks, Marjorie. Would you also please make me a copy of this?" Steve handed her the article.

"That's your copy," Michelle said.

"I'll take that back then." Marjorie handed him the article again and turned to leave.

"Marjorie, can I ask you to stay for a minute? We need to open Professor Siegel's will. Would you grab your journal and serve as a witness?" Propping his elbows on his desk, Steve held the will with both hands while waiting for Marjorie's return. She came back armed with a green legal-sized journal and sat down in the large leather chair next to Michelle.

"Okay. It's 10:45 a.m. on Thursday, October 16, 1997. Present are Ms. Michelle Siegel, daughter of the decedent, Professor Felix Siegel; Ms. Marjorie Weldman, paralegal; and Steven J. Stilwell, executor. This is the first reading of the will of Professor Felix Siegel, who died in Israel on October 14, 1997." Marjorie recorded Steve's recitations in the journal as he removed the will from the folder and began to peruse the document.

"As I remember, Ms. Siegel, your father did have some specific burial instructions. I believe he desired to be buried in New York." Steve scanned the will, looking for the relevant paragraph while Michelle stared at the purse in her lap.

"Yes," he continued, "your father wanted to be buried in the cemetery used by Temple Beth Israel in Great Neck, Long Island. I take it you're familiar with that synagogue?"

"Yes, of course, but he had to be buried in Israel. That's why I want a memorial in New York. Is there anything else?"

"No, that's it."

"Then is there any reason why you can't go over the rest of the will now? I'm his only surviving family, you know."

"Let me take a look at the rest of the document before I answer that." Although Steve had a vague recollection of the will's provisions, he couldn't remember any of the specific bequests. After rereading the dispositions, though, he nodded. "I don't see any reason why we can't do this now. Perhaps you can help me locate the other individuals named in the will."

"I'll do what I can."

"Okay, then, it's fairly simple." Steve marked the applicable provision with his finger. "Mr. Tadeusz Zalinsky, Mr. Teodor Rudnik, and Mr. Emil Weisentrope each receive five hundred thousand dollars, and Temple Beth Israel receives two hundred fifty thousand dollars. You get everything else in your father's estate."

"Does each man get five hundred thousand or do they get five hundred thousand in total?"

"They each get five hundred thousand." Steve looked up to see Michelle's reaction. There was none; only a follow-on question as she continued with her eyes locked on her purse.

"What happens if any of the men died before my father?"

"Then you get his five hundred thousand dollar share."

"I guess you've told me what I need to know," Michelle said as she gathered her things to leave. "I won't take up any more of your time."

"Could I ask you to stay just a minute more?" Michelle's desire for a quick exit after learning the terms of the will surprised Steve. Suddenly she didn't seem the grieving daughter.

"What is it you need?" Michelle replied, easing back into her chair, apparently realizing her attempted departure had been too abrupt, considering the circumstances.

"Can you tell me who the men in your father's will are and where I can find them?"

"I believe they're his friends from the war, although I've only met one of them—Mr. Weisentrope." Michelle glared at her purse again and began to repeatedly buckle and unbuckle its strap. "I think he lives in Germany, although the name of the city escapes me. I don't know where the others are. Strange, isn't it? My father leaves these men one-and-a-half million dollars and I don't even know them."

"It does seem a little odd. Didn't he ever talk about them?"

"My father rarely talked about the war, Mr. Stilwell. He was a Jew at Auschwitz. He didn't have a lot of fond memories."

"I'm sorry. I wasn't trying to be insensitive. Anyway, this is the wrong time to be asking you these questions. You've got a lot of things you need to take care of. Marjorie will give you a sheet of dos and don'ts that will help us probate your father's will as quickly as possible. Also, if you could check at home to see if you have the addresses and phone numbers for your father's friends, I'd really appreciate it."

"He has an address book in his desk at home. I'm sure it'll have what you need. I'll check it tonight and fax it to you tomorrow." Michelle got up and started to make her way to the door.

"Please call if you have any questions at all," Steve said, following after Michelle. She was already opening the door to the outside. She turned her head not quite far enough to see Steve, but far enough to acknowledge that she'd heard what he'd said.

"I will," she replied. With that, she was out the door and on her way.

"That is one rude woman," Marjorie said as she walked back into Steve's office to retrieve Professor Siegel's will. "She never said thank you. Did you notice that?"

"I'm not sure she knows how," Steve said as he walked toward his chair. "But in her defense, her father was just blown up in a terrorist attack. She's got to be under some terrible stress. I can't believe she actually had the presence of mind to check to see if her father left any burial instructions in his will." Steve sat down and began to shuffle some papers on his desk. Then he remembered he had to finish proofing a will for a signing ceremony later in the day.

"Marjorie, let's go ahead and establish a probate file for Professor Siegel's estate. Also, would you remind me to follow up with Ms. Siegel tomorrow if she hasn't called by fourteen hundred, excuse me, two o'clock?"

"Aye, aye, Captain," Marjorie said as she saluted and started to leave the office. "Once a Navy man, always a Navy man." Marjorie disappeared into the reception area and Steve got back to work. He only had a couple hours left to prepare for his afternoon appointments.

13

———∿∿———

Friday, October 17
Williamsburg

THE TELEPHONE RANG and Marjorie answered after the first full ring. Steve tried to listen from his desk, hoping the caller was Michelle. It was already 10:45 and he hadn't received her fax. He knew she had more important things to do than provide him with a few telephone numbers and addresses. Still, he predicted she'd call soon. She seemed like the type who wanted to know how much money she had coming and when she would get it. Perhaps it was a harsh and needlessly judgmental assessment, but he knew it was true. Plus, he was curious as to Professor Siegel's relationship with his three friends. What at first seemed like nothing more than a routine will had become quite intriguing.

"Mr. Stilwell," Marjorie called over the intercom, "it's Ms. Siegel on line one."

"I knew it," Steve said, half out loud. "She couldn't wait until after the memorial." He put a cap on his cynicism in favor of a more lawyerly demeanor. "Hello, this is Steve Stilwell."

"Hello, Mr. Stilwell. It's Michelle Siegel."

"Yes, Ms. Siegel."

"I've got the information you requested. Would you like me to read it to you now or wait until I can fax it?"

Steve was surprised by Michelle's considerate approach. He felt bad about thinking she was acting only out of greed.

"Sure, go ahead and read it. I've got a pen and I'm ready to copy."

"Okay," Michelle began. "The first individual is Teodor Rudnik. He lives on Nudderth Street in Danbury, London. Did you get that?"

"Got it. Go ahead."

"The next man is Tadeusz Zalinsky. He's listed on Buttermill Road in Cleveland, Ohio." Michelle provided telephone numbers for both men.

"Got it," Steve confirmed without waiting to be asked.

"The last man is Emil Weisentrope. I've got an address for him, but no phone number. Is that all right?"

"That's fine. Just give me what you've got."

"Okay. Mr. Weisentrope's address is Apartment 4C, 13-281 Tabelstrasse, Düsseldorf, Germany. That's it."

"Great. I'll try contacting these men today."

"Steve, can I ask you a quick question?"

"Of course," Steve replied, surprised by Michelle's familiarity. "What is it you need?"

"How long will it take to do what you need to do with the will?"

"That's hard to say. It'll depend on how easy it is to track down these men and liquidate your father's estate. I'd say at least six months, but more likely it'll be a year before we can wrap up everything completely."

"You've got to be kidding me! What could possibly take so long?"

"Well, we've got to probate the estate. That requires me to go to court to get the court to approve the dispositions I make under your father's will. Anything you do in court simply takes time."

"Are you telling me I've got to wait a year before I can get anything out of this?" Michelle's question sounded more like an indictment than an interrogatory.

"No, but you'll have to wait that long to get everything you've got coming to you under the estate. Let me try to explain. Your father left your interest in the form of a remainder. That is, he gave you everything he didn't give to someone else. So in order to determine exactly what you get, I have to inventory everything your father owned, pay all the expenses of the estate, make the dispositions to the other beneficiaries, and then give you the rest. It simply takes time to do all that."

"When will you start?"

"Like I said, I'll start contacting the other beneficiaries today."

Although this was the Michelle Steve expected, he was still amazed at her callous attitude. Her father was buried less than seventy-two hours ago and all she could think about was how quickly she could get her hands on her share of his estate. There was no sadness in her voice and no sense of loss—only pure, unadulterated greed. It made Steve want to drag out the probate process just to spite her. But that would mean putting up with her longer than necessary, and no way did he want that.

"Ms. Siegel, I promise you, I'll move on it as quickly as possible, and I'll keep you informed on where we are."

"Look, Steve. I just want this whole thing done so I can move on with my life."

"I think we're set then," Steve said, trying to terminate the call. "You can expect to hear from me again next week."

"Thank you, Mr. Stilwell," Michelle said, her voice softer. "Goodbye."

Steve hung up the phone. *What a strange woman.* His thoughts drifted to his own family. He hoped his two sons would at least pretend to mourn his death. Plus, there was damned little money for them to be concerned about.

Michelle slowly hung up the telephone in her hotel room. Dealing with the police in Israel, returning to the United States, making the memorial arrangements and directing the resolution of her father's estate had kept her too busy to think about what had happened. Now, just a couple of hours before the memorial, she had her first opportunity to really think about her father's death. She sunk back into a deep crevasse in the hotel chair's plush cushions and gazed out the window, not looking at anything in particular. Her father was really gone. Tears began to well up in her eyes. She would be strong for the memorial; people expected that. For now, though, she was by herself. She could picture her father walking to the car in the hotel parking garage. She could almost hear him telling her to hurry up so they wouldn't be late for lunch. Now she realized she'd never hear her father's gentle voice again. For the second time in a week, Michelle Siegel cried.

14

***

Saturday, October 18
Berlin, Germany

THE SETTING SEEMED better suited to an impressionist's canvas than a clandestine meeting. A solitary gray concrete park bench stood guard on a grassy knoll overlooking the lake. The nearly fluorescent yellow foliage of a large elm tree swayed slowly over the bench, with the sounds of the not-so-distant Berlin congestion drowned out by the back and forth *whoosh* of the tree's dying leaves. There were only a few short hours of daylight left, and the ducks in the water joined up in little formations near the reflection of the sun to retire to some safe harbor at the end of a long day.

With military precision, two figures simultaneously appeared at opposite ends of the lake. Both figures' gaits were out of step with their surroundings. They walked with determination, with boldness, with purpose, the synchronized *click, click, click* of their heels on the paved walkway echoing around the lake. Gradually the sound became more pronounced.

The first figure left the pavement and walked on the grass

toward the bench. He wore a gray business suit, only slightly darker than the bench itself. He also wore a gray hat with a black band just above the brim. It marked him as one of an older generation, at the pinnacle of his power, but soon ready to turn that power over to some young protégé with new ideas—ideas he could never embrace. But for now, the power was his. When he got to the bench, he sat down and crossed his legs. He didn't look at the other figure approaching him. There would be time for that in a moment. Now, even if just for a few seconds, he intended to enjoy the view.

The second figure left the walkway less than a minute after the first. He, too, climbed the grassy knoll toward the bench. He dressed casually: a green windbreaker, a button-down shirt, blue slacks, and well-polished wingtip shoes. His neatly parted hair, heavily greased so that every hair remained firmly in place, also marked him as a man in his prime, but his power was not nearly as apparent. He approached the bench and sat down a comfortable distance from his counterpart.

Neither man said a word or looked at the other. They were like strangers—strangers who knew each other all too well. The man in the gray suit reached into his suit coat and pulled out a package of American cigarettes. Digging into his pants pocket, he retrieved a silver and gold lighter and lit a cigarette, taking a deep drag as he flipped the lighter closed and returned it to his pocket. He tilted his head back as if to better appreciate the speckled sunlight through the elm tree, but instead let a long, steady column of smoke escape from his lips. He spoke to the man in the windbreaker without looking at him.

"How are you, Hermann?"

Hermann Borne didn't know how to respond. He wasn't in the mood for conversation, yet this was perhaps his oldest and dearest friend. He was one of the Five. Hermann knew he needed to speak. "These are difficult times, Werner." Werner Klecken nodded and took another guttural drag on his cigarette.

"Tell me, Werner, what were you able to do for our man in Damascus?" The conversation was slow and deliberate. A chess game between two masters, each phrase calculated to evoke the desired response.

"These things take time, Hermann, these things take time."

"How much time?" Hermann asked, now staring at the tree line on the other side of the lake.

"Time, Hermann. My guess is a week to ten days." The extended silence after his response told him Hermann desired further explanation. "My men are good, Hermann. I know them personally from my days in the Foreign Ministry. They were on my staff in Amman. Bidel is from the East. He did work for the Soviets for twenty years. He is good, Hermann. He's the best. When Bidel is done, your man will have a new life. No one will question his documents."

Hermann sat silently, staring across the lake. Finally, he spoke. "Do the others know?"

"They know," Werner replied, "and they support you." Werner made an effort to change the direction of the conversation. He noticed a haggardness in Hermann he had not seen before.

"How is your father, Hermann?" Again, silence followed as Hermann searched for a suitable answer. Dealing with his father was an intensely personal responsibility. Still, the Five remained loyal to him, so he felt he owed them an explanation, however limited. Once he began to speak, much more came out than he intended.

"He hasn't spoken a word since he arrived last December," Hermann said in a voice so quiet and filled with melancholy Werner had to strain to hear it. "He just sits there, hour after hour, day after day, looking out the window." Hermann shifted his weight to his right side, away from Werner. His eyes remained fixed on some vague point across the lake. He continued after a moment, this time without any instigation, "I know he hears me. The doctors say he's alert and understands everything I say. He can get out of his wheelchair and walk short distances, but I've never seen him do it. Once he gets up in the morning, he motions for his attendant to wheel him in front of the window, and he just sits there. Every time I walk into the room, he's there. It's starting to haunt me."

"Why don't you put him in a home, Hermann?" Werner spoke softly and with the compassion of an old friend. "There are suitable places, good places. They can care for your father. It will be better for both of you."

"I can never send him away again. He was gone for fifty years, for God's sake!" Hermann clenched his fists and, for the first time, turned his head and looked directly into Werner's eyes. "I can't … I won't just throw him away!"

"I wasn't suggesting—"

"Yes you were, Werner. Yes you were." Hermann's eyes were wild. He glared at Werner even after he stopped speaking. Werner turned his head away, but continued to try to reach Hermann. He could see the man was nearing the edge.

"What about your wife, Hermann, and your son? Don't you want them to come back? And what about you? You can't keep going on like this."

Werner's reference to Sonja and Peter filled Hermann with rage. He slammed his open hand on the bench and let loose an impassioned "Enough!" startling even the pigeons pecking near the bench. "Can't you see it, Werner? My father was robbed of his life fifty years ago by some … Jews! They took his life away. They took him from my mother. They took him from *me*! How can I let this go? I turned my back on it for fifty years. FIFTY YEARS!" Hermann slammed his hand on the bench again and continued to glare intensely at Werner. "Until those bastard Jews pay, how can you ask me about my family? *They* ruined my family!"

"Does your father even know what you're doing for him?"

"I'm not doing it for him, Werner, can't you see? I'm doing it because it's the right thing to do for my family." Hermann turned his head and began to look back over the lake. His voice mellowed ever so slightly. "I should have done it twenty-five years ago."

"So what happens when it's over, Hermann? Do you think killing a few old Jews is going to make your father talk or bring your wife and son back?"

"Since when do you care about a few old Jews?"

"I don't; you know that. It's you and your family I'm worried about. I want you sharp again, Hermann. Like in the old days. Don't you remember all those Thursday night meetings?"

"I remember."

"Do you, Hermann? Do you really?"

"I said I remember."

"Well, I remember, too. And so do Horst, Henschel, and Felder. Thirty-five years ago, we took a pledge to the Five—to us, Hermann—and to Germany. We've never forgotten that, or what our fathers did during the war."

"What is it you want, Werner? Do you want out? Is that what you want?"

"No. We made a commitment and we're in. What I want is your word, Hermann."

"What are you saying?"

"I want you to promise me that when this is over, you'll get your father professional help, even if that means moving him out of your flat."

"And if I don't?"

"I want your word that you will. I won't take no for an answer."

Hermann didn't respond immediately. He didn't want to admit a problem existed, let alone one he was incapable of solving himself. That would mean admitting weakness, or even worse, defeat. He considered saying he would get his father help without really intending to do so, but he couldn't do that to the Five. He valued their trust, so he thought long and hard before he spoke. Werner remained quiet as well. After several minutes of soul searching, Hermann finally replied, "All right, Werner. You have my word."

Werner smiled and leaned over toward Hermann. He put his hand on his friend's shoulder and then patted him on the back as if he had just scored the winning goal. "That's good, Hermann. That's good. Now we can finish our business."

Hermann didn't return the smile or the gesture. He was ready for the conversation to move on.

"What do we have left, Hermann?"

"One more. But we can't begin work until Strauss' papers are complete."

"They'll be finished soon enough. By the way, where is the last one?"

"In America."

"Have you given Strauss the assignment yet?"

"No, and I won't until he's ready to go. I don't want to risk something going wrong, something that might tip off the old Jew."

"Good then," Werner replied. "By the way, when you make the assignment, use the same contact as before." Werner flicked what was left of his cigarette onto the grass. Then he reached into his suit coat and pulled out the pack for another. "I've got to be going now. You know how to get a hold of me."

Hermann nodded.

Werner stood up slowly. "Goodbye, Hermann." When he didn't get a reply, he looked down at Hermann, still sitting on the bench and gazing over the lake, already lost in thought. It would do him no good to try and elicit a farewell from his friend.

Werner pulled the silver and gold lighter from his pants pocket and lit the new cigarette now dangling from his mouth. He inhaled deeply and looked back at Hermann one more time. He wasn't sure how much longer Hermann could hang on. He tried to convince himself that once the last job was done, Hermann would return to normal. Seeing him sitting so statuesque on the park bench made that difficult to believe.

Deciding he could wait no longer for a goodbye, Werner retraced his steps down the hill toward the pavement. Soon the *click, click, click* of Werner's heals faded away.

Hermann didn't move; he couldn't move. He was heavy with hatred—hatred he could not control. He remained on the park bench, motionless, even as the sun went down. Only when a light came on, illuminating the path near him, did he take notice of his surroundings. He hadn't even realized Werner was gone. The air was humid and held a bit of a fall chill. He got up and began to walk back the same way he came. This time there was no military precision. Instead, he walked slowly around the lake until he disappeared into the darkness.

15

Monday, October 20
Düsseldorf, Germany

Detective Hans Schueller walked into his office at 5:30 on Monday morning. "*Guten Morgen*, Max," he said to the night shift Duty Detective.

"*Guten Morgen*, Hans," Max replied. Max looked as though he'd had a rough night, judging from the state of his desk. Papers were strewn all over, one of his drawers was open about four inches, and three or four half-filled Styrofoam coffee cups sat abandoned on the edges. Even his computer's screen saver looked worn out, with the many speckles of fast-moving light appearing much duller than usual. Yet all of this looked good compared to Max himself. His medium-length and slightly greasy brown hair was matted back on his head from his repeatedly running his fingers through it from front to back. His shirttail flapped freely behind him, and he desperately needed a shave. Schueller felt fortunate he had not drawn duty that night, given the visible toll it had taken on Max.

"Looks like you had a busy night, Max."

"Not so bad," Max replied, sounding unconcerned.

Schueller grabbed his empty coffee mug as he walked by his desk, stopping only when he stood directly in front of the coffee maker. On the bottom of the coffeepot was burned and blackened sludge—the remains of Max's last pot of coffee. Schueller rolled his eyes in frustration. He came in early every morning to stay caught up and organize his work for the day. He hated it when he had to devote his most productive hours to cleaning up after someone else's carelessness. Even more disconcerting: this was not Max's first run-in with stupidity.

"Come on, Max. It looks like you had a real rough one. What happened?"

"Actually, nothing. I didn't get a single call."

"So what the hell have you been working on all night?"

"I've got to get a report out on the Bauer case. Belmar wants it by five this afternoon. I thought it'd be a quick job, so I saved it until last night. Turns out it wasn't so quick." Max forced a fake smile.

"You need some help?" Schueller hoped Max would say no. The office worked as a team and Schueller was a team player, meaning he often put in some serious personal time. Today, though, he wasn't in the mood.

"I might just take you up on that," Max replied, much to Schueller's chagrin. "But I'm not quite ready for it yet. If I need a push to get this thing done, though, I'll ask you to lend me a hand."

"You got a deal," Schueller answered. He couldn't help smiling. Now, even cleaning the coffeepot didn't seem so bad.

Schueller worked on the pot in the sink next to the coffee maker. After about five minutes of determined scrubbing, polishing, and drying, the coffeepot met even his high standards. He filled it with water and began making a fresh pot. Once the brew was in progress, he returned to his seat to get the day underway.

He turned on his computer and logged in to the system. The

monitor displayed a calendar and a graphic depiction of an old-fashioned alarm clock. The clock showed it was already 5:50 and he had yet to complete a single task. He could feel his body temperature rising. He had to get back on track, especially after a couple of days out of the office. Besides, Belmar would arrive in half an hour and he wanted to be caught up in the event Belmar threw any new work his way.

He began going through the mail in his inbox. Within fifteen minutes, he had worked his way down to a manila interoffice mail envelope lying face down. He started to reach for it, but as he did, his eye caught his empty coffee cup and he realized he was working without his mandatory shot of morning caffeine. With a smooth motion akin to that of a man feigning an itch after being rebuffed in an attempt to shake someone's hand, he veered his outstretched arm from his inbox to his coffee cup. He walked over to the coffee maker and poured himself a jet-black cup. He added a pack of non-dairy creamer, stirred the concoction, and returned to his seat. Just as he sat down, Belmar walked in.

"*Guten Morgen*," Belmar said as he strode back toward his office.

"*Guten Morgen*," Max and Detective Schueller replied in succession. When Belmar reached his office door, he stopped and turned toward Max.

"How's the Bauer report coming, Max?"

"Fine," Max exaggerated. "I'll have it to you later today."

"Good," Belmar answered as he turned and vanished into his office.

With Belmar settled in, Schueller took a sip of his coffee and grabbed the manila envelope in his inbox. As he began to open it, his telephone rang. He picked up the receiver and wedged it between his ear and shoulder, freeing his hands to open the envelope while he talked.

"*Guten Morgen*. Detective Schueller speaking." He unfastened the envelope's tie string as he spoke and removed some pictures and a typewritten cover sheet.

"Hans, it's me." It was Detective Schueller's wife. "I'm on my way to drop the girls off at school and I'm late, so I've got to talk fast." Detective Schueller peered into the envelope to make sure he'd removed everything. Satisfied, he tossed the envelope face down into his out-box.

"What is it?"

"I forgot I've got to go to the doctor's office this afternoon. Can you pick up the girls at six?"

"Sure," he replied, spreading the pictures out on his desk.

"Great, honey. I've got to go. Bye."

Schueller heard the phone click as his wife hung up. He held the receiver in front of his face and stared at it as if it had done something wrong. Then he, too, hung up.

Finally able to focus, he carefully studied the pictures. The subject was a blond, blue-eyed man in his early thirties. He appeared in very good shape and was well dressed. The cover sheet identified the man as Wilhelm Strauss, a thirty-three-year-old German citizen entering the United States on September 30, 1997. It also provided the subject's travel itinerary and a detailed inventory of everything the U.S. Customs inspectors found when they searched him upon his entry.

Schueller set the paper next to the row of photographs and again focused on the blond, blue-eyed man. Nothing jumped out at him. In fact, he wondered why he had the photographs. He wasn't working any cases with suspects in America.

"Perhaps Belmar is testing me," he thought to himself. "He probably knows who this guy is and is waiting to see if I'll ask about him." He gathered up the pictures with the cover sheet, walked to Belmar's office, and knocked on the open door.

"Come in," Belmar said without looking up from the report he was reading. Schueller stood quietly in front of the man's desk until he was acknowledged.

"Hans, please, sit down." Belmar leaned forward with his elbows on his desk. "What can I do for you?"

"I just finished reviewing the photographs you gave me and I was wondering what you want me to do with them."

"What photographs?"

"The pictures of the German national who entered America about three weeks ago. You didn't give them to me?"

"No, I didn't. Let me take a look." Belmar took the pictures and turned them around until all three were right side up. Then he set them side by side, just as Schueller had done. He scrutinized every feature on the suspect's face in each of the pictures. "I'd say these are reprints of the same picture, wouldn't you?"

"Looks like it to me."

"Where'd they come from?"

"Found them in my inbox this morning. I thought maybe you gave them to me."

"Not me. Did they come with any sort of explanation?"

"Just this sheet from Headquarters. It says the pictures came from the American Customs Liaison Office in Bonn."

"Why'd they send them to us?"

"Beats me. Looks like the stuff Counter-Narcotics would normally deal with, not us."

"Let me see that, Hans." Belmar took the paper and gave it the same studied look he gave the photographs. When he finished, he rocked back in his chair with his hands behind his head, shifted his jaw to the right, and looked up at the ceiling.

"Hans," Belmar began, only to pause before continuing with his thought, "there is something here that rings a bell, but I can't quite figure out what it is."

Schueller nodded.

"We've got to think, Hans. We've got to think." Belmar again stared silently at the ceiling. Then he planted his chair back firmly on the floor and picked up the cover sheet.

"I want you to go over every detail of this cover sheet carefully with me. Think, Hans, think. Between us, something will have to register."

"Yes, sir."

"Okay. Here goes. Name: Wilhelm Strauss." Belmar paused to see if the name evoked any reaction from Schueller. When it didn't, he continued, "Thirty-three-year-old German national entering the U.S. on September 30, 1997." Belmar again paused, this time for a bit longer. Still nothing. "Suspicion of narcotics trafficking. Entered U.S. with seven thousand eight hundred and forty-five Deutschmarks and five thousand U.S. dollars." Schueller shook his head. Belmar went on. "Contact departed Düsseldorf—"

"That's it!"

"What, Hans, what?"

"When did you say the suspect left Düsseldorf?"

"September thirtieth. Why?"

"What was the day that old man was killed? Wasn't he shot that same morning?"

"You mean Weisentrope?" Belmar asked. Hans nodded. "I think he was, Hans, now that you mention it."

Schueller didn't wait for Belmar to ask him to explain the connection. "The old man was shot in the morning. This guy's flight left Düsseldorf in the afternoon. That gave him plenty of time to get to the airport." Schueller had more to say, but he looked at Belmar to see if his theory was striking any chords. It was. Belmar leaned forward in his chair and picked up one of the pictures.

"Go on, Hans."

"Well, remember that eyewitness we interviewed? Frau Hintle or something like that?"

"Hinkle, wasn't it?"

"That's her. Didn't she say the man she saw was a tall, blond guy?"

"I think so. Let me grab the file quick." Belmar went over to the dented gray metal file cabinet and pulled the Weisentrope file from the drawer. He did a cursory flip through the file as he returned to his chair, where he began to give it a more thorough reading.

"Here's Frau Hinkle's account," Belmar said, pulling her statement. He laid the file on his desk and read the statement out loud to confirm Schueller's hypothesis. Vague though the description was, it matched the man in the picture in every detail. "You know, Hans, there's only one way to tell for sure."

"I'll make the arrangements."

"Good. Let's get out there as soon as we can. I really want to get this bastard."

"So do I, Detective Belmar. So do I."

16

Williamsburg, Virginia

"HELLO, MAY I please speak to Mr. Teodor Rudnik?" Steve asked as he strained to hear over the static on the telephone line.

"Who is this?" an elderly woman asked suspiciously. Her English accent made it difficult for Steve to understand.

"My name is Steve Stilwell, and I'm a lawyer calling from the United States. Is this Mrs. Rudnik?"

"Yes."

"Mrs. Rudnik, may I please speak to your husband?" There was silence on the other end of the line, interrupted only by the occasional pop of a static burst. "Mrs. Rudnik, are you still there?"

"What did you say your name was?"

"Stilwell, Steve Stilwell." Steve enunciated every word, recognizing that if he was having trouble understanding Mrs. Rudnik, she was probably finding it just as difficult to understand him. "Mrs. Rudnik, I'm sorry to say that an old friend of your husband's has died. I represent his estate. Your husband was mentioned in the will, so I need to speak to him if he's available."

Still no response.

"Mrs. Rudnik?"

"Yes."

"Mrs. Rudnik, may I speak to your husband?"

"How do I know you are who you say you are?"

"I'll tell you what. Let me give you my telephone number in America. You can call me back collect. Just ask your telephone operator to help you make the connection. I'll pay for the call. Then you'll know you're talking to a lawyer in the United States." Steve knew the scheme wouldn't actually verify who he was, but he hoped it would give Mrs. Rudnik enough confidence to continue speaking with him.

"Very well, then. What's your number?" Mrs. Rudnik asked skeptically.

Steve gave her his number. "Mrs. Rudnik, will you or your husband be able to call me right back?"

"I'll do what I can. Goodbye."

Steve heard Mrs. Rudnik hang up the receiver. "Damn." He figured there was no way she was going to call him back. He'd have to try again later. First, though, he'd turn his attention to the other names on the list. The next name was Tadeusz Zalinsky in Cleveland, Ohio. Steve dialed the number and waited for Mr. Zalinsky to answer. After the third ring, an answering machine informed him that the Zalinskys could not come to the phone right now. Steve left his name and number, but nothing more. He hated leaving messages. He always ended up calling back anyway.

"Mr. Stilwell," Marjorie called over the intercom. "You have a collect call from London on line one. Do you want me to accept the charges?"

"You bet!" Steve shouted loud enough to be heard without the intercom. "Go ahead and put the call through right away." He picked up line one before the first ring stopped.

"Hello, this is Steve Stilwell." Steve used his most formal greeting to assure the Rudniks that they were speaking with an American attorney. After a moment, a hollow "hello" came across the line.

"Is that you, Mrs. Rudnik?"

"What is it you need, Mr. Stilwell?"

"I'd like to speak to your husband, if I might." Steve fought off the urge to speak the Queen's English with a British accent.

"I'm afraid that's impossible. Teodor recently passed away."

"I'm sorry, Mrs. Rudnick, I couldn't understand what you said."

"I said my husband's dead, Mr. Stilwell. Teodor is dead."

This time Steve understood perfectly well. He was embarrassed for having asked her to repeat something so painful. Still, he needed more information, and pressed on as delicately as he could.

"I'm so sorry to hear that, Mrs. Rudnik. Do you mind if I ask you when he died?"

"I might. Why do you need to know?"

"Mrs. Rudnik, let me speak plainly. Your husband was apparently a very good friend of Professor Felix Siegel, an American college professor. Professor Siegel has died and his will contains a bequest to your husband. The catch is, your husband had to survive Professor Siegel. If he died before Professor Siegel, your husband, or in this case, his estate, gets nothing. Does that make sense, Mrs. Rudnik?"

"Perfect sense, Mr. Stilwell," she answered, her voice no longer wavering. "Tell me, when did Felix Siegel die?"

Steve hoped Mrs. Rudnik wasn't going to make things difficult for him by providing him with false information. Any conflict at this point would mean a much more tedious process of verifying the date of Mr. Rudnik's death. He hoped for the best.

"He was murdered in Israel on October 14, just six days ago."

"My dear God," Mrs. Rudnik gasped. "Did you say he was murdered?"

"I'm sorry to say I did. He was killed by a terrorist bomb in Haifa." Steve thought he heard the faint echoes of Mrs. Rudnik sobbing. "Mrs. Rudnik, are you all right?"

"Teodor was murdered two months ago. Someone robbed him and then shot him in the head. He was gone so fast." She began to cry openly.

"Mrs. Rudnik, I'm so sorry. I really don't know what to say, other than that I'm terribly sorry."

Mrs. Rudnik composed herself briefly. "Is there anything else you need?" Her voice quivered and once again began to fade.

"If you don't mind, did they catch the individual or individuals responsible?" Steve didn't need this information. He simply wanted to know because he hated whoever killed Teodor Rudnik, just as he hated the terrorists who killed Professor Siegel. The perpetrators were animals—animals that needed to be judged and punished with the full force and effect of the law.

"They've caught no one," Mrs. Rudnik answered, composing herself. "They don't have any idea who did it."

"I'm sure they'll find his killer. And I do apologize for asking you to discuss these very personal matters with me, but I appreciate your candor. Please don't hesitate to call me again collect, just like you did today, if you have any questions or if there is something I can help you with." Steve was quite sincere with his offer, although he knew there was little chance she would ever take him up on it.

"Thank you," came a faint reply.

"Goodbye, Mrs. Rudnik."

Steve hung up the phone. He felt terrible. His call had forced Mrs. Rudnik to relive the pain of her husband's death. Even worse, the information she provided told him Teodor Rudnik's estate would get nothing from Professor Siegel because Teodor

Rudnik died before the Professor. He felt like a naval officer assigned to inform some young wife that her husband had just been killed in the line of duty. He had to take a break; he had to do something uplifting to get his mind off Mrs. Rudnik and the Professor. He got up to speak to Mr. Smythe, but he was on the telephone. It was up to Marjorie.

"Boy, did I just have a depressing phone call," Steve said, trying to pique Marjorie's interest.

Marjorie looked up from her computer screen, leaned back in her chair and pretended to be interested. "Who were you talking to?"

"That lady from England, Mrs. Rudnik."

"Was she the collect call I put through?"

"Exactly. Her husband was one of Professor Siegel's beneficiaries."

"She had to be happy about that. Doesn't her husband get half a million dollars?"

Steve paused because he thought he heard Mr. Smythe hang up his telephone. When he glanced into Mr. Smythe's office to see, Marjorie leaned forward and used her computer's mouse to double-click on the spell-check symbol of her word processing program. When Steve started to turn his head back toward her, she quickly let go of the mouse and again sat back in her chair, smiling.

"He would have, except that he was murdered two months ago. And my call made her live the whole ordeal over again."

Marjorie's eyes widened and she let out an awkward little laugh. "You know, Mr. Stilwell, we never had anything like this before you came. You've only been here a month and you've already gotten one client killed and a beneficiary murdered. What's next?"

That wasn't the response Steve was looking for, although, when he thought about it, he really didn't know what he was looking for. He decided the best thing to do was just get back to work. He shrugged his shoulders and returned to his desk. He hadn't called the rabbis at Temple Beth Israel yet. They already knew, of course, about Professor Siegel's death, because they conducted the memorial. What they probably didn't know about was Professor Siegel's generosity. Steve called Marjorie and she connected him with a rabbi at the synagogue. As Steve suspected, he was unaware of the Professor's gift.

"We shall all miss him," the rabbi said. "He was a kind and loving man."

"I could tell that from just the few times I came into contact with him," Steve added.

"You know," the rabbi continued. "He deserved a more fitting end."

"No one deserves to die like that," Steve said, perhaps more emphatically than intended.

"Of course not. What I meant was, this man lived through Auschwitz. He was the only member of his family to survive the war. Yet he was able to put those years behind him and build a new life in America. Now, once again, he's the victim of man's cruelty to man. When will it stop?"

"I don't know, Rabbi, I just don't know." Steve had hoped the phone call to the synagogue would be uplifting, yet it made him feel even worse. He wanted to distance himself from Professor Siegel's memory so as not to become emotionally involved in his client's life. He tried the tactic all the time doing legal assistance in the Navy. The problem was, it didn't work then and it wasn't working now.

"Mr. Stilwell, are you still there?" the rabbi asked after Steve's last response trailed off into silence.

"I'm sorry, Rabbi. I'll get back to you to coordinate Professor Siegel's gift."

"I truly appreciate your assistance, Mr. Stilwell."

"Goodbye, Rabbi." Steve hung up the phone. He sat quietly, thinking about Professor Siegel and Teodor Rudnik. The rabbi's point hit home. Sure, nobody deserved to die like they did, but these two men in particular deserved to die in peace.

Marjorie broke his concentration with an exaggerated knock on his door.

"Mr. Stilwell, would you mind if I cast an idle speculation?"

"Of course not. What's on your mind?"

"What do you think of Professor Siegel's daughter?"

"She's all right, I guess. A little formal, perhaps, but all right."

"Is that what you really think?"

"No, not really. She's actually a self-centered, spoiled, ill-mannered … person!"

"That's what I thought. So what does she get out of all this?"

"What do you mean?"

"I mean, doesn't she get to keep Mr. Rudnik's five hundred thousand dollars since he died before her father?"

"Yeah, so what?" Steve replied, seeing where Marjorie was headed but not wanting to go there.

"So, first Mr. Rudnik was murdered and then Professor Siegel. And you saw how she treated her father. I think she's involved somehow."

"You can't be serious, Marjorie. There's a huge difference between being a bitch and being a murderer." Marjorie was getting him worked up and the most fitting, if not appropriate word, worked its way out. "I'm sorry, Marjorie. I didn't mean to say it that way."

"Oh yes you did, and you were right." Marjorie matched his passion word for word. "And that's exactly why I think she did it. She's been like that since the moment we met her—brash, cold, and unfeeling. I don't know how she did it, but somehow she's involved. Just call it a woman's intuition."

Steve laughed and shook his head. "Do you really think Michelle Siegel is capable of planning the murder of two people in two countries and then having them carried out? I just don't see it, Marjorie." Not wanting to discuss the matter further because it bordered on the ridiculous, he changed the direction of the conversation. "But you did remind me of something. I promised to notify Ms. Siegel of any significant developments affecting her father's estate, and Mr. Rudnik's death certainly qualifies. Would you get her on the phone for me?"

Steve's cue worked and Marjorie left his office. Although he liked Marjorie and valued her opinion, he could just hear the Williamsburg police laughing at him if he went to them with such a story. Besides, he had better things to do than to listen to such nonsense. He had to update Michelle on the status of the case and finish work on a few wills. That would get his focus back where it needed to be.

17

~~~

Düsseldorf, Germany

BELMAR RAPPED ON the brass doorknocker three times and then took a step back, fidgeting with the handle on his briefcase. Detective Schueller checked his watch; it was already 6:10 p.m. After discovering the man they believed to be Emil Weisentrope's killer, they had to wait the entire day before Frau Hinkle was available to view the photographs. Belmar heard what sounded like a woman in heels approaching the apartment door from the inside. A moment later, the door cracked open and a short, stocky woman peered cautiously outside to see who was knocking.

"Yes?" the woman said, eyeing the two men waiting just outside her door.

"Frau Hinkle?"

"Yes?"

"I'm Detective Schueller, and this is Detective Belmar. I spoke to you earlier today about showing you some pictures."

"Oh, yes," Frau Hinkle said pleasantly as she opened the door. "Please come in."

"Thank you," Detective Schueller added as both men went inside. "We appreciate you seeing us on such short notice."

"It's no problem at all, really." Frau Hinkle closed the door and escorted the men to the living room. "Please, have a seat. May I get you something to drink?"

"No thanks," Detective Schueller responded. "This will only take a minute or two."

Belmar opened his briefcase and pulled out a manila folder with six pictures in it. All were of medium-built blond-haired men, but only one was Wilhelm Strauss. He arranged the pictures on the coffee table in front of Frau Hinkle, who sat down opposite the men. It was now Belmar's turn to lead the discussion.

"Frau Hinkle, do you remember the last time we spoke?"

"Of course. You're the two detectives who asked me some questions about the person I saw the morning that poor old man was shot to death."

"Exactly. I need you to take a look at these photographs and tell me if you recognize any of them."

Without hesitating, Frau Hinkle reached out and pointed to the picture of Strauss. "That's the man I saw that morning."

Belmar and Detective Schueller looked at each other but neither smiled ... yet. They still needed to ask a few confirming questions.

"Are you sure that's the man?" Belmar asked.

"Positive."

"How can you be so sure?"

"I'll never forget his face. He looked so angry at me, even though I'd never seen him before. All I wanted to do was go in my shop and get away from him."

"Well, I'm glad you remember him," Belmar said as he started to gather up the pictures. "We really appreciate your help."

"So who is this man, anyway? Someone I need to be afraid of?"

"Oh, no ... not at all. He's not in Germany anymore and he

doesn't know you exist. You don't have a thing to worry about," reassured Belmar as the two men walked back to the front door. "We'll get back in touch with you soon. Thanks again for your help."

Frau Hinkle leaned out the door after the detectives walked out of her apartment. "Please let me know if there is anything else I can do."

"We will," Detective Schueller said, waving over his shoulder as the two men walked toward the stairwell. Frau Hinkle smiled and closed the door.

"We've got our killer, Hans." Belmar grasped his briefcase with both hands. "Now all we have to do is find him." They began to walk down the stairs.

"Do you think he's still in America?"

"Hard to say," Belmar replied. "It'll depend on why he went there in the first place. If he lives there, our chances of finding him are good. If he had work there or was on his way to someplace else, it'll be tough. But at least we know what he looks like."

"What do we do if we find him? I mean, we don't have enough evidence to ask the Americans to extradite him. All we've got is a statement by a single witness who can put him near the murder at about the right time. But nobody saw him do anything."

Belmar knew Hans was right. There was a big difference between knowing who the killer was and having enough evidence to bring him to trial. They had to get more on him, but how? Right now, they didn't even know where he was. That was where they had to start. They reached the ground floor and walked out of the building toward their car, parked about a block away.

"Hans, I want you to work this with the Americans. It's only about noon there now, so you might even get somewhere this evening." Then Belmar added, "We've got to run with this case before it gets too old. The longer it takes, the tougher it's going to be to find this guy. Were you able to get back in touch with your wife to pick up the girls?"

"I was … I'm all set. I'll try to confer with the Americans as soon as we return."

"Good, Hans. That's good."

* * *

Williamsburg, Virginia

STEVE COULDN'T REACH Michelle after his conversation with Marjorie earlier that morning. He was glad, because the intervening hours gave him a chance to think about what Marjorie had said. He had half a mind to flat-out ask Michelle if she was involved in the killings, but he knew that was utterly foolish. He'd just have to let the police do their job. If she was involved, the law would catch up with her … eventually.

Now it was late Monday afternoon and he was prepared to speak to Michelle. He dialed her number, hoping to check one more item off his to-do list before he closed up shop for the day. The phone rang four times, but just as he was about to hang up, Michelle answered.

"Hello?"

"Hello, Ms. Siegel. This is Steve Stilwell."

"Yes, Mr. Stilwell," Michelle said as though irritated by the interruption—the familiarity of the day before now gone. "What is it you need now?"

Steve bit his lip. Michelle was the primary beneficiary of an estate he was managing, so he decided to put up with a certain level of rudeness as long as it didn't become too flagrant. "Actually nothing. I promised you an update on your father's estate, so here it is. This morning, I contacted the wife of one of your father's friends, Mr. Teodor Rudnik. It seems Mr. Rudnik was killed about two months ago."

"So, what does that mean for me?"

Steve couldn't bring himself to answer Michelle's question.

There was no sorrow in her voice, no sense of loss. Not even a measure of respect for one of her father's best friends who was brutally murdered. In fact, she didn't ask how Mr. Rudnik died. Was it because she already knew?

"Mr. Stilwell," Michelle began even more callously. "I asked what happens under the will now that Rudnik is dead?"

"You'll get his share," Steve said bluntly.

"What about the other two? Have you contacted them yet?"

"I contacted the synagogue. It gets two hundred fifty thousand dollars. I also tried Mr. Zalinsky; he's the one from Ohio. All I got was his answering machine."

"What about the one in Germany?"

"You mean Mr. Weisentrope?"

"If he's the one in Germany, then yes."

"I have no way of contacting him by telephone. We tried to get a number for him, but couldn't find one. I'll put a letter together tomorrow."

"A letter? You've got to be kidding me."

"No, actually I'm quite serious." This time Steve's voice gave away his anger. Michelle picked up the signal and re-charted her course.

"I'm sorry. I didn't mean for it to come out that way. It's just that I want to get this thing behind me. The longer it takes, the longer I'm going to be reminded of my father's death. I just want to get the will taken care of and move on with my life."

Once again, a few kindly spoken and possibly sincere words repaired Steve's outlook toward Michelle. He knew she must be going through some hard times, so he rededicated himself to putting up with her.

"I know you do, and so do I. But without a telephone number, the only way I can get in contact with Mr. Weisentrope, short of going there, is to send him a letter or an overnight package."

"That's it!"

"An overnight package?"

"No. We'll go over there and take care of this ourselves."

"You can't be serious, Ms. Siegel. It'll cost you a fortune to send me there, and what if he isn't available? Then you've wasted my time and your money."

"Look, Mr. Stilwell," Michelle said, taking charge. "We're talking about half a million dollars here. I don't care if it costs a few thousand to get this thing over with right away."

"It'll be more like eight to ten thousand," Steve replied, hoping Michelle's greed would cause her to rethink her foolish idea. How could she conclude he was serious when he mentioned going to Germany?

"I'll authorize the expenditure," Michelle answered.

"You'll have to do more than that. You'll have to pay for it yourself. As executor, I can't allow such a frivolous expense just to save a few days."

"It's hardly frivolous, Mr. Stilwell. Think about it. Even if you send an overnight package, there's no guarantee the old man will respond to it right away. In fact, he might never respond. Sending a letter by mail is even worse. But if you go in person, you can wrap it up in a day or two. You'll actually save money."

"Going there won't save money, Ms. Siegel, and I won't authorize the expenditure out of the estate." Steve was adamant. Then he threw out one more point to drive the issue home. "Besides, what if I get over there and the man isn't living at the address you gave me?"

"He'll be there. He's lived there for a long time and he's an old man. My father wrote him all the time, almost weekly. I'm sure he'll be there."

Steve clicked on his computer calendar, searching for other reasons not to go. His week was essentially clear because he'd left it open to catch up on some will drafting. He had a few appointments, but they could be rescheduled. Then the best rebuttal argument hit him.

"Even if I could go, I don't speak German. I wouldn't be able to talk to the man even if I found him." Michelle jumped on his argument with the skill of a veteran cross-examiner.

"So, how, then, were you going to send Mr. Weisentrope a letter? If you're assuming the old man doesn't understand English, wouldn't getting the letter translated add even more time, with still no guarantee of a response?"

"You haven't answered my earlier question, Ms. Siegel," Steve responded, now quite irritated that Michelle was mounting a significant challenge to his judgment. "How will I speak to him when I find him? As I said before, I don't speak German."

"*But I do*," Michelle said, defiantly tossing her trump card on the table. "I'll go with you, and I want to leave tomorrow. Can you go?"

"My schedule's clear, but as I said before, I won't authorize payment of these expenses out of the estate." This was not a matter of pride to Steve or some power play he was trying to pull. He felt ethically bound to hold his ground.

"I'll pay for it then," Michelle said.

"Excuse me?"

"I said, I'll pay for the trip. Now, can you be ready to leave tomorrow?"

Michelle had him and he knew it. One by one, she'd refuted each of his arguments and finally gotten him to admit his schedule was free. It looked like he was going to Germany.

"I'll have Marjorie make the travel arrangements," Steve said, still not understanding how he had been so completely outmaneuvered. "Do you have any airline or hotel preferences?"

"No," Michelle replied in a voice so uncharacteristically pleasant Steve was sure she would gloat all the way to Europe. "Just try and get a morning flight out of D.C. Make the tickets business class, and ask her to get the best rates possible."

"I'll charge you a thousand dollars a day, plus expenses."

"Fine. I'll expect a call from you as soon as you have the tickets so I can get to Washington tonight if I have to. Is there anything else?"

"No," Steve answered. Then he heard "goodbye" and the call ended. The experience reminded him of being dismissed by a senior officer after receiving clear-cut instructions to complete a mission he disagreed with. Still, Michelle won the day, so he was ready to go get the thing done. First, though, he had to set Marjorie to work on the travel arrangements, and then he would have to tell his wife. Neither discussion would be pleasant, but there was no sense putting off the inevitable. He dragged himself away from his desk and walked out to where Marjorie was gathering her things to go home.

"Marjorie, you're not going to believe what just happened." He was right, but she began making the travel arrangements anyway.

18

~~~

Wednesday, October 22
Düsseldorf, Germany

STEVE ARRIVED IN the hotel lobby at 9:25 a.m. He was dressed in a business suit and looked well rested after the previous day's flight to Düsseldorf. Michelle arrived fifteen minutes later, just as Steve was getting ready to call her room. For the first time since he'd met her, she looked bad, though 'bad' for Michelle was a relative term. He could see in her bloodshot eyes the agony of a sleepless night, so he braced himself for the wrath of Michelle now aggravated by no sleep and a bad hair day. He didn't have to wait long.

"Why didn't we use some common sense and schedule this later in the day? I mean, we knew they were six hours ahead of us here. We should have slept in."

"And a good morning to you, too, Ms. Siegel."

"I'm sorry, I didn't get much sleep last night."

Steve was certain Michelle noticed his jaw drop. He equated Michelle saying "I'm sorry" with the fall of the Berlin Wall or the dissolution of the Soviet Union. As he stood there, at a loss for words, she elaborated.

"I've simply got to have a cup of coffee in the morning, and this time change has only made it worse."

"I believe I saw the dining room over there, Ms. Siegel," Steve said, pointing to his right. "I'm sure we can get some coffee and breakfast."

"Great," Michelle replied unenthusiastically. "By the way, please call me Michelle."

Steve wanted to ask Michelle to repeat herself, not because he hadn't heard her, but because he had. Could this be coming from the same woman who despised everything about attorneys? He decided not to respond to her invitation. He thought a period of silence would allow her to realize what she'd said, and in fairness, give her the opportunity to rescind it. To his astonishment, though, Michelle made no effort to amend her statement. Either she meant what she said or was too embarrassed to admit her mistake. Since he couldn't imagine Michelle being embarrassed, he presumed she meant it.

The two walked into the dining room and took a seat near the entrance at a table for two. Steve helped Michelle with her chair and then sat down across from her.

"I'm not very hungry this morning," Steve said, reaching for one of two green silk-covered menus. Michelle took the other, but didn't open it.

"Why *did* we start this early?" Michelle asked again.

"I wanted a full day to try and get this wrapped up. If we can talk to Mr. Weisentrope this morning, we can be back on a plane tonight or tomorrow at the latest. It also gives us time this afternoon in case we can't find him right away."

The waitress walked over and began to address Steve in German. Steve looked at Michelle and shrugged.

"What would you like to order?" Michelle asked, rescuing him.

"A glass of orange juice and a bowl of fruit. Any kind is fine."

"Coffee?"

"No, thanks."

"You really should try some German coffee. There's none quite like it anywhere. It's very strong. I'm sure you'd like it."

Not wanting to discourage what appeared to be Michelle's first goodwill offering, Steve agreed to try a coffee, even though it didn't sound good to him. Michelle placed his order and ordered some toast and a cup of coffee for herself.

"So what's the plan for today?" Michelle clasped her hands together on the table and leaned forward toward Steve in anticipation of his response.

"I thought we'd go straight to Mr. Weisentrope's," Steve replied, also resting his arms on the table but maintaining his distance. "I'm sure we can catch a cab from here."

"Then what?"

"Then we'll knock on his door and talk to him."

"What if he's not there?"

"Then you've just given me an all-expense-paid vacation to Germany." Recalling that Michelle had dismissed that possibility when he raised it two days before, Steve couldn't pass up the opportunity for the not-so-subtle *I told you so*.

"Don't start gloating yet," Michelle cautioned. "If I didn't think we'd get what we need, I wouldn't have offered to pay for the trip."

"I just hate to see you waste your money. There were far easier ways. But we've been over that ground before, and we're here, so we need to make the best of it. I take it from your fancy for German coffee that you've been to Germany before?"

"I have, but that's not how I learned to like the coffee. My father brought my mother and me to Germany when I was about ten years old. That's when I met Emil Weisentrope. My father wanted to show us where he was born, even though his family moved to Czechoslovakia while he was still a boy. We visited there, too. I can still remember the puppet shops in

Prague. They all sold brightly painted Pinocchio marionettes, and my father bought me one. I think I still have it somewhere. It's funny how I can still remember the details of the trip. It's like it just happened."

Michelle's reflective mood softened everything about her. It was a side of Michelle Steve hadn't seen before, a side he didn't mind traveling with or talking to. He decided to see where the conversation might go.

"You've still left me hanging on the coffee. Where did you acquire your taste for German coffee?"

"Oh, that came in college. I dated a boy whose family lived in Germany. He told his parents he missed the smell of coffee from home, so they used to send him German coffee at school. We'd save it for the coldest winter mornings. It smelled so good."

"Where did you go to school?"

"Columbia, where else?" Michelle posited, the softness gone from her voice. "That's where my father taught, that's where I was expected to go, and that's where I went. In fact, once my parents heard Columbia would admit women, they actually made me change my plans and wait a year before starting college so I would be part of Columbia's first coed class."

Realizing he struck a nerve, Steve searched for a way to steer the conversation back to its more pleasant beginnings. Before he could say anything else, though, the waitress returned with their order and meticulously arranged it in front of them. Michelle began with a sip of her coffee and a small bite out of the corner of one of her pieces of heavily buttered toast. Steve followed with a spoonful of fruit and waited to see if Michelle would pick up the conversation where she left off. When she didn't, he finished the rest of his fruit and slowly worked on his coffee while Michelle ate. The silence made him uncomfortable, although it appeared to suit Michelle just fine. After finishing her toast, Michelle took a sizable sip of coffee, and as she set it down, announced that she was ready to go. As the one most familiar with German currency, she paid the bill and the two walked back to the lobby and arranged for a cab.

The ride took only twenty minutes, even in the morning rush hour traffic. The driver let them off on Tabelstrasse in front of what used to be Emil Weisentrope's four-story, soot-stained brick apartment building. Michelle took care of the fare.

"Not very impressive, is it?" Steve commented.

"What did you expect, a mansion?"

"I don't know, something more German-looking. I mean, this could be any old street in America. Shade trees along the sidewalks, apartments lining both sides of the street. I feel like I'm in Chicago."

"Well you're not," Michelle proclaimed. "Do you know which apartment Weisentrope lives in? I want to get this over with."

"I've got it written down," Steve said, opening his leather organizer. He flipped to the notes section and found where he had written Emil Weisentrope's address. "It's apartment 4C."

Steve walked to the front door and opened it for Michelle. He followed her into the ground floor hallway, which accessed only the main floor apartments. Michelle searched for a stairway entrance and found it midway down the hall. "It's this way," she announced, and she started up the stairway with Steve not far behind. Two flights later, they emerged on the second floor.

"There's 4C over there," Michelle said, motioning with her hand. The two walked over and stood in front of the door. "How do you want to do this?"

"When someone answers, why don't you tell Mr. Weisentrope who you are? Then introduce us and I'll tell you what to say after that. If you interpret, I'll handle the rest. Are you ready?"

"Ready," Michelle replied, nodding.

Steve knocked on the door. Within a moment or two, a young woman holding a baby appeared and greeted them in German. She was not at all what they expected, and Michelle hesitated before introducing herself and Steve and asking if they could speak to Emil Weisentrope. The woman looked puzzled and then responded to Michelle in German. When the woman finished speaking, Michelle didn't immediately respond. She looked off balance and uncertain of what to do next. She asked the woman something else and the woman nodded.

"What's she saying?" Steve asked. He was losing patience with Michelle for not translating for him.

"She says Emil Weisentrope died about three weeks ago." Michelle looked Steve straight in the eyes.

"Are you sure?" Steve asked, not believing what he had just heard.

"I'm sure. I've already asked her twice."

"How did he die?"

"I'll have to ask." Michelle looked back at the woman standing patiently at the door. She spoke at length; the woman answered with a correspondingly long narrative, all the time gently rocking the sleeping baby in her arms. When she finished, both she and Michelle turned to relay the information to Steve.

Michelle's translation was slow and unemotional. "She says Weisentrope was murdered about three weeks ago after somebody tried to rob him. She wasn't here at the time, but she heard about what happened from the neighbors in the building."

"Does she know for certain when he died?"

"She doesn't know the exact date, but is certain it was more than two weeks ago. She moved here on October 8, not realizing that the former resident had just been murdered. So she knows he died sometime before October 8."

"Tell her thank you. That's all we need."

Steve's mind raced back to his conversation with Marjorie, where she insinuated that Michelle had a hand in the death of her father and the beneficiaries under her father's will. What seemed so preposterous just a few days ago was now gaining credibility right before his eyes. He tried desperately to shift Marjorie's theory to the back of his mind. He had no proof anyway—nothing solid to hang his hat on. Nothing, that is, except three dead men and an additional one million dollars for Michelle. It suddenly occurred to him that could be why Michelle didn't object to paying him so handsomely to fly to Germany. He had to think. He had to run through all his dealings with Michelle to see if there were any other indicators.

"Steve, what's wrong?"

"I'm sorry, Michelle. Did you say something?"

"As a matter of fact, I've asked you twice what we need to do next and you just keep staring at the door. And you didn't even say thanks or goodbye to that woman. That was rude." The two continued talking as they retraced their steps out of the building and onto the street where the cab had dropped them off.

"I'm not sure what to do next," Steve said, ignoring Michelle's admonition. He couldn't share his suspicions with her. But what if she wasn't behind the killings? What if she was a target as well? Could he be a target too? He needed time to think. "Let's catch a cab back to the hotel. Maybe on the way back I can figure something out."

"There isn't anything else we need to do in Germany now that Weisentrope is dead, is there?"

Once again, Steve detected no compassion in Michelle's voice. She showed no more emotion in response to Emil Weisentrope's death than she did when she ordered their breakfast that morning. No surprise, no shock, no anger, no curiosity. She didn't even have the courtesy to refer to Emil Weisentrope as Mr. Weisentrope. She had to know something. But what?

"We need to obtain proof of Mr. Weisentrope's death," Steve replied curtly.

"What kind of proof?"

"A death certificate is best." Steve tried to deflect Michelle's probes for information by reminding her they needed a cab back to the hotel.

"Yes, of course," Michelle said as she looked around for a telephone. She saw one in front of a small shop just a couple of doors down. "There's a phone right over there." She motioned to Steve to head in that direction. As they began walking toward the telephone, Michelle surprised Steve with a new line of questions.

"Don't you think it's odd that my father and two of the men listed in his will have been murdered within the last three or four months?"

"It's unbelievable," Steve replied, avoiding eye contact. "Simply unbelievable." Before he had a chance to continue, Michelle interrupted.

"Here comes a cab. Try and flag it down."

Steve looked up and saw a red cab coming down the street toward them. He raised his hand and began waving at the cab to get the driver's attention. His efforts paid off as the cab swerved over to the curb. Steve opened the door for Michelle and she got into the back. While Steve walked around the cab to get in on the other side, Michelle gave the driver the necessary instructions to return them to the hotel. As soon as Steve shut his door, the cab driver started driving.

"I take it he knows where we're going?" Steve asked.

"No, actually, I thought he could drive around until we tell him he's close to the place." The driver laughed, indicating he understood English well. Steve did not laugh, indicating he found no humor in their situation. Recognizing Steve's somber mood, Michelle channeled the conversation back to before Steve asked her to find a cab.

"So what do you think's going on?"

"How the hell do I know?" Steve snapped. He usually wouldn't be so terse with a client, or a former client's daughter, for that matter. But he just didn't feel like talking to Michelle, let alone telling her that he thought if there was any connection between the killings, she was it. Michelle, though, wasn't ready to let the matter drop. Now she was the one who found the silence uncomfortable.

"It can't just be coincidence, can it?"

Steve didn't answer. He couldn't understand why she was pushing it, unless she meant to deflect suspicion away from her. It wasn't going to work. The situation seemed too obvious. He continued trying to mentally identify other signs that Michelle might be involved in the killings. Michelle, on the other hand, pressed with her questions.

"What about the last guy?"

"What last guy?" Steve asked, again trying to send a vibe that he didn't want to continue the conversation.

"The last guy from Ohio. Have you been able to get in contact with him yet?"

"You mean Mr. Zalinsky?"

"Whatever," Michelle said, not realizing her lack of concern for the man's name only heightened Steve's suspicions. "Is he still alive?"

"I don't know. I haven't been able to get in touch with him yet. All I've been able to do is leave a message on his answering machine."

"You need to get in touch with that man right away to make sure he's all right."

"And what if he's not all right?"

"You're the lawyer," Michelle responded, obviously miffed. "You tell me."

"Then there's something here bigger than both of us, and getting your father's will through probate will be the least of our worries."

Michelle didn't have time to figure out what Steve meant because their cab came to a sudden stop under the awning of their hotel. "Here we are," the driver said in English, but with an accent reminiscent of Professor Siegel's. "That will be twenty Marks."

Michelle reached into her purse to get the cab fare while

Steve exited the cab to open her door. Before he could reach it, the cab driver had it open for her. Michelle paid him and he repeatedly thanked her.

As they walked into the lobby, Steve decided on a plan of action. Because he could see Michelle preparing to speak again, he jumped in first so she wouldn't preempt his idea.

"Let's go up to our rooms for a few minutes. I've got a couple of calls to make. Then we can meet back here in the lobby." Steve looked at his watch. "It's 11:20 right now. I say we meet down here at 12:15. We'll go and get a quick bite to eat and then we'll try and get some answers."

"What do you have in mind?"

"Just a couple of quick inquiries," Steve replied, not wanting to disclose anything given his suspicions about Michelle.

"Do you need me to interpret for you?"

"No, not this time."

"Whatever you say. I guess I'll see you in about an hour."

"Aren't you going up to your room?" Steve asked, noticing Michelle wasn't heading toward the elevators.

"I'll be up in a few minutes. I want to hit the newsstand first."

"All right. I'll see you in a little while." With that, Steve made his way to the elevators. He hoped Mr. Zalinsky wasn't dead. If he was, Steve felt confident Michelle was involved. The key, though, was Mr. Zalinsky. Steve would be back in his room in a matter of minutes and then he would know for sure.

19

STEVE SAT ON the edge of his hotel bed and prepared to dial the telephone. He opened his organizer and flipped to the "Z" tab, where the only contact listed was Tadeusz Zalinsky. With phone number in hand, he read the telephone's pullout menu to see how to place a long-distance call to the States. Feeling short on time and even shorter on patience, he was quickly frustrated by his inability to make the seemingly simple overseas call. "Dammit," he said out loud. "A law degree and I can't even make a phone call by myself." Finally after several failed attempts, he resorted to the hotel operator to put through his call.

Following a brief period with an echo, the telephone began its slow, rhythmic ring. *Ringhhh.* Steve was sure the price of the operator-assisted overseas call would be staggering, but then remembered Michelle was footing the bill. *Ringhhh.* With no answer yet, he began to fear the same fate had already befallen Mr. Zalinsky. *Ringhhh.* He started to compute the time difference to see if that could account for Mr. Zalinsky's failure to answer. *Ringhhh.* It was 11:40 a.m. in Düsseldorf. That made it … just then, someone answered.

"Hello?" a groggy voice said at the other end of the line.

"Hello, is this Mr. Zalinsky?" Steve dared not try to pronounce Mr. Zalinsky's first name.

"Yes," the somewhat more alert voice responded.

"Thank God you're alive!" Steve blurted out before he realized what he was saying.

"Of course I'm alive. Who the hell is this?" Mr. Zalinsky spoke with a discernible, but well-worn, Eastern European accent. His voice was animated.

"Mr. Zalinsky, my name is Steve Stilwell, and I'm calling from Düsseldorf, Germany."

"You're what?"

"I said my name is Steve Stilwell, and I'm an attorney calling from Germany."

"Listen, if you're selling something, I'm calling the police."

Steve knew he had to take control of the conversation or he'd lose his chance to get a word in before Mr. Zalinsky hung up. Mr. Zalinsky didn't give him the opportunity.

"Do you know what time it is here?" he growled.

"I'm sorry, Mr. Zalinsky, but I can assure you I'm not selling anything. In fact, it's quite the opposite. I'm calling to tell you that you've inherited half a million dollars."

For a moment, there was silence.

"What did you say?"

"I said, Mr. Zalinsky, you've inherited five hundred thousand dollars." Steve finally had Mr. Zalinsky's attention.

"What's the catch?" Mr. Zalinsky asked, his voice filled with skepticism.

"There's no catch," Steve said, now no longer concerned that Mr. Zalinsky would hang up. "I'm sad to say that an old friend of yours died recently and left you the money through his will."

"But who could that be? I don't have any rich friends."

"What about Professor Felix Siegel?"

"Dear God!" Mr. Zalinsky cried out with a sudden sadness. "I haven't seen Felix in over forty years!"

Steve didn't say anything. This was one of those occasions when listening was more important than speaking. Nothing he could say would be the right thing anyway. The line sounded dead for what seemed like an eternity; then Mr. Zalinsky spoke.

"How did it happen?"

"He was killed by a terrorist bomb in Israel about two weeks ago."

"I heard about that, but I didn't pay attention to the name. I had no idea it was Felix. I can't believe he's gone. It seems like just yesterday we were …." Mr. Zalinsky's voice trailed off in despair.

"I'm sorry to be the one to bring you this news." Steve wanted to speak to Mr. Zalinsky in greater depth, but he had to get off the phone and back to dealing with Emil Weisentrope. Anyway, now that Steve knew Mr. Zalinsky was alive, he no longer had any concern for his safety. All of the other beneficiaries under Professor Siegel's will predeceased the Professor. If Michelle was really trying to increase her share of the inheritance by killing the other beneficiaries, the timing of their deaths made sense. With her father dead, though, there was nothing she could do to take Mr. Zalinsky's share away from him, short of contesting the will. So Steve knew Mr. Zalinsky was safe.

"Who did you say you were again?" Mr. Zalinsky asked.

"My name is Stilwell, Steve Stilwell. I'm the attorney handling Professor Siegel's estate."

"How can I take this money, Mr. Stilwell? Doesn't he have a family?"

"He has a daughter, and he made sure she was well taken care of. But you obviously meant a lot to him. He really wanted you to have it."

"Did he tell you that?"

"Yes, he told me when we wrote out his will. He told me he wanted you to have the money."

"It still doesn't seem right. I mean, I haven't spoken to him for many years."

"That must not have been important to him, Mr. Zalinsky. If you don't take it, I'm sure he would be disappointed."

"Do I need to do anything?"

"No, not now. In fact, I've got to get going. Let me give you my office number so you can contact me if you have any questions. Otherwise you can expect to hear from me in the next two or three weeks." Steve gave Mr. Zalinsky his office telephone number and apologized for waking him up. "Goodbye, Mr. Zalinsky."

"Goodbye."

Steve hung up and returned his attention to Emil Weisentrope. He still needed confirmation that Emil Weisentrope was dead. He required written proof in order to remove him from consideration for Professor Siegel's estate. If he were in the United States, he'd simply get Mr. Weisentrope's death certificate. He assumed Germany also issued the equivalent, but didn't have a clue how to obtain such a document. The logical place to start was the American Embassy in Bonn, but without a contact at the embassy, he was just another American needing immediate assistance. That could take hours or even days. If he could get in touch with the naval attaché, though, that would solve his problems.

This time Steve didn't try placing the call by himself—he went straight to the hotel operator and had her connect him with the Navy Judge Advocate General's Office at the Pentagon. The Admiral's aide, a Navy captain, was an old friend. Steve knew he'd be arriving at the Pentagon any minute now, if he wasn't already there. The captain could get him the name of the naval attaché in Bonn, and probably even a direct telephone number.

"Judge Advocate General's Office, Captain Remaker speaking."

"Joe, this is Steve Stilwell. How the hell are you?"

"Steve Stilwell. I don't believe it. What in the world are you doing up at this time of the morning? I thought when you retired you got to sleep in for the rest of your life."

"Listen, Joe, I've got to make this quick. I'm in Germany and I'm in a bit of a hurry. I need to ask you for a favor." Steve didn't want to get tied up in a long conversation. He wanted to talk to the naval attaché right away, if possible, and that meant keeping this conversation short. Captain Remaker must have sensed the urgency.

"Sure, Steve, whaddya need?"

"I need the name and telephone number of the naval attaché in Bonn. I think there's an attaché section at the Pentagon that should have the info readily available. Do you think you could get it for me?"

"Do you think there's anyone there at this time of the morning?"

"You are."

"Good point. Let me put you on hold for a second."

Steve hoped Joe Remaker would come through. He held on for what seemed like forever, but actually it was only a couple of minutes. Finally Joe's voice broke through the silence.

"Steve, you still there?"

"Yeah, Joe. Were you able to get anything?"

"You ready to copy?"

"Shoot."

"Captain Hank Turnbull, T-U-R-N-B-U-L-L." Captain Remaker also provided Steve with the attaché's direct office number.

"Joe, I'm forever in your debt," Steve said rather hurriedly.

"I'll catch you later," Joe answered, "but I want a full report when you get back in town."

"You got it, and I'll throw in a beer to boot. Talk to you later, Joe." With that, Steve hung up the phone and looked at his watch; it was 12:10 p.m. He had five minutes to make one more call and get down to the lobby to meet Michelle. He knew he wasn't going to make it and had no way to contact her. She would just have to wait a few minutes. The next call was simply too important to put off. If they were going to get out of Germany tomorrow or the next day, he had to get in touch with the naval attaché. With a little luck, the naval attaché would point him in the right direction. All he needed to know was where to go and what to ask for. It seemed like such a simple request.

* * *

Damascus, Syria

THE TELEPHONE RANG three times before Wilhelm Strauss picked up. "Hello," he said in English. He was not expecting a telephone call so he approached the conversation with caution.

"Mr. Strauss," a Middle Eastern sounding man said.

"Yes?" Strauss didn't recognize the voice. He thought it was the front desk clerk, but wasn't sure.

"Go to the lobby and look through the glass front doors. You will see a red Mercedes-Benz parked on the opposite side of the street. Walk out of the hotel and the car will pull up to you. Get into the back seat; you will be given further instructions at that time. Do you understand?"

"Yes, but …." Before Strauss could finish, the caller hung up. Was this finally the new identity he'd asked his client to arrange for him after his rough handling by U.S. Customs in Washington, D.C.? Or was it a setup? He'd been in Damascus long enough to be at risk and had the strangest feeling someone, perhaps even his client, was zeroing in on him. But why? Maybe his client felt it time to eliminate any trace of the killings. Maybe he was just paranoid.

Strauss looked out his window and onto the street below. He was on the opposite side of the building from the lobby and could see nothing. He had to make a choice and it had to be now. He decided to give the Mercedes a try. He grabbed his passport, wallet, and room key and headed for the door. Within two or three minutes he was in the lobby approaching the main entrance. His eyes swept the lobby like a ship's radar, hoping to detect a warning sign before anything bad started to go down. He saw nothing. The coast was clear.

When he reached the front door, he stopped before going outside. He wanted to scope out the situation before committing himself. To the right, about twenty-five meters up the road, was a late-model red Mercedes with someone sitting in the driver's seat. There were numerous other cars parallel-parked on both sides of the road and only a few other vehicles moving along the street in both directions. To the left was more of the same, but no red Mercedes. So far, the telephone call checked out. Seeing no obvious warning signs, he walked past an ornately dressed bellhop and stood under the hotel's green awning down by the road. His right foot no sooner hit the sidewalk than the red Mercedes began pulling out of its parking space and heading toward him.

Strauss' heart pounded. Although he saw only the driver in the Mercedes, he pictured a gunman popping up on the driver's signal and riddling the sidewalk with bullets. He also remembered how he killed Professor Siegel and wondered if the Israelis had tracked him down. Still, he couldn't just walk away.

The Mercedes continued slowly toward the hotel until it stopped in front of the awning. The driver looked directly at him. With his adrenaline pumping, Strauss approached the car at an angle so he could see inside before opening the passenger side's rear door. He knew once he got into the car, there was little he could do to defend himself, because he carried no weapon and would have no freedom to move. He was about to become very vulnerable.

He reached for the back door of the Mercedes. Nothing happened. As soon as he saw there was no one hiding on the floor or crouched down in the front passenger seat, he decided to commit. He climbed into the back seat and closed the door. He was at the mercy of the driver.

The driver never looked back. It was as if he didn't want to see Strauss' face close up. Instead, he pulled the car back on to the main thoroughfare. He silently navigated out of downtown and onto a busy road leading from the city. Once he established himself in the flow of traffic, he began to reach under the front seat with his left hand while continuing to drive with his right. The move was slow and almost imperceptible, but Strauss noticed the driver's left shoulder begin to dip and realized he was making a move to pick up something off the floor. Strauss started to breathe more deeply and could feel sweat breaking out on his forehead. He had to react now.

His first thought was to choke the driver, knowing they would crash. The alternative was to do nothing and possibly take a bullet in the head. As he leaned forward to make his move, he caught the speedometer out of the corner of his eye. They were traveling at over one hundred kilometers per hour. He faced near certain death if the car crashed, yet he wasn't even sure his life was really in danger. He decided to take his chances and let the situation play out.

Strauss sat back in his seat and focused on the driver's left shoulder. After bottoming out, it started to rise slowly until it was level with his right shoulder. Suddenly, the driver brought something over his right shoulder and thrust it toward Strauss. Strauss instinctively fell to his left, expecting to feel the burning sensation of a bullet searing into his body. Instead, he felt nothing. He looked up and saw the driver trying to hand him a small leather binder. Embarrassed, but at the same time relieved, he sat up and took it. He could see the driver's bearded face in the rearview mirror break into a wide smile. With a rather sheepish return grin, he shifted his attention to the binder. He hoped it contained the documents he needed for his new identity. This time his instincts proved correct.

Inside the binder was a tablet of paper with nothing written on it. When he held the binder up to explore its other features, a German passport fell out from behind the tablet and into his lap. Inside the passport he also found a driver's license clipped to the page opposite his picture. Now it was his turn to smile broadly, thrilled he could finally leave Syria. Then he remembered to look at the name on the passport to find out his new identity—Karl Vernhausen. It matched exactly the name on the driver's license. Even more impressive, his pictures on the driver's license and passport were very recent, yet he hadn't posed for either shot. His client was a capable and powerful person, indeed.

Strauss looked over the passport more closely. It contained an entry stamp for Syria and an unexpired and unstamped visa for entry into the United States. He surmised this meant America was his next destination, although the visa could have been included simply as a ploy. In any event, the passport looked good and he was satisfied.

"Put old passport and driver's license back in book," the driver said in gruff, broken English.

Although Strauss was surprised to hear the driver speak, he complied. He didn't want to have anything on him that referenced his old identity. Reaching into his pocket, he pulled out his wallet and old passport. He thumbed through the passport, and finding that it contained nothing, placed it in the binder behind the paper tablet. He did the same with his old driver's license. He then went through every other item in his wallet to eliminate any trace of his former self. Finding nothing, he put his new driver's license away in his wallet, leaned forward, and tossed the binder into the front passenger seat. With Wilhelm Strauss now gone forever, he gave the driver a thumbs-up to indicate mission accomplished.

When the driver saw the thumbs-up, he returned the signal and flashed a smile into his rearview mirror. "Karl Vernhausen" could finally relax. He sank back into the soft leather seat and stretched his legs out as far as they would go. Within an hour, he'd be free to start making arrangements to get out of Syria. All he needed was an Internet connection and new instructions from his client.

20

———～———

Düsseldorf, Germany

BELMAR HASTILY SHIFTED the papers around on his desk in an effort to make it look neater. Actually, it was already well organized as far as he was concerned. Every paper was either in an appropriate pile or a proper folder, although to the untrained eye, it might look like his desk was a mess. But Belmar knew where everything was and that was all that mattered. Today, though, he needed his desk to look respectable—well, at least semi-respectable. The same went for the desks of the detectives sitting in the outer office. Belmar looked up briefly from the clutter and into the detectives' pit. The office was a flurry of activity, with junior detectives stashing papers and half-eaten lunches into drawers and filing cabinets. None wanted to be the one Belmar singled out as not having done a good enough job.

Belmar looked back at his desk and saw that all of his rearranging had made little difference. "To hell with it!" he said, loud enough for the detectives in the pit to hear. What could Headquarters expect him to do on such short notice, anyway? Here it was, almost 3:15 p.m., and they wanted him to meet with some American attorney without even telling him why. All they said was that the visit had been requested by the naval attaché at the American Embassy. He had no idea what case the American naval attaché could possibly be interested in. He wasn't working any cases involving American sailors, and none of the other detectives had any cases even remotely involving Americans.

Frustrated, but with everything done he intended to do, he sat back and started going through his inbox. This by itself was an all-day project, given the ten-inch stack of papers and reports he'd let build up. Before he'd received the call from Headquarters, he'd planned to have the task finished before going home. Now the chances of that happening looked slim.

Shortly after he sat down and began reading, the pit became uncharacteristically quiet. Belmar looked up to see why and saw a beautiful woman standing in the middle of the pit, apparently waiting for someone to speak to her. A man dressed in a business suit stood behind her. Belmar got up to greet them, but before he reached his door, Detective Schueller was shaking hands with the woman and introducing himself. When she responded in fluent German, albeit with a slight American accent, Belmar was impressed. He cut in on Detective Schueller's introduction with more confidence than he ever could have done in a social setting. The conversation began in German.

"May I introduce myself? My name is Detective Günther Belmar." Belmar held out his hand and Michelle shook it with a firm grip.

"I am pleased to meet you, Detective Belmar. I am Michelle Siegel. Also, please let me introduce Mr. Steve Stilwell. I will interpret for him today."

Up until this point, Steve had been slightly off to Michelle's right. He had yet to say anything and merely stood there smiling. When he heard Michelle mention his name, he extended his hand toward Belmar and they shook hands.

"I am pleased to meet you, Mr. Stilwell," Detective Belmar said in textbook English. "I take it you do not speak German?" Belmar wasn't trying to embarrass his visitor, but simply wanted to establish how the conversation should proceed.

"I'm sorry to say I do not," Steve replied. "I only speak English, and some say I don't do that very well."

Steve chuckled as he spoke, but Belmar didn't laugh. Belmar was mission oriented and right now his mission was to find out what the Americans wanted and send them on their way. Humor was not a part of the equation.

"Please, come into my office." Belmar gestured for Michelle and Steve to follow, and Steve stepped back so that Michelle could lead the way. When all were inside, Belmar offered Michelle a chair. Steve sat down in the other chair next to her. Now Belmar was embarrassed about the condition of his desk, but there was nothing he could do about it. He could, however, be as hospitable as possible.

"Would either of you like something to drink?" Belmar asked before returning to his seat. Steve looked at Michelle and waited for her to respond first.

"Nothing for me, thank you," Michelle replied.

"I could go for a Coke," Steve answered.

"There's no need for you to go for it, Mr. Stilwell," Belmar replied, not quite understanding the American's enthusiasm to get the drink himself. "I can have it brought to you."

"That would be great," Steve said, his mouth twitching at the corners to hold back the laughter.

As Belmar sat down, he picked up his telephone and ordered Steve's drink. Then he looked at Michelle and rocked back in his chair. "Miss Siegel, your German is excellent. Where did you learn to speak it?"

"My father was German," Michelle said, making direct eye contact with Belmar. "He insisted I learn it as a child."

"Good for him. Does your father live in America?"

Michelle looked down at her knees. "My father is dead."

"I'm very sorry, Ms. Siegel. I didn't know."

"Of course you didn't," Michelle said, regaining eye contact, "but we didn't come here to discuss my father."

"Yes," Belmar acknowledged. "What is it exactly that I might help you with?"

Steve used Belmar's question as the opportunity to direct the remainder of the conversation.

"Detective Belmar, I'm an American attorney and I represent the estate of Ms. Siegel's father, Professor Felix Siegel. Professor Siegel died about ten days ago in a terrorist bombing in Israel. He left a substantial sum of money to a friend who lived in Düsseldorf. We came to Düsseldorf this morning to inform Mr. Weisentrope about Professor Siegel's death and—"

"Excuse me," Belmar interrupted. "Did you say Weisentrope?"

"Yes, but—"

"Emil Weisentrope?" Belmar was struck by the apparent coincidence, not yet recognizing Emil Weisentrope's death was precisely why Steve and Michelle were in his office.

"Yes, that's him," Steve said, finally able to complete a sentence.

"Then you must please wait a minute while I check something." Belmar stood up and walked over to his active case filing cabinet. He opened the drawer, thumbed to the Weisentrope file, and pulled it out with one hand while shoving the drawer closed with the other. He walked back to his desk and set the one and a half inch thick file in front of him. Not saying anything, he sat down, centered the file on the desk, and opened it. After glancing over the file summary sheet, he finally spoke.

"I'm sorry to tell you that Emil Weisentrope is dead."

"I was afraid you were going to say that," Steve said. "We spoke to the woman this morning who moved into his apartment after he died. She couldn't tell us much."

"I'm afraid I can't tell you much either, as the case is still open."

"I take it then he was murdered?" Steve asked.

"It was more than a murder, Mr. Stilwell. It was an execution." Belmar's voice rang with the frustration of a detective at a dead end.

"Can you tell me when he died?"

"Of course." Belmar looked down again at the summary sheet in the file. "He was killed on the thirtieth of September."

"I really only need one more thing."

"And what is that?" Belmar thought Steve was getting ready to ask for details he couldn't disclose.

"All I need is an official document that confirms Emil Weisentrope died on September 30, like a death certificate or autopsy report."

Belmar looked back at the file and began to flip through the documents fastened to the right side with a two-prong fastener. About three-quarters of the way through, he paper-clipped a page and then continued flipping through the remaining documents. He clipped two more pages before reaching the end of the file.

"I have three documents that might help you. They're in German, of course."

"That's no problem," Steve responded. "I'll have them translated when we arrive back in the States."

"Then why don't you take a look at them and tell me which one you want. I can tell you what information each one contains." Belmar flipped the file open to the first paper-clipped page. It was Emil Weisentrope's death certificate. Then he added, "Is the main thing you are looking for the date of death?"

"That's correct," Steve said as he walked around Belmar's desk and began to stoop over the file to look at the documents. "The other information would be—"

Steve stopped mid-sentence and stared at the *other* side of the file, while Belmar waited for him to finish his sentence.

"Would be what, Mr. Stilwell?"

"Let me think for just a second," Steve said, peering over at Michelle. When he saw she was looking down at the floor, apparently paying little attention to the goings on, he lapsed back into silence.

"Take all the time you need," Belmar said, perturbed. He could feel the work in his inbox piling up as he waited for Steve to speak.

Steve's face lit up. "Detective Belmar, if you give me a piece of paper and a pen, I'll write down exactly what I need and then you can give me the documents that contain the information. How does that sound?"

"If you think it's that complicated, we can do it that way." Belmar pulled out the center drawer of his metal desk just far enough to display a stash of pens and dull-tipped pencils. He took a pen and handed it to Steve, together with a yellow legal pad. Steve scribbled out a note.

> I have information about Emil Weisentrope's killer, but I can't say it in front of Michelle. I think she's involved!

Belmar looked at the message in disbelief. Now it was he who was speechless. How could this American lawyer have any information that could help his case? His first impression was that Headquarters had set him up with a wingnut just to mollify the American embassy. But what if this guy did know something? More important, what could it be? Belmar had to know, but first he had to come up with some unobtrusive way to get Michelle out of his office.

"Excuse me, Mr. Stilwell, why don't you relax and have a seat for a moment. I want to see what happened to the drink you requested. I'll be right back."

Belmar had an idea. He wasn't sure if it would work, but

it was worth a try. He looked over at Michelle and saw her looking up at him.

"Please excuse me, Miss Siegel. I assure you I'll be back in just a minute." With that, Belmar walked out into the detectives' pit, where neither Michelle nor Steve could see him.

Belmar's departure raised Steve's level of concern. He hoped he did the right thing by telling Belmar. His information was more than speculation; it was strong circumstantial evidence. He also hoped this wouldn't delay his departure tomorrow, but he was preparing for the worst. This had been such a bizarre case from the very beginning. What started as his first will client now had him sitting in a German police station ready to pin a murder on his client's daughter.

"What in the world is taking so long?" Michelle inquired, looking over her shoulder to see where Belmar had gone. Before Steve could answer, Belmar returned with Steve's drink and Detective Schueller.

"Miss Siegel, Mr. Stilwell, please let me introduce Detective Hans Schueller." After giving Steve his drink, Belmar stepped back so that the parties could shake hands.

"I believe we spoke when we walked in," Michelle said as she and Steve took turns shaking Detective Schueller's hand.

Belmar continued. "I can see this process is going to take a little longer than I originally thought, as I've got to get clearance to release the document you require. I wonder, then, Miss Siegel, if you would do us the honor of allowing Detective Schueller to show you around our station while I get Mr. Stilwell what he needs? It's not every day we are visited by a beautiful American model, and we would love to show you around and get you a cup of good German coffee."

"I'm very flattered, but I'm afraid I'm not a model and I really don't mind waiting until you finish with Mr. Stilwell."

"Please, Miss Siegel, everyone will enjoy meeting you," Detective Schueller added in German.

"Why don't you go, Miss Siegel?" Steve said, trying not to

sound too much in favor of the idea. "I'm sure you'll enjoy it. It'll certainly be better than sitting around here while I wait for a copy of a death certificate."

Michelle smiled as if she deserved the attention and then gave in. "Well, I suppose I can't object when it's three against one. Shall we go, Detective Schueller?"

"That's the spirit!" Steve said, a little too enthusiastically. Michelle shot him an *I'll deal with you later* look similar to the one his wife often gave him. He smiled and shrugged as Michelle and Detective Schueller left the office.

"Please, you will call me Hans," Steve heard Detective Schueller say as they disappeared out the office door. Steve's face became stern. He didn't know where to begin, so he simply took a deep breath and started to speak.

"Detective Belmar, I couldn't talk in front of Ms. Siegel. But when I walked around your desk and looked in your file, I saw the picture on the left side of the folder." Steve paused for a second to see if Belmar showed any interest in what he was saying.

"So?"

"So, I saw that man with Michelle Siegel just before her father was killed. I take it that's the man you think killed Emil Weisentrope?"

"Mr. Stilwell, you must appreciate my position—"

"Detective Belmar, you know as well as I do that the man in the picture is your prime suspect. He has to be."

"Why do you say that?"

"Because it can't be Emil Weisentrope. He was an old man. He was in Auschwitz with Michelle Siegel's father during the war. The man in the picture is far too young. More importantly, I saw him with Michelle on the day her father signed his will."

"Go on."

"All I have is circumstantial evidence to back what I am about to say." Steve hesitated for a moment to see if he really wanted to go on. For a second he thought he should tell the

American authorities before he told the German police. But then, there was no crime in America—the murder took place Germany—so he decided to continue. There was no turning back.

"I believe Michelle Siegel is somehow involved in Emil Weisentrope's death." Steve could almost see the words leaving his mouth and floating toward Belmar. When they hit Belmar's face, Belmar's expression changed to one of disbelief.

"Mr. Stilwell—"

"Would it make a difference if I told you that because Emil Weisentrope died before Michelle's father, Michelle inherited the half-million dollars her father left to Emil Weisentrope?" Steve paused to make sure Belmar understood. "Let me say that again. Michelle Siegel's father left Emil Weisentrope five hundred thousand dollars. But because the man died before Michelle's father did, she receives Emil Weisentrope's share."

"Mr. Stilwell," Belmar interjected again, "as a lawyer, you should know that's not enough to build a case on."

Steve nodded. "There's more. Just before Michelle's father left for Israel, I went to her father's house so he could execute his will. Michelle was there, too. After her father left, the man in the picture knocked on the front door and Michelle let him in. She said they were strangers, but she ended up going out to dinner with him that night. Ten days later, Michelle's father is killed and Michelle inherits millions of dollars."

"That is interesting, but it's still not enough. Your embassy would be up in arms if I arrested her on that."

"Then let me tell you something else even more interesting. Michelle's father left three of his friends half a million dollars apiece. His friends were Emil Weisentrope, Teodor Rudnik, and Tadeusz Zalinsky. You know what happened to Emil Weisentrope. And now you know that Michelle's father was murdered. But did you know about Teodor Rudnik?"

"I've never heard of him."

"Well, he was murdered a little over two months ago

in England. And because he died before Michelle's father, Michelle gets his half-million too."

"How did Rudnik die?"

"He was shot during a robbery."

Belmar sat straight up in his chair. "Where was he shot?"

"I'm not sure where he was when—"

"I'm sorry," Belmar interrupted. "Where on his body was he shot?"

"If I remember correctly, it was a gunshot wound in the head." Steve was pretty sure of his answer, but exactly where Mr. Rudnik was shot hadn't been as important to him as the fact that Mr. Rudnik had been shot at all.

"That's the same way Herr Weisentrope was killed. Maybe we *are* talking about the same killer." Belmar rubbed his chin and thought for a moment. "You know I'll have to verify everything you've told me with INTERPOL. I hope you are telling the truth, Mr. Stilwell."

"It'll check out," Steve said, knowing he was correct. "Besides, why would I lie?"

Belmar ignored Steve's question and responded with one of his own. "What about the last guy, was he killed too?"

"You mean Zalinsky?"

"Whoever the third friend was."

"That's the only part I can't explain. He's still alive. If he had died before Michelle's father, then Michelle would have taken his share too. But for some reason, she let him live and now there's nothing she can do to keep him from getting the money."

"Tell me, Mr. Stilwell, why did Professor Siegel leave these men so much money, anyway? Wouldn't most people leave it to their daughter rather than their friends?"

"That's precisely my point. That's why Michelle had to be involved. She must have thought she was entitled to the money."

"Is that everything?"

"There is one more thing. Almost immediately after

Professor Siegel died, Michelle came into my office to see when she could start collecting her share of her father's estate. In fact, that's why I'm here today. She didn't want to wait for the normal process. She wants as much money as she can get, as soon as she can get it."

"Give me the name of the one who is still alive," Belmar directed as he prepared to write.

"It's Zalinsky, Tadeusz Zalinsky."

"Did you warn him?"

"About what?"

"About the murders and the danger he's in. Isn't it obvious?"

"I don't think he's in any danger. Now that Professor Siegel is dead and Michelle's inheritance is fixed, I don't think there'll be any more killings."

"What if you're wrong?"

"I'm not. Michelle and the man in that picture are the keys to the murders." He leaned forward, almost to the point of being able to put his arms on Belmar's desk. "So what's your plan?"

Belmar came to his feet and painted a quick smile on his face. He walked around the corner of his desk and began speaking as he approached the door.

"I hope you enjoyed your tour, Ms. Siegel."

Michelle remained focused on Detective Schueller. "Thank you, Hans." She extended him her hand.

Hans took Michelle's hand and grinned the grin of a married man. "It was my pleasure," he replied, speaking loud enough for those in the pit to hear. Then he bowed a gentleman's bow and withdrew from the room.

"Thank you for arranging the tour, Detective Belmar," Michelle said. "I enjoyed it."

"I'm glad you liked it," Belmar responded, as he once again stood behind his desk and opened the folder containing the documents he was considering copying for Steve. "I'm afraid we've done a bit too much talking here and we still have to copy these pages." Belmar motioned for Michelle to take a seat.

"Please, sit down and relax while I make these copies. It will only take a minute." Belmar gathered up the Weisentrope file and left the room as Michelle sat down.

"So, what did you talk about?" Michelle asked.

Steve wasn't sure if she really wanted to know or if she was just making idle conversation. He guessed it was the latter and tried to shift the topic back in her direction.

"We spoke some about the case, but the big question is, how was your tour?"

"I really enjoyed it. The detective, Hans, was very sweet. But I am ready to get going." Michelle sat back in the chair and brushed her hair off of her shoulders as Belmar walked back into the room and handed the documents to Steve.

"I trust you'll be able to get these translated," Belmar said as he stepped to the side of his desk. The fact that he remained standing cued both Steve and Michelle that it was time to go. Steve stood up and shook hands with Belmar and Michelle did the same.

"Thank you very much for your time, Detective Belmar. You've been most helpful, especially on such short notice." Steve began to ease out the door with Michelle trailing.

"Thank you, Detective Belmar," Michelle added.

"Let me show you out of the station," Belmar said, heading for the door.

"Would you mind if I asked Hans to show us out?" Michelle spoke with an enticing smile. "I want to thank him again for showing me around."

"Of course," Belmar answered. He poked his head out the door and spoke a few phrases in German to Detective Schueller. Detective Schueller shot to his feet so quickly that his chair slammed into the wall behind his desk. One of the other three detectives in the room rolled his eyes toward the ceiling. Schueller would never let them hear the end of this.

"I hope you enjoy the remainder of your stay in Düsseldorf," Belmar added. "By the way, where are you staying?"

"The Reiman Hotel," Michelle answered.

"Very nice. I know you must be comfortable there. Do you know when you'll be leaving?"

Michelle deferred to Steve.

"We'd like to get a flight out tomorrow, but we'll have to see what's available."

"Well, if I may be of any assistance to you, please give me a call."

"Thank you, Detective Belmar," Steve said.

With that, Detective Belmar nodded to Hans that it was okay to leave. Hans walked over to the two Americans and with his best English, managed to reproduce the phrase Michelle used a few minutes before to begin her tour, "Shall we go?" Michelle offered her arm and the two left the room with Steve following close behind. He was already thinking about arranging their return flight to Washington. He'd get Michelle to help him book it as soon as they arrived back at the hotel. In twenty-four hours, they would be on their way home.

* * *

Damascus, Syria

Wilhelm Strauss, now Karl Vernhausen, walked into his hotel room and fastened the door's chain lock behind him. He didn't want to chance being disturbed by a cleaning lady on her afternoon rounds. He walked over to the chair in front of his computer and plopped down in the middle of it. Even though nothing had gone wrong, getting his new passport had drained him mentally and physically. Still, he had one more thing to check before he made his way out of Syria.

He reached up and moved his laptop's trackball just enough to get the computer screen to reappear. Having lost his previous connection, he reinitiated the logon sequence by hitting the refresh option. Because he was in Syria, he expected the process to take a long time, but now, because he wasn't in a hurry, he gained access immediately. He clicked on the pull-down menu and went directly to his client's Web page. Less than fifteen seconds later, the password screen appeared. He hit the all-caps key and typed in JINENIGHEILEN from memory. After double checking the spelling, he hit *enter* and sat back to see if his situation had changed.

Slowly, a color image formed on the screen, filling in from top to bottom. Biographical data followed. He pulled out a pen from his computer case and copied the information on to a piece of hotel stationery. Then he folded the paper, tucked it in his wallet, and shut down the computer. The sooner he got to the airport, the sooner he'd be out of Syria. He packed his belongings with a vengeance and was ready to go in fifteen minutes.

His biggest fear in checking out was that the front desk clerk would ask to see his passport. He'd had that happen before, only this time his check-out passport didn't match his check-in documentation. He approached the clerk with a cover story ready to go but didn't have to use it. The checkout clerk never asked for identification and he didn't offer any. The clerk did refer to him as Mr. Strauss, but he was ready for that and answered politely. When he finished paying for his room, he left both the checkout clerk and Wilhelm Strauss behind. From that point on, he would answer only to Karl Vernhausen.

Carrying his modest amount of luggage by himself, he walked to the concierge to arrange for a cab to the airport. A bellhop escorted him to the front entrance where they found several cabbies swarming under the green awning. The bellhop spoke enough English to act as a go-between for him and the first cab driver in line. After tipping the bellhop with U.S. dollars, he was on his way.

Usually, he liked to pay attention to the surroundings in cities he passed through. Not so with Damascus. He had absolutely no interest in seeing any more of the city, so he rested his head on the top of the back seat and closed his eyes. He was awakened some time later by a smiling cab driver trying to coax him out of the cab at the airport. His U.S. dollars paid the cab fare and then some, and the smiling cab driver repeatedly thanked him while he set his bags on the curb. Baggage handlers descended upon him, but he waved them off. No one touched his baggage unless it was absolutely necessary, and it rarely was. Instead, he slung his bag over his right shoulder, picked up his computer case, and walked into the Damascus International Airport.

He walked along the line of airline ticket counters in search of a flight to America. He immediately got into the shortest line to see if any flights were available. Unbelievably, there was a plane leaving in four hours with connections to Chicago's O'Hare airport. From there he would have access to anywhere in the United States. He purchased a first-class ticket and headed for the gate.

Even better than the early flight was the success of his new passport. The flight attendant and a Syrian immigration official never gave it or his U.S. visa a second thought. Three hours and thirty-four minutes later, he lifted off the ground in a 747 and said goodbye to Damascus forever. He was on his way to kill Tadeusz Zalinsky.

21

———— ❧ ————

Thursday, October 23
Düsseldorf, Germany

GETTING READY IN the morning was a long, drawn-out process for Michelle. Her appearance was important to her, for she saw herself as a seasoned businesswoman and wanted to make sure that was consistently the image she presented to the world. In a few short years on Wall Street, she had developed keen business acumen and a reputation for being able to drive projects through to successful conclusions. Of course she knew she was attractive and saw nothing wrong with using that to open doors. But impressing people with her looks was less important than convincing them of her authority and ability.

Michelle wanted—no, needed—affirmation of her business persona because it was business that allowed her to escape her family shackles. Working in the city after college, living away from home and earning her own money for the first time, she had finally become her own person, rising or falling on her own merit. But the combination of an abusive marriage, the rape, and her divorce had proved too much to handle, so she'd left work and returned home until she could get back on her feet. The shackles reappeared, though, as her father redoubled his efforts to prevent her from being hurt again. With her father gone, Michelle saw returning to the business world as her salvation. This time she would be a player with working capital, not just an entry-level manager. She was ready to put her Columbia business degree to the test.

At 8:45 a.m., she was primping her hair in front of the bathroom mirror. Every now and then she turned the hairdryer toward the mirror to defog it. The bathroom had no exhaust fan, and it was still steamy from the shower she'd taken twenty minutes before. She'd already put on her makeup and jeans and a light blue Angora sweater; all that was left to finish was her hair. She was supposed to meet Steve at 9:00 a.m. in the lobby for breakfast and a couple of hours of shopping. Afterward they planned to check out of the hotel and head to the airport for their flight home. Their flight departed Düsseldorf at 5:45 p.m., and after a plane change in Frankfurt, would bring them into Washington, D.C., just after 9:00 p.m.

Michelle worked in a touch of styling gel and used the hairdryer and a brush to finesse her hairstyle to perfection. The whine of the hairdryer's motor was so loud she barely heard the knocking on her hotel room door. In fact, had the bathroom not been situated near the door, she probably wouldn't have heard the knocking at all. While still drying her hair with one hand, she stopped brushing long enough to glance at her watch. It wasn't even 8:50. She distinctly remembered telling Steve to meet her in the lobby at 9:00. Plus, she didn't like him coming by her room. She much preferred meeting him in the lobby. In any event, he was just going to have to wait until she finished getting ready.

As she started blowing her hair off her shoulders, the knocking started again, this time more insistent. Although that made her want to make Steve wait even longer, she decided it would be better to tell him she would be ready in a few minutes and to wait for her in the lobby. She turned off the hairdryer and checked herself in the mirror one last time; she was satisfied with what she saw. Two steps later she was around the corner and standing in front of the door. She unfastened the chain lock, turned the deadbolt, and yanked the door open to communicate her dismay at having been bothered prior to the agreed-upon time.

To her surprise, she saw not Steve, but Detective Hans Schueller and two other detectives from the Düsseldorf police. At first she thought Detective Schueller had found out where she was staying and was trying to hit on her, but she dismissed that thought because he was there with two other men. Then she thought she must have done something wrong, but had no idea what it was. She fought to maintain her composure and spoke to the detectives entirely in German.

"Hans, what are you doing here? It's not even nine o'clock."

"I am very sorry to disturb you, Miss Siegel, but I need to ask you to come back to the police station for a little while."

"I'm sorry, Hans, but I can't. I'm meeting Mr. Stilwell for breakfast at nine o'clock and then we're going shopping. You know we're returning to the United States this afternoon."

"You don't understand, Miss Siegel, but you *must* come with me."

"What in God's name do you need me for?" Michelle blurted out, unable to grasp what was happening.

"We just need you to answer a few questions," Hans replied, trying his best to be patient. "Please, Miss Siegel. Gather your things and come with us to the police station."

"What do you mean *gather my things*? Do you expect me to pack up and check out just so I can go with you to answer a few silly questions? You can't be serious, Hans."

"I didn't mean for you to pack all your belongings, but you should get what you think you'll need for the day."

"The day! I'm leaving this afternoon. I demand to speak to

my embassy." Just as she finished, she saw Steve walk out of his room. When he turned to lock his door, he looked over to where Michelle was standing and made eye contact with her. They were about twenty-five feet apart.

"Steve, thank God you're still up here. Would you come here for minute and explain something to these men?"

Steve approached Michelle and the three detectives. He recognized the detective who gave Michelle the tour the day before, but not the other two. Although they might have been in the detectives' pit when he and Michelle walked through, he hadn't noticed them. He walked up to the group to see why Michelle was so spun up, although unlike Michelle, he had an idea what the cause might be. He hadn't really thought through all the repercussions of his discussion with Detective Belmar. Deep down, though, he knew once he informed Belmar of his suspicions, Belmar could not allow Michelle to leave the country because extraditing her from the United States could take up to a year.

What he hadn't thought through was how Belmar would take care of what needed to be done. He also hadn't thought of what Michelle would do if she found out he was the one who tipped off Belmar. He hoped she wouldn't figure it out on her own, although she certainly had all the information she needed to link him to her arrest. What he naively envisioned was being able to walk a fine line between Michelle and Belmar, feeding Belmar the information he needed to solve the murders but appearing to Michelle as a trusted ally. A lot depended on how Belmar presented the situation to Michelle. A lot more depended on luck.

"What's going on here?" Steve asked, half smiling.

"These *detectives* are telling me I need to go with them to the police station."

Steve could see that even the Germans, who spoke little or no English, recognized Michelle's negative emphasis on the word "detectives." He knew he had to step in before she dug herself a hole she couldn't get out of. With all her apparent sophistication, she couldn't recognize a situation where it was in her best interests to at least feign civility. Cooperation now could make the difference between liberty and incarceration.

Steve thought he could make inroads for Michelle by speaking to the detective he recognized from the day before, but he couldn't remember the detective's name or whether he spoke English. He had to go through Michelle to get answers to both questions.

"Ms. Siegel, could you remind me of the name of your escort at the police station yesterday?" Steve spoke softly, but not so softly that the detectives would think he couldn't be trusted. He made sure they could hear everything he said, even if they might not be able to understand it.

Michelle made no effort to speak calmly or softly. Instead she spoke loudly, enunciating each syllable as if she were making a public address in a crowded auditorium without a microphone.

"It's Schueller, Hans Schueller."

After hearing Michelle's response, Steve didn't bother asking her whether Detective Schueller spoke English. He was afraid she'd use the opportunity to belittle the detective. Besides, it was easy enough to find out on his own.

"Detective Schueller," Steve began, attempting to gain the detective's attention. "Could you tell me what's going on here?"

Detective Schueller didn't answer. Instead, he looked to Michelle to translate what Steve had said.

"Michelle, I think Detective Schueller wants you to translate for him," Steve said when he realized Michelle was too preoccupied to notice the detective's need. She relayed Steve's question without looking at Detective Schueller, and then translated his response for Steve.

"He says I've got to go down to the station to answer some questions." Michelle paused and huffed a bit before continuing. "I'm not under arrest, but if I refuse to go, he has instructions to arrest me. He says he can't tell me any more than that. Now, Mr. lawyer, what the hell do I do?"

It was all Steve could do to keep from walking away. Michelle had been condescending and unfriendly since the day they met. How nice it would be to see this rich, spoiled, rude woman suffer. Her current attitude only reinforced his thoughts. But it simply wasn't in Steve's DNA to abandon her, especially since he was the one who brought about the situation. Of course, she was the one involved in the brutal deaths of at least three old men. Still, he felt some semblance of responsibility for her.

"Ask him if I can ride with you to the police station."

Michelle did as directed and then translated Detective Schueller's response.

"He says that's permissible, but one of his detectives must accompany us."

"Tell him that will be fine. Grab what you need to take to the police station and let's get going. Maybe we can still make our flight this afternoon."

"You're not going to let them take me, are you?" Michelle asked with more anger in her voice than panic.

"We don't have a choice. This is Germany, Ms. Siegel, not America. You've got to at least pretend to cooperate. Otherwise, this could be a long and painful experience. Let's try not to let that happen, for both our sakes."

Michelle's eyes widened. It was the first time Steve had spoken so bluntly to her.

"I'll also give the embassy a call as soon as we get to the station," Steve reassured her. "I'm certain this will be over in no time." In reality, though, he knew it wouldn't be.

* * *

Berlin, Germany

HERMANN BORNE UNLOCKED the door to his flat and went inside. He tried to pull the door closed too quickly and it got away from him. The slam echoed throughout the apartment.

"Hello, father," he called, still standing in the foyer. There was no reply, only silence. He fastened the chain lock and walked into the living room. There sat his father, perched in his wheelchair, looking out over the Spree River. "I'm home, father," he announced again, hoping to gain some sign of recognition or acknowledgment. Even a twitch or a flinch at the sound of his voice would be welcome. But the words evoked no response. They never did. It was as if Hermann were living in a horrible, recurring dream that haunted him day after day. But this dream was reality.

Hermann's reality only fueled his hatred and impatience. He walked from the living room back to his study and turned on his computer. He cursed under his breath at the time it took to boot up, even though the start up sequence lasted only a few seconds. At last the computer screen displayed Hermann's tailor-made desktop menu. He launched his email account. There was one new message from the password-defined user JINENIGHEILEN. Hermann's pulse throbbed as he opened the message. It was short, but it gave him what he was looking for: "arrived cleveland ohio beginning work tomorrow." Hermann read the message four or five times for its soothing effect. Then he deleted it, leaned back in his chair, and closed his eyes.

"Soon," he said in a barely audible voice. "Very soon." He slid forward in his chair and rested his head on the desk, using his hands and arms as a pillow. He shut his eyes and tried to rest, but his mind began to wander. He thought he'd be able to relax with the jobs now all but complete. Instead he felt his hatred growing in intensity. He feared something would go wrong that might allow the last one to escape. He had to be able to tell his father what he had done. That, he believed, would make his father talk and show some respect. Anything less than complete and total success would be unacceptable, both for him and his father. Of course, he hadn't told his father what he was doing. Plans could not possibly impress such a man. But actions—completed actions—might.

Now more excited than when he'd laid his head down, he keyed the computer to enter his Web page. He had to send a message; he could afford to wait no longer. He typed "COMPLETE IMMEDIATELY!" just below Tadeusz Zalinsky's picture and exited the screen. He felt his heart racing and he was breathing harder than usual. In the ten minutes since sitting down to relax, he had worked himself into a frenzy. There was no escaping it. He could not rest, no, he *would* not rest, until the last man was dead.

22

Düsseldorf, Germany

"PLEASE COME IN and sit down, Miss Siegel," Belmar said as if nothing had changed since their pleasant meeting the day before. He walked from behind his desk to greet Michelle as she entered his office. The scowl on her face told him she was not taking the unscheduled visit well.

Michelle did not sit down. Instead, she stood in front of one of the guest chairs facing Belmar's desk, while Steve stood in front of the other. Upon entering the office, Steve said nothing, waiting instead for Belmar to address him. He didn't want to make it look like he had orchestrated the visit.

"Good morning, Mr. Stilwell," Belmar said.

"Good morning, Detective," Steve replied. "May I ask why you have summoned us this morning?"

"Actually, Mr. Stilwell, I didn't summon you at all. I really only need to speak to Miss Siegel."

"May I ask what about?" Steve inquired.

"Are you Miss Siegel's attorney?"

"Well, no." Steve knew his answer would leave Michelle

feeling abandoned, but he really had no choice. He was already representing her father's estate and had to be careful not to conflict himself out of that representation. Still, he hated for the issue to come up this way, rather than in a one-on-one discussion with Michelle.

"Then I'm afraid I'm going to have to ask you to leave, so I can speak with Miss Siegel in private."

"I'd like to notify our embassy, then," Steve responded, hoping to bolster Michelle's confidence.

"Of course." Belmar spoke in German to Detective Schueller, who was standing in the doorway leading to the detectives' pit. Detective Schueller motioned for Steve to follow him. Before leaving, Steve tried to reassure Michelle.

"Will you be okay?"

"Does it matter?"

"It does to me," Steve replied, rather than letting it drop.

"I'll be fine," she said, trying to appear unshaken. "Just get a hold of the embassy and tell them what's going on."

Steve nodded and glanced at Belmar. Belmar gave him a confirming look, and then Steve left with Detective Schueller for the phones in the detectives' pit. When Detective Schueller returned alone, Belmar commenced the questioning.

"Miss Siegel, I'm sure you're wondering why I asked you to come here this morning."

"Actually, Detective Belmar, I don't recall being *asked* to come here at all."

Belmar didn't flinch. "I'd like you to tell me about your father's relationship with Emil Weisentrope. How did your father know him?"

"They met at Auschwitz," Michelle answered. Then she looked Belmar right in the eye, and in a surprisingly defiant tone for one being questioned in the custody of a foreign police department, added, "They both survived your country's attempt to exterminate the Jews."

Belmar couldn't let Michelle see that her response cut him

deeply. It wasn't the time or place to explain he had personally vowed to get to the bottom of Emil Weisentrope's murder precisely because the man had been persecuted during the war. Belmar was not of the old Germany. But he couldn't dwell on the point. He had to find out if Michelle was blowing smoke to cover her role in the old man's death. That meant remaining focused and not allowing his personal sensitivities to get in the way. He moved on with the interrogation, but at a faster pace.

"Did they ever see each other after the war?"

"A couple of times."

"Didn't your father leave him five hundred thousand dollars in his will?"

"Yes."

"But I thought you said they only saw each other a couple of times?"

"That's what I said."

"Did they correspond at all?"

"Yes."

"How did they correspond?"

"They wrote to each other."

"How often?"

"To tell you the truth, Detective Belmar, I never really kept track."

"So let me ask you then, Miss Siegel. Don't you find it a little strange that your father left five hundred thousand dollars to a man he only wrote to every once in a while, instead of leaving the money to his only daughter?"

"Is there a point to these questions, Detective Belmar? I mean, I hope you didn't call me to your office and risk me missing my flight back to the United States just to satisfy your curiosity as to why my father might leave an old friend some money." Michelle sat back in her chair, crossed her legs, and with her arms clamped across her chest, added, "And I hope you are ready to explain this to my embassy."

Detective Belmar was surprised by Michelle's brashness. He

hadn't seen this side of her the day before. He couldn't tell if it was a guise or genuine indignation. He decided he better get to the point, especially now that Michelle was obviously upset but still in control.

"Okay, Miss Siegel, I suppose I owe you an explanation. First, though, I have one more thing to ask you about." Belmar stood up behind his desk and opened the Weisentrope file. Wilhelm Strauss' picture was loose inside, staged for quick access at the most opportune time. Belmar picked up the photograph and looked it over silently for a few moments to allow the suspense to build.

Michelle stared at the back of a photograph like a cat ready to pounce on its unsuspecting prey. She became so engrossed in trying to figure out what it might be that she jumped when Belmar finally spoke again.

"Miss Siegel," he began as he walked around his desk to hand the picture to her, "tell me, do you recognize the man in this picture?" After Belmar passed it over to Michelle, he and Detective Schueller focused like lasers on her face to detect any measurable reaction.

Michelle took the photograph and rotated it until it was right side up. "This isn't Emil Weisentrope," she said with a quizzical look.

"I didn't say it was. We were hoping you would recognize him."

"What if I do?" Michelle asked cautiously.

"Then why don't you tell us who he is?"

Michelle did not respond. In fact, she couldn't respond. She just sat there, glaring at the picture. Twice she looked up at Belmar, only to find his piercing eyes riveted on her. He gave her no way out.

"Well, Miss Siegel?"

"All right, I recognize him." Michelle shifted in her chair and pulled her hair back into a ponytail, only to let it fall free again. Belmar did not let up.

"Who is he?"

"His name is Wilhelm Strauss."

Belmar looked away from Michelle and directly at Detective Schueller. First, he hadn't expected her to immediately admit knowing the man. Second, and even more surprising, was that the name she gave matched the name provided by U.S. Customs. Belmar thought it would be harder than that. In fact, this was the first indication that Michelle really didn't know why she was there. Then again, he knew Michelle was aware Steve saw her with Strauss, so she had to tell the truth or risk Steve exposing her as a liar. Belmar decided to press his unexpected good fortune and see what additional information he could glean from her.

"How do you know Wilhelm Strauss?"

"Detective Belmar," Michelle began, shifting from patience to exasperation in the space of two words, "before I answer any more questions, I want you to tell me what is going on here."

"We're just trying to obtain information that will help us with our investigation."

"What investigation are you talking about?"

"Why, the Weisentrope investigation, Miss Siegel," Belmar said, matter-of-factly. "What other investigations are you aware of?"

"Only the investigation into my father's death."

"Oh, yes. I'm sorry," Belmar apologized. "We aren't involved in that investigation ... *yet*." Belmar ended on an intentionally cryptic note.

"So what does this picture have to do with Mr. Weisentrope's death?"

"That's what we were hoping you could tell us," Belmar answered.

"How should I know?"

Michelle's intransigence and her apparent ignorance of the link between Strauss and Emil Weisentrope's death led Belmar to conclude that either she really had nothing to do with the murder or she was an incredibly effective liar. He decided to take the next step and make the connection for her.

"Miss Siegel, Wilhelm Strauss is the man who murdered Emil Weisentrope."

Belmar couldn't have predicted the effect his words had on Michelle. She gasped and covered her mouth with her hand, frozen in shock. Her radiant complexion paled and she sat all the way back in her chair.

"I'm sure you must be mistaken," she said defensively.

"And why is that, Miss Siegel?"

"He didn't seem like he could kill someone," she answered, searching for the right words and finding them impossible to come by.

Belmar sensed blood and began to close in. "It sounds like you knew him well."

"I met him once," Michelle answered in an attempt to distance herself from the murderer. "He came to my father's house in Tappahannock, Virginia, asking about the neighborhood. As a matter of fact, Steve Stilwell was there when he came by. You can ask him." Michelle's face flushed with realization. "But then, I suppose you've already discussed that with Mr. Stilwell, haven't you?"

Belmar ignored her question. "When was it that you met him?"

"It was just before I left for Israel. I think it was around the first Friday in October."

Belmar began paging backward through his desk calendar. "That would make it sometime around October third?"

"You're the one with the calendar," she answered, returning to her former brash style. Her anger toward Steve had reinvigorated her.

"Is that the only time you ever saw him?"

"I saw him the next day, as well."

"Miss Siegel, you said you saw Wilhelm Strauss at your

father's house on October third and fourth. If he was only interested in learning about the neighborhood, why did you spend so much time with him?"

"Look, I slept with the man. Does that make you happy? We had wild sex one night after my father left for Israel. Now you can go tell all your detective buddies you got the American model to admit she had sex with a man she hardly knew. I think it's time for me to leave now." Michelle stood up to make good on her announcement.

This was not the direction Belmar had expected the interview to proceed, and he didn't have any questions in mind to follow Michelle's revelation. Her attempted exit, however, gave him a rallying point.

"Please sit down, Miss Siegel. I can appreciate that this is an embarrassing situation for you, but we need to ask you some more questions before you can go."

"Why don't you ask Wilhelm Strauss?"

"Because we need to ask you. Now please sit down."

Michelle did as instructed but maintained a rigid, uncompromising posture. "I want to speak with someone at the U.S. embassy before I answer any more questions."

"We informed your embassy this morning that we'd be questioning you today." Belmar hoped that would be enough to keep Michelle from terminating the session.

"That's just great, Detective. But *I* want to speak with them before we go on."

"As you wish." Then Belmar dropped the bombshell. He had rehearsed it several times before Michelle arrived, knowing the reaction he would get. The rehearsals paid off, for the announcement came across as if there were absolutely no other alternatives.

"Under German law, I can arrest you and hold you in custody because, as a foreigner, you are a flight risk. Your case would then be examined by a judge who will decide whether or not you will remain in our custody. The other option we have, and the one I recommend, is that you give me your passport and agree to voluntarily stay, at your own expense, of course, until we complete our investigation. The choice, Miss Siegel, is yours."

"This is absurd. I've done nothing wrong." She spoke again, still forcefully, but lacking her former brashness. "What can you possibly hold me for?"

"Why, murder, Miss Siegel. Complicity to murder."

* * *

MICHELLE'S REUNION WITH Steve in the detectives' pit was not one Steve would soon forget. He had just finished speaking to the naval attaché and was sitting at Detective Schueller's desk when Michelle emerged from Belmar's office. She made a beeline toward him with a look on her face that made his skin crawl. He braced himself for what he thought would be an unpleasant exchange; however, Michelle had no exchange in mind. She let loose, even before she came to a complete stop in front of Detective Schueller's desk, with an accusation loud enough to cause people walking by in the hallway to turn their heads to see what was going on.

"Listen, you bastard. I don't know what you told these Nazis about me, but you better un-tell it fast, or so help me, when I get back to the States I'll make sure the only will you ever write again will be your own!"

"Michelle, let me ex—"

"You'd better explain. You'd better tell me why I'm under arrest when you're free to go." Then she turned her attention back toward Belmar, who by this time was standing just outside his door with the other detectives in the pit, watching the show. Her tirade increased both in volume and intensity.

"I demand to speak to someone at my embassy this instant. I cannot believe this is happening. Detective Belmar, have one of your men get me in touch with the U.S. embassy."

Steve could stand no more of it. He'd put up with this rude, insolent woman long enough. He was going to give her one chance and one chance only to come around, or he was through with her. He felt somewhat responsible for her predicament, but he would only help her now if she cooperated. He got up, walked around the desk and stood dangerously close to her. He spoke quietly to force her to concentrate on what he was telling her.

"I need you to listen very closely to what I am about to say."

"I—" Michelle began.

"Shhhhhhh!" Steve blurted out angrily. "The reason you're being held is because you were with the man they believe killed Emil Weisentrope just days after the old man's death. They also know that you will get an extra five hundred thousand dollars because Emil Weisentrope died before your father. If that isn't enough, they know that the same killer probably murdered Teodor Rudnik a few weeks before he killed Emil Weisentrope, and that also made you five hundred thousand richer. What that means is, you're lucky you're not already in jail. They've cut you some slack, which I'm not sure you deserve. So take my advice, Ms. Siegel. You'd better start treating these men with a little respect or you'll find yourself under arrest and waiting for months to stand trial."

Michelle was speechless. After a few seconds passed, she sat on the corner of Detective Schueller's desk and looked down at the floor. Her voice was sullen and barely audible. "I had nothing to do with these murders, Mr. Stilwell, so help me God."

"For your sake, I hope not," Steve replied, not recognizing that Michelle was reaching out for help. She decided to take a less subtle approach.

"What should I do?"

"Give these men your passport and agree for the time being to remain at the hotel for five days. If you don't, you'll leave them no choice but to arrest you. They won't want to let you go now because it would be too difficult to extradite you, especially when they've got you here already. In the meantime, I'll work with the embassy to get you in touch with a local lawyer. And above all, you've got to be civil to them. You haven't endeared yourself by calling them Nazis. To put it bluntly, they're the ones holding all the cards."

Michelle didn't wait to hear any more. She set her purse on the desk and opened it up as wide as it would go, pulling out her passport. At first Steve thought she was going to toss it on the floor in a final act of defiance, but she'd evidently taken to heart what he'd said and suppressed her first instinct. After one last look at her passport's cover, she handed it to Steve.

"Give it to whomever you've got to give it to."

Steve nodded and walked across the room, feeling almost disappointed that Michelle had given in. He handed her passport to Belmar, who passed it, in turn, to Detective Schueller. Steve knew it was time to make their exit.

"Thank you, Detective Belmar, for allowing Ms. Siegel to stay in her hotel. I'm sure she'll be available as the need arises."

"Will you still be departing this afternoon?" Belmar asked.

"I'm afraid I must."

"Very well, then. I'll have Detective Schueller drive you and Miss Siegel back to your hotel. Would you be sure to give Detective Schueller a number where we can reach you during the course of our investigation?"

"Certainly."

"I'm sorry for the inconvenience, Miss Siegel," Belmar said. "I can assure you we will move to resolve your situation as quickly as possible."

Michelle responded with a subdued "thank you" and nothing more. She retrieved her purse and began to walk to the door. Steve shook hands with Belmar and followed Michelle, who by now was in the hallway. Detective Schueller trailed them both.

Steve was ready for a long, quiet, embarrassingly uncomfortable ride back to the hotel. He knew what would likely happen in five days if Michelle sought to leave, but he didn't dare tell her. If Detective Belmar didn't gain any more information, either pointing to or away from Michelle, the Germans would have no choice but to arrest her. That was fine if Michelle was involved in the killings. But what if the events so far really were coincidence? Then it could be up to a year before Michelle saw the light of day again, and it would be his fault. That meant only one thing. He had five days to either prove or disprove Michelle's involvement in the murders. But how could he even begin to do that? Right now, he didn't have a clue. What he did know was that he had a six-hour plane ride ahead of him, and that would give him some time to think.

23

———~∞~———

Friday, October 24
Williamsburg

"From what I can tell, it sounds like she deserves to be in jail," Sarah commented as she poured Steve his second cup of coffee. Rarely did Sarah see him off to work, but she'd woken up early this morning to hear about his trip to Germany. He'd tried to fill her in during the ride home from Dulles Airport the night before, but the combination of jet lag and the late arrival caused him to doze off before they cleared the outskirts of Washington. Now Sarah pressed him for details about Michelle's arrest, but getting information on such a juicy subject was like pulling teeth. She set the pot back on the coffee maker and sat down at the kitchen table, waiting for a reply to her last comment. All she got was a nod and an "Mmmm," which in no way satisfied her curiosity.

"Steve, why don't you stay home and get some sleep? Mr. Smythe doesn't expect you back today, anyway."

"Can't do it today," Steve replied as he finished off his bowl of bran flakes and a glass of orange juice. "Would you mind putting my coffee in a thermal cup? It's already 6:45 and I'm gonna be late."

"Late? Your office doesn't open until nine. How can you be late?"

"You know what I mean," Steve said as he collected a plastic bowl of fruit salad for lunch and waited by the door for his coffee. Sarah handed him his covered cup and gave him a heartfelt kiss goodbye. Though not as young as she used to be, she was still a beautiful woman, he thought.

"I'll get home a little early tonight and tell you about my trip. I promise."

"That's not what I need you to promise, Steve."

Sarah's response stopped Steve halfway out the door. He couldn't leave on that note, even though he felt the Siegel case yanking him toward his car. "What do you mean?" he asked, dreading the answer because it was clear where the conversation was going.

"You know what I mean, Steve." Sarah brushed the bangs of her slightly graying but still rich brown hair away from her eyes and reached out and touched Steve on the arm. "I see you getting sucked in again, the way you did when you were in the Navy. You said it would be different once you retired."

"It's just this one case. Once it's done, there'll be plenty of time for us. I promise."

"Don't you see, Steve? It's always just one more case, or one more deployment, or one more issue. You've already missed the boys' growing up. You can't ever get that time back. Do you want to fritter away what time we have left, too?"

Sarah's response cut deep because Steve knew it was true. Although he voiced well-intentioned and honest devotion to his family, the Navy always came first. In a sense he felt trapped. It wasn't like he could just walk away from a tough assignment because it was taking up too much family time. His units had missions to accomplish, and he was a key member of the team, so they relied on him. But Sarah relied on him, too. She trusted him, over and over again, every time he said things would get better and he'd be able to spend more time at home. Now he saw a flicker of doubt in her big green eyes, eyes that implored him to make her a priority again, like she was when they first married.

"Honey, you know I love you."

"I know you do. And I love you, too. But it's going to take more than nice words from here on out. I need to see a difference, Steve. I can't just keep waiting."

Steve reached back inside the door, set his fruit salad and coffee on the counter, and gave Sarah a big hug. "You are beautiful, you know," he said, kissing her on the cheek. "And I'm really lucky to have you." He hugged her even tighter, picking her feet off the ground until she protested, laughing.

"I know you are," she said, smiling. "I just hope you heard what I said this time. Now, go on, go to work." Sarah leaned forward and softly kissed Steve on the lips. "There's more to life than work, you know."

"Thanks honey," Steve replied, retrieving his fruit salad and coffee. As he opened his car door and started to climb in, he added, "Maybe we can go out to dinner tonight and talk."

"I'd like that," Sarah answered, barely completing her sentence before the car door closed. She pushed the garage opener button and waved as Steve backed down the driveway.

THOUGH CONCERNED THAT he was on thin ice with Sarah, Steve was already focused on Michelle's situation by the time his car reached the stop sign at end of the street. He started running through every aspect of his meetings with the Professor and Michelle to see if he'd overlooked some minute detail that might give him insight into Emil Weisentrope's murderer. All he knew was the killer's name, Wilhelm Strauss, and that he'd visited Michelle's house on Friday, October 3rd. He surmised Strauss cleared U.S. Immigration sometime between Emil Weisentrope's death and the day he showed up at Michelle's door, but he didn't have a contact at the Immigration & Naturalization Service, or INS, to confirm when Strauss came through. He could try Captain Remaker again at the Judge Advocate General's Office, but he hated to use all of his silver bullets on his first case. Still, the case was important enough to justify the request.

Steve called Captain Remaker as soon as he arrived at his office. Captain Remaker was sure he could come up with a contact at INS, but it would take time, perhaps the rest of the day. He understood the urgency and promised to hurry.

Next, Steve scoured the Internet for information. He searched for the name Wilhelm Strauss and came up with several thousand Internet hits. He had no way to narrow the search without losing potentially valuable data, so he began the tedious process of reviewing each site to see if it contained useful information. He had only cleared the first 200 hits by the time Marjorie arrived at 7:45.

"Welcome back!" Marjorie said enthusiastically as she set her purse and lunch on her desk and strolled into Steve's office. "How was your trip?"

"You're not going to believe this, Marjorie," Steve answered, pausing long enough to look up at her from behind his computer screen. "Emil Weisentrope, the man we went over there to see, was murdered three weeks ago. He was shot in the head."

"My dear God!" Marjorie said, gasping at the thought. "Mr. Stilwell, you've got to get away from that woman. I'm telling you, she's dangerous. No. She's more than dangerous … she's evil."

"I'm afraid the German police have already taken care of that."

"I hope they arrested her."

"Not exactly. But they took away her passport and she can't leave the country. My guess is they'll take her into custody within the next few days."

"Hallelujah!"

"You know, Marjorie, something just doesn't add up." Steve began to think out loud. "I'm not convinced she's involved."

"Don't be taken in by that pretty face, Mr. Stilwell. You've seen how she treats other people."

"Being rude is far cry from being a murderer. Plus, why would she leave one man alive?"

"You mean she missed one?" Marjorie couldn't help but chuckle. There was no changing her mind on this.

"The guy in Cleveland. His name is Zalinsky. Tadeusz Zalinsky. I spoke to him from Germany. He's very much alive, and now he's half a million dollars richer." Steve spoke with a degree of satisfaction, recognizing that even if Michelle was innocent, Mr. Zalinsky's five hundred thousand dollar share was out of her reach forever. "That's the part that doesn't make sense. Why would she let Zalinsky live? Wouldn't she want him killed before her father so she could take his share as well? Plus, Michelle's too smart for this. She had to know that when someone started to track down the beneficiaries, they'd find a pattern."

"But the police haven't put the deaths together, just you," Marjorie noted, still clinging to her theory that Michelle was the mastermind behind the killings.

"The Germans have," Steve corrected, "because I told them." As the last word came out of his mouth, he heard the tiny *bleep* from his computer signaling that he'd been disconnected from the Internet. As long as he touched nothing, he could pick up where he left off by simply hitting the refresh function. He leaned back in his leather chair and put his hands behind his head, elbows outstretched. Maybe talking this out with Marjorie would do him some good.

"You know, Mr. Stilwell, she might have left Mr. Zalinsky alone because he lives in the United States. These other men lived in other countries. She probably figured it would be harder to connect her with those deaths."

"Not her father. He lived in Virginia."

"But he was killed in Israel. And didn't you tell me the police report said Michelle was walking out to his car with him and then suddenly left to get her passport? She had to have known there was a bomb in the car. It can't be any clearer than that."

"There's one more detail you don't know about." Steve knew this would be the icing on the cake. "The day I witnessed the execution of Professor Siegel's will, a man called on Michelle and they went out to dinner."

"So?"

"So, it was the man the German police believe killed Emil Weisentrope."

"I hate to say it, Mr. Stilwell, but you're wasting your time if you spend any more of it on Michelle Siegel. By the way, I left your schedule open for today. There are some first drafts in your box for you to take a look at, and I'm going to start scheduling appointments for you again next Monday ... that's the twenty-seventh." Then she added, "I know you're going to keep working on that woman's case anyway, so I'll let you get back to it."

"Thanks, Marjorie." She was right. He probably was wasting his time. But he had to satisfy himself that Michelle really was behind the killings. He grasped the arms on his chair and rolled forward as far as he could up to his desk. Clicking on the refresh button, he started going over the remainder of the Internet hits. It would be a long morning of Internet searches and dead ends. All he could hope for was that Captain Remaker would come through with an INS lead and a way to locate Wilhelm Strauss.

THE DAY PROVED almost a total loss. Steve found nothing of use on the Internet to track Wilhelm Strauss. The only ray of hope was Captain Remaker's return call.

Captain Remaker wasn't able to give him a contact at INS because the INS official didn't want to pass information directly to a private attorney. But the official was willing to pass the information to Captain Remaker because he worked for the Navy. Captain Remaker shared the information with Steve with the understanding that Steve would never divulge its source. Those were easy terms and Steve readily accepted.

The information severely damaged Michelle Siegel's case. It confirmed that Wilhelm Strauss entered the U.S. through Dulles Airport in Washington, D.C., on the evening of September 30—the same day Emil Weisentrope was murdered. More distressing: Wilhelm Strauss' departure port was Düsseldorf, Germany—the site of Emil Weisentrope's death. Only three days later, Wilhelm Strauss knocked on Michelle Siegel's front door.

The most damning information, however, concerned Wilhelm Strauss' departure from the United States. INS records showed he departed Dulles Airport on October 7, onboard a nonstop flight to Tel Aviv. A little over a week later, Professor Siegel was killed in Haifa. This convinced Steve that Wilhelm Strauss committed all three murders. Interlocking details linked Wilhelm Strauss with both Emil Weisentrope and Professor Siegel's deaths, and the methods used in Emil Weisentrope and Teodor Rudnik's cases were too similar to be coincidence. As far as Steve was concerned, Wilhelm Strauss was the triggerman.

Yet for some reason Steve wasn't convinced Michelle was the mastermind behind the killings. He just couldn't explain why Michelle would let Tadeusz Zalinsky live. If she was dumb enough to believe she could get away with murdering her father and two of the beneficiaries under his will, then she wasn't smart enough to throw any would-be investigator off of her trail by letting one of the beneficiaries live. But with no one else standing to gain by the deaths of the beneficiaries, the arrows kept pointing to Michelle.

The situation so perplexed Steve that he couldn't leave the issue at work. Following up on their conversation that morning,

Sarah tried to strike up a casual conversation with him at their favorite Italian restaurant, but his mind was far away, trying to identify the link between the beneficiaries and someone else with a motive to kill. He dragged her in to see if her outsider perspective could help him solve the puzzle, but she fared no better. All they could discern was that the victims had been friends. They had, after all, been confined at Auschwitz and had rarely, if ever, seen each other since. They had communicated, but infrequently. Only Emil Weisentrope and Professor Siegel carried on a regular correspondence. Steve made a mental note to obtain their letters, in case they provided any useful clues. Perhaps the men had alienated someone, and that someone had set out to kill them. The thought seemed so preposterous he almost convinced himself he was spinning his wheels. But he wasn't ready to quit … yet.

Steve went to bed early, hoping a good night's sleep would help him think better in the morning. He drifted off to sleep quickly, but his rest was short lived. Around 10:00 p.m., one of his old fraternity buddies called and asked Sarah to wake him so he could tell Steve he would be in Williamsburg the following week. Knowing Steve would want to talk to his friend, Sarah roused him out of bed, and they spoke on the phone for about fifteen minutes. He tried to go back to sleep after the call, but with an hour of sleep already under his belt and the echo of a million crickets resonating throughout his room, he could do little more than toss and turn. After forty-five minutes of staring at the ceiling and praying for sleep, he finally gave up and got out of bed just as Sarah was coming to join him. With no one still up to talk to and an aversion to primetime television, he decided to try the Internet one more time. He had nothing to lose but a little more sleep.

Steve walked into his study armed with a cup of hot tea and a fistful of strawberry-filled cookies. After taking a sip of the tea and tossing an entire cookie into his mouth, he fired up the computer and navigated to a search engine on the World Wide

Web. Because he had exhausted every possible combination and keyword involving Wilhelm Strauss, he decided to focus on Professor Siegel. His initial search using the Professor's name gave him over five thousand hits, twice what he'd gotten with Wilhelm Strauss. He discovered, though, that unlike the Web hits for Wilhelm Strauss, many of the hits on "Felix Siegel" actually pertained to the Professor. The first thirty or so were newspaper articles concerning the professor's untimely death. Steve plodded through these one at a time, hoping to find something pointing either to or away from Michelle. He found nothing.

The next set of hits dealt with the professor's professional achievements and was too big to work with. Although Steve knew the professor was a distinguished scholar at Columbia University, he hadn't realized what a prolific writer he had been. Hit after hit linked to one of the professor's articles, to another scholarly article citing one of his works, or to a critique of one of his publications.

"Perhaps he came across something during his research and writing and someone needed to have him killed," Steve said to himself. "This could be the break I've been looking for." He started going through the articles one at a time, but quickly saw the process would take him weeks. Out of frustration, he began to page rapidly through the list of Web hits, hoping the one he needed would jump out and cut his search short. The problem was, he had no idea what he was looking for, so he could easily pass by the Holy Grail and never realize he'd missed it. He looked down at his watch to see what time it was.

"Shit!" It was 2:18 on Saturday morning. He'd wasted almost three hours with nothing to show for it. Even worse, his plans to get up early and go into the office to finish the will drafts he'd neglected on Friday were slipping away fast. He saved the list of hits to a disk so he could print it out later at the office. Once he had the hard copy in front of him, he could better narrow his search to the sites most likely to bear fruit.

After he removed the disk, he moved the mouse and clicked on the screen to shut down the computer. He knew he should end his session for the evening and get a few hours of sleep, but he really wasn't tired. Working on the computer always made him more alert, especially when he worked on something that interested him. This issue was becoming more than an interest; it was an obsession. He decided to work for one more hour, running a couple of quick searches to see if he would get lucky, or at least get on the right track. Instead of focusing on Professor Siegel, though, he switched his emphasis to Teodor Rudnik and Emil Weisentrope. He reasoned that, because these men lived overseas and had seemingly uncommon names, he might be able to zero in on a relevant website more quickly than trying to comb through the many hits for Professor Siegel.

Before he started on his new round of searches, he headed for the bathroom and then on to the kitchen. He needed another fistful of cookies and a drink to keep him going at this time of the morning. As he tiptoed through the hall back to the study, Sarah turned on her reading light to see what was causing the hardwood floors to creak. As soon as she realized Steve wasn't in bed with her, she checked the time on her alarm clock.

"Steve, it's almost three o'clock," she wailed.

"Sorry, honey," Steve answered, not stopping to talk. He knew if he did he'd be on the receiving end of a one-way conversation with a tired and irritated wife. He walked into his study and closed the door. Then he loaded the CD player on the bookshelf with an Eagles CD and hit random play. As he sat down, the music played at just the right volume to keep him both awake and relaxed. Finally ready to begin, he keyed up the Web browser and ran a search under Emil Weisentrope. Amazingly, the first hit to appear was from an English language newspaper published in Germany. It ran a story about the old man's death but provided no additional substantive information, other than that the death could have been the result of a resurgence of skinhead activity in Düsseldorf. The search also revealed a thousand other Web hits, most of them on the name Emil. The search was still too broad to be useful. He tried another search using Teodor Rudnik's name—another 654 hits and again, no standouts.

Steve rocked back in his chair with his hands clenched behind his head. There had to be a way to narrow the search. More out of an urge to doodle on the keyboard than from any conscious decision, he typed "Weisentrope" in the search field, followed by "Rudnik." Why hadn't he thought of this earlier? He quickly entered "Siegel" following the other names and inserted "AND" between each name to ensure any hits he got included all three. After double-checking the spelling of each name, he clicked *search*. Ten seconds later, four hits popped up. Now he had a list he could work with.

The first site was a Holocaust registry listing the names of individuals who survived Nazi concentration camps. The registry listed all three names, although no other information was provided. Steve bookmarked the site and returned to his search results to scan the next hit. He clicked on a link to the U.S. Holocaust Memorial Museum and found himself in the middle of a page with "Siegel" highlighted in blue. None of the other names were readily apparent, but he assumed they were somewhere in the text. The text was in the form of a trial transcript, with Felix Siegel responding to a series of questions posed by a prosecuting attorney. Steve scrolled to the top of the screen and saw he was looking at a page identified only as "The Doctor's Trial." He scrolled back to the beginning of the testimony and began to read slowly.

Felix Siegel identified himself as a prisoner at the Auschwitz concentration camp in Poland. He described living conditions so deplorable Steve couldn't fathom how he survived. Several minutes into his testimony, Felix Siegel began to describe his function at the camp, beginning in August 1944. He and several others were slave orderlies on a medical ward where German "doctors" conducted human medical experiments. He believed he and his fellow orderlies were chosen for their youth and relative vitality, although they all feared their health would at some point make them subjects of the evil experiments they now watched in horror. Their main function was to provide a minimal degree of attention to those on the ward incapable of caring for themselves, yet still valuable enough to the Germans to be kept alive. The victims the Germans believed were no longer useful were removed from the ward and killed ... if they weren't already dead.

In an emotional passage, Felix Siegel testified that as he tended to patients in one room, he heard bloodcurdling screams coming from a victim across the hall. Although he dared not look to see what was happening, about two hours later he was tasked with cleaning the victim's room while the victim, still strapped to his bed, writhed in pain. The victim was little more than a boy, probably not much older than Felix himself. His bed was covered with blood and what appeared to be flesh and bone fragments; it was Felix's job to clean that up. As he approached the young man, he could see that the fragments weren't bone pieces at all, but bits of ground glass. Felix learned later that the victim had been shot in the shinbone with a rifle at point-blank range. Afterward, he was brought onto the ward, where a German "doctor" forced ground glass into the wound and infected it with gangrene. Ten days later Felix carried the victim's lifeless body off the ward.

Then, in yet another passage that cried out in anguish and pain, Felix described how he could still hear the poor boy's screams every time the night grew still. He could see the young face looking up at him, silently imploring him for a rescue they both knew could never come. Felix's nightmares were filled with guilt, futility, and utter despair. Worse yet, the nightmares didn't end after he stopped working as an orderly or after his own suffering became so intense he could focus on little else.

It was during this time of hopelessness that Emil Weisentrope, Teodor Rudnik, and Tadeusz Zalinsky reached out to Felix and gave him the strength to carry on. They offered him their bread when he grew weak, and their courage when it seemed easier for him to just give up and die. But most important, they made him promise that if God allowed him to survive, he would make the "doctors" pay for the incalculable suffering they'd caused. That was why Felix and the others testified at Nuremberg; they had to make sure justice was served.

Steve immersed himself in the transcript, losing track of time and purpose. Until now, he'd only known the unspeakable horror of the Holocaust through books and movies. The trial transcript and his association with Professor Siegel brought the horror to life. Now it was more than nameless faces in a history book. Now it was real. It was Professor Siegel and Emil Weisentrope and the other beneficiaries under the will. Now it involved people he knew, or felt he knew, even if only through the written bequests of an aging client.

Two and a half hours later, Steve was too tired to move, but still felt driven to read the transcript through to the end. It was as if skipping even a single word would dishonor those who had come forth to testify. So he read on. At 5:45 a.m., he reached the end of the defense's case and felt true anxiety as the military tribunal prepared to announce its decision. Now, fifty-one years after the trial, Steve sat on the edge of his seat demanding justice and accountability for the Nazi "doctor." He read the tribunal's decision out loud slowly, as if he were announcing it in the chamber for the very first time:

"Heinrich Borne, Military Tribunal ONE has found and adjudged you guilty of war crimes and crimes against humanity, as charged in the indictment heretofore filed against you. For your said crimes on which you have been and now stand convicted, Military Tribunal ONE sentences you, Heinrich Borne, to imprisonment for a term of fifty years without parole, such sentence to be served at a prison directed by higher authority, and to commence this twentieth day of December, 1946."

After reading the transcript, Steve had an emotional stake in the outcome. Although pleased Borne received fifty years, he felt as though the death penalty would have been more appropriate. Still, the panel had spoken, and the decision was final. He read the tribunal's findings one last time to try and close the wound in his soul Professor Siegel's testimony had so passionately wrenched open.

"That's it!" he exclaimed, rising to his feet so abruptly that the folding chair he was sitting in flew backward and landed on the floor with a crash. The revelation jolted him like a bolt of lightning. He could hardly control himself. He had to tell someone, but there was no one to tell. He looked at his watch. It was almost six o'clock—time to get ready for work. But there was no way he could go to the office without talking to someone first. He had to tell Sarah what he'd found out. He burst out of his study and down the hall toward the master bedroom.

"Sarah," he shouted even before he entered the bedroom. "Sarah," he yelled again as he pushed the door wide open just in time to see his startled wife sit straight up in bed.

"What's the matter?" she said, clutching her pillow against her chest. "What is it?"

"Michelle isn't behind the murders," Steve announced, trumping his wife's fear with his own excitement. "Michelle is innocent."

"You better have more important news than that," Sarah answered, her distress quickly segueing into anger. She looked over at her nightstand and stared at the clock for a second before looking back at him. "Do you know what time it is?"

"I'm sorry," Steve said quickly before returning to the matter that had gotten him in trouble. "But listen to what I've found. The Germans have the wrong person."

"Do we have to do this now?"

"Please, sweetie. I promise you can go right back to sleep."

"All right, but remember this, 'cuz it's gonna cost you big

time." Sarah propped her pillow against the headboard. Then she settled back, let out a huff, and waited for Steve's revelation while rubbing the sleep from her eyes.

Steve was too fired up to sit down and speak coherently. The words escaped faster than he could control. "I've been running some searches on the Internet. I ran Professor Siegel's name and the names of the two other guys who were murdered, and I got hooked into a site at the Holocaust Museum."

"Can you at least give me the condensed version?"

"Okay. Look, the Holocaust Museum had a transcript of a trial of a Nazi doctor. Guess who the witnesses were?"

"Your client and the other two men who died," Sarah said unenthusiastically.

"Not bad," Steve said, surprised that Sarah had guessed correctly, "but that's not all. The trial took place in 1946 and the doctor got a fifty year sentence." Steve paused, waiting for Sarah to make the connection.

"So?" Sarah asked.

"So?" Steve shouted. "Don't you see what that means? That means the doctor was released from prison in 1996. That's right before the killings started."

Sarah, to her dismay, began to wake up. Although this made her answers more coherent, it signaled the end of any possibility she would go back to sleep.

"Why would he do it?" she asked.

"Revenge, of course."

"Revenge for what?"

"Revenge for testifying against him fifty years ago."

"That seems a little far-fetched, doesn't it? And are you sure he was actually released from prison?"

"I haven't checked that yet."

"Is he even alive?"

"I don't know that either."

"Sounds as if you should have prepared a little better before you woke me, counselor. Plus, who do you think has a better chance of pulling something like this off? Some ninety-year-old war criminal who probably doesn't have a penny to his name, or a rich woman who'll get a lot richer if a few people around the world inexplicably die at about the same time? Seems pretty clear to me."

Steve heard what his wife said, but he was already thinking about calling Detective Belmar to tell him what he'd found. "I need to give the German detective a call," he announced.

"Why don't you find out if the doctor is alive first? Knowing that could keep you from looking stupid."

"Right." He knew Sarah had a good point and it was easy enough to do. "Thanks, honey." He walked over to her, kissed her gently on the forehead, and whispered, "Sorry to wake you up." Then he rushed out the door, leaving Sarah wide awake and feeling a little used.

"Why did I marry a lawyer?" she exclaimed, and then she rolled over to try and eke out another hour of sleep.

Steve was back at his computer in a flash. He ran an Internet search for the name Heinrich Borne and waited. Within fifteen seconds he had 442 hits. He scrolled down to the first one and double-clicked on the link to a Berlin English-language newspaper. The December 20, 1996, headline said it all: *Convicted Nazi War Criminal Released Today*. The article was short and stated only that a frail, eighty-eight-year-old Heinrich Borne was released from prison and that he'd been involved with some of the heinous medical experiments conducted during the war. The article said nothing about where Borne was staying after his release, but he *was* alive. Steve ran back into Sarah's room and announced his findings, once again forgetting that she was trying to sleep.

"He *is* alive. I knew it!"

"What?" Sarah groaned as she sat up in bed. This time she sounded more exasperated than angry or fearful.

"The Nazi doctor. He's alive, and he was released from prison last December!"

"That's great, Steve. Now why don't you let me get some sleep?" Sarah fluffed up her pillow, stuffed it beneath her head, and rolled on her side, facing away from Steve.

"Sorry," Steve said, crushed by Sarah's lack of interest. Giving up on her, he started toward the door and once there, began to close it quietly.

Suddenly Sarah sat up in bed again and shouted, "Steve!"

"Yes?" Steve knew he was in trouble.

"Supposing you're right about this Nazi. What about the last guy under the will? If he testified, isn't he in danger too?"

"My God! I forgot about Tadeusz Zalinsky. I've got to get a hold of him quickly." He actually sprinted from the room back to his study.

Sarah looked over at her clock; it was 6:22 a.m. Her alarm would go off in thirty-eight minutes. She plopped her head down on the pillow to try to sleep, but she could hear every *tick* and *tock* of the clock, as if someone were sending drum signals announcing that her sleep for the night was over. She decided to listen to the signals and sat up one last time. She would deal with Steve later.

By the time Sarah turned on the hot water for her shower, Steve was anxiously waiting for Tadeusz Zalinsky to pick up his phone. *Two rings. Three. Four. Five.* Then, just as the answering machine started to kick in, a grouchy, scratchy voice answered the telephone.

"Hello," the voice said with an accent Steve recognized as Mr. Zalinsky's. "Wait a minute until the answering machine shuts off." After an elderly woman's voice on the answering machine told Steve to leave a message and the machine beeped, the scratchy voice continued, "Go ahead."

"Hello, Mr. Zalinsky? This is Steve Stilwell, the attorney for Felix Siegel's estate."

"Mr. Stilwell, I don't know what time it is where you are, but here in Cleveland it's 6:30 in the morning."

"I'm very sorry about that, Mr. Zalinsky," Steve said

hurriedly, "but there've been some new developments and I needed to talk to you right away. I have reason to believe you may be in danger."

"What? What kind of attorney are you? Why are you calling me at this time of the morning to tell me crazy things?"

"Mr. Zalinsky, you've got to listen to me. Do you remember when I told you Professor Siegel was murdered?"

"Yes, of course."

"And that Teodor Rudnik and Emil Weisentrope were murdered too?"

"So I'm next, right?" Mr. Zalinsky made no attempt to hide his sarcasm. "What do you want from me, Mr. Stilwell? Why are you bothering me?"

"Let me just ask you one question," Steve implored. "Just answer me this one question, and after you answer it, I'll leave you alone if you want. Will you give me a chance?"

"What's the question?"

Steve took a deep breath. This could mean the difference between saving Mr. Zalinsky's life and having one more dead heir. He pressed on.

"Let me ask you then. Have you seen in the last couple of days a blond, blue-eyed man, early thirties, about six feet tall, with a German accent?" Steve believed—and hoped—the answer would be no, but he had to ask the question to be sure.

For a moment it was so quiet Steve thought Mr. Zalinsky had hung up or walked away from the receiver. Then Mr. Zalinsky broke the silence, this time without the grouchy, irritated early morning voice of just moments before.

"Yes, I've seen him."

"When?!"

"Just last night, at my house."

"At your house? What was he doing at your house?"

"He wanted to know about the neighborhood. He said he was thinking about buying the vacant house across the street, but he wanted to see if there were any problems in the neighborhood first. I only talked to him for a minute, though, because I had a neighbor over visiting with me."

Now it was Steve's turn for silence. He couldn't believe he'd actually located the hitman. But if he didn't act quickly and get Mr. Zalinsky's attention, there would soon be a fourth victim in this bizarre scheme for revenge. He decided to take the straightforward approach and tell Mr. Zalinsky what he knew. Then he'd let Mr. Zalinsky in on his plan; that is, as soon as he came up with one.

"That man you saw last night," Steve began slowly, "was the man who killed Emil Weisentrope."

"That's preposterous."

"The German police have a picture of him." Then Steve added what he hoped would convince Mr. Zalinsky that he was in grave danger. "Not only that, but just before Professor Siegel was murdered, that same man knocked on the professor's door asking about *his* neighborhood. I know it's true; I was there." Steve waited for a few moments to let the information sink in. He also started to think about his options for dealing with the threat. With the hitman closing in, Steve knew he had no time to lose. But before he could develop any concrete ideas, Mr. Zalinsky started speaking.

"Why do you think this man is trying to kill me?"

"It's a long story, Mr. Zalinsky. But I believe it has something to do with a war crimes trial you testified in fifty years ago."

"Do you mean Dr. Borne?"

"Yes. He got out of jail late last year, shortly before these murders started. He's got something to do with the killings. I just don't know what it is yet."

"Let's say I believe you. What do I need to do?"

"I haven't thought that far ahead," Steve said honestly. "Does anyone else live with you?"

"Just my wife. But she's off visiting our daughter in Colorado. She won't be back for another two weeks."

"Good. That makes it a little easier. Here's what we can

do. How about you come and stay with me in Williamsburg, Virginia, until we can convince the police that you need protection? Pack enough stuff for a week. You'll be safe here. I'll catch a plane up to get you today."

"Why should I trust you?"

"Because you have to."

"If I do, when will you get here?"

Steve could tell Mr. Zalinsky was getting nervous.

"I can be there this afternoon. If that man comes around again, or if you think anything is going wrong at all, call the police immediately. I'll fill them in when I get there."

"How will I know who you are?"

"I'll be wearing a white and blue golf shirt and a pair of khaki pants. If you'd like, I'll call you from the airport as soon as I get in."

"Mr. Stilwell, can I be frank with you?"

"Certainly," Steve answered, curious about what was coming next.

"I'm an old man. I really don't want all that money you told me about. You can have it. What would I do with it anyway? All I want is to live with my wife and get to visit my grandchildren. If I tell you to keep the money or give it to the man who came to my house last night, will all of you leave me alone, please?"

Steve felt tears welling up in his eyes. He hadn't focused on the human side of what was happening … the disrupted lives, the fear, the mistrust. To him, it had been a simple question of finding the killer before he killed again. Mr. Zalinsky's plea brought the situation into perspective.

"I'm afraid not, Mr. Zalinsky. This really isn't about money. I think it's about what happened fifty years ago, and we've only got a short time to stop it." Steve didn't expect Mr. Zalinsky's reply.

"Then thank you, Mr. Stilwell, for helping me."

"I'll do the best I can, Mr. Zalinsky. I'll see you later today."

After Steve hung up the telephone, he leaned back in his

chair and for the first time all night, tried to relax. He looked at the clock. It was almost seven. He could feel sleep creeping in as he eased even farther down into the chair. His eyes grew heavy and he was almost gone. His mind, though, continued to work. His brain repeated a message over and over, like a ship broadcasting an SOS. *Call Detective Belmar. Call Detective Belmar.* When he realized what he was hearing, he shook his head to ward off the sleep. He not only had to call Detective Belmar to give him his latest theory, but he also had to make airline reservations to Cleveland. First, though, a shower was in order. He remembered a saying from his Navy days that a shower was worth three hours of sleep. Today he hoped it was true.

24

Sunday, October 26
Cleveland, Ohio

K ARL VERNHAUSEN DROVE toward Tadeusz Zalinsky's house at thirty-five miles per hour. It was 2:00 a.m., and all the neighbors were sound asleep, safe and secure in their darkened houses. Only the streetlights cut through the blackness, but even these were few and far between.

After passing Zalinsky's house and verifying the area was clear, Vernhausen drove to a vacant house he'd found the day before. As he approached, he shut off the car's lights and turned into the driveway without using a turn signal. He inched the car forward all the way to the garage, which was set back on the lot just behind the house itself. He shut off the car and disengaged the cabin light, so as he eased the car door open, the night remained intact. Then, after silently slipping outside, he dashed for the shadows and vanished behind the sprawling branches of a ten-foot juniper tree.

Vernhausen had an ideal view of the neighborhood from behind the tree. More important, no one could see him surveying the area. He reached into his back pocket and pulled out the rope one last time just to make sure he'd brought it with him. Strangulation was his primary option, provided he could surprise the old man in bed. If that failed, he had a knife, too. But his scouting reports told him that he didn't have to worry; he'd find the old man sleeping and could kill him in bed without a struggle.

Now came the difficult part. He had to get across the street and down to the old man's house without being detected. He initially thought he could cross the street and move surreptitiously through the backyards until he reached the old man's house, but fences and dogs made that impossible. He also had to take care to avoid catching the eye of a passing motorist. He decided to take the direct approach, hoping that the sparse, early morning traffic would work in his favor.

Vernhausen worked his way behind the garden's shrubs, at times on all fours, until he reached the corner where the distance was the shortest to the old man's yard. Once in place, he crouched in the ready position, poised to sprint across the street as soon as he saw a break in the traffic. His first opportunity came less than five minutes later. After a blue Camaro passed on the street in front of him and the car's taillights began to shrink into insignificance, he jumped up and ran across the street to the sidewalk on the other side. In a flash he was in the old man's front yard, then around the side of the house, past a green Lincoln, and into the backyard. The entire sprint took less than fifteen seconds. No other cars appeared and no telltale lights went on in the neighbors' houses. Not even the neighborhood dogs sounded the alarm. He was in position for the attack.

Although Tadeusz Zalinsky took care to leave his front porch light on every night to do his part for the Neighborhood Watch, he never left any lights on in his backyard. The result was a backyard tailor-made for Vernhausen's work. He crept along the wall until he reached the back door, keeping as close to the house as humanly possible. Without a sound he turned the knob on the screen door and opened it. Next was a wooden door, the upper portion of which consisted of nine rectangular windows in a tic-tac-toe board pattern. He stepped up onto the back step and squeezed between the screen door and wooden door leading into the house. He tried the doorknob to the wooden door, but this time the door was locked.

A locked door with glass panes was no match for Vernhausen. He reached into his pocket and removed a small suction cup with a nylon cord attached. Next came a container of super adhesive, which he used to apply a thin coating of glue to the concave portion of the suction cup. He stuck the suction cup to the glass pane nearest the doorknob and pulled a small glasscutter out of his pocket. He pressed his left hand against the glass to eliminate the chance of any squeaks and slowly traced a five-inch diameter circle around the now permanently affixed suction cup in the bottom corner of the nine-by-twelve inch window. After tracing all the way around, he placed a rag against the pane and tugged sharply on the nylon cord. With barely a sound, the circular section of window popped out and dangled by its nylon tether.

Vernhausen set the cutout glass on the ground next to the back step. Then he stuck his black leather gloved hand through the hole in the window and reached over to the doorknob. He turned the lock and pulled his hand back through the glass. Again he tried the door, only this time it opened. He was in.

Vernhausen found himself in Tadeusz Zalinsky's kitchen. The room was dark and it was difficult to see. He didn't dare use a flashlight; the old man or a neighbor would see that for sure. That meant scrutinizing every step before he moved. He began by surveying the kitchen. The only objects of concern were the kitchen table and the chairs at the far end of the room near the hallway. As he walked in that direction and passed the refrigerator, he saw a flashing red light on a device sitting on the countertop. He froze. Had he tripped an alarm? He turned his head slowly to study the device more carefully, only to discover it was nothing more than an answering machine announcing a previously recorded incoming call. He breathed a sigh of relief and continued on his way.

Vernhausen recognized the layout once he reached the hallway. He'd scoped it out when he spoke to Zalinsky from outside the front door the evening before. The first part of the hallway opened into the living room. Farther down were the bedrooms. He knew Zalinsky would be asleep in one of them—he just didn't know which one. He began to move down the hallway toward the bedrooms. He wasn't distracted by the pictures of grandchildren adorning every inch of wall space on both sides of the hallway. Neither did he notice the pristine condition of the living room nor the aging hall rug frayed around the edges that absorbed the sound of his footsteps as he continued silently on his way. His total focus was on locating and killing the last of his client's victims. He would let nothing get in his way.

He crept along until he was just outside the first of the two bedrooms. He paused and pulled the rope from his back pocket, wrapping one end tightly around his right hand and the other several times around his left, leaving about fifteen inches dangling between his clenched fists. Then he peered into the room and searched for his target with the precision of a high-powered radar.

The bed was empty and Zalinsky was nowhere to be seen. That meant he was asleep in the second bedroom across the hall.

Moving to the other bedroom, Vernhausen stopped just outside the door. It was open perhaps an inch, but from where he was standing he could see nothing inside the room. He slipped past the opening to the other side of the door, but still no bed was visible. That meant Zalinsky was asleep on a bed behind the door and he would have to get almost completely inside the room before he could make his move. With every moment of delay increasing the probability of detection, he could afford to wait no longer.

Vernhausen felt his senses come alive as instinct took over. His breathing grew heavy and loud and the rope became taut in his hands. As the door slowly opened, his eyes scanned the darkness in an ever-widening arc. Suddenly, the end of the bed appeared. He moved toward it rapidly, staying shielded behind the door as long as possible. Then the door creaked, announcing his presence. With but a second of surprise left, he shoved the door open and lunged for the bed with his outstretched arms.

The bed was empty! His heart raced even faster than before. In the blink of an eye he had shifted from predator to prey. He searched the room wildly to find his target before his target found him. Then he saw it.

He should have noticed it right away, but the excitement caused him to miss the crucial detail. The bed was still made. He took off a glove and touched the center of the bedspread with the palm of his hand. It was cold. Now he became concerned that Zalinsky had really been in the first room and he had overlooked the old man.

Vernhausen eased out of the second bedroom and crossed the hall back to the first. The door remained wide-open, leaving him a clear view of the entire room. That bed was made too. "Somebody tipped the old man off," he muttered as he unwound the rope from around his left hand. He entered the room and began to search every nook capable of hiding a grown man. He started with the closet and then looked under the bed. He moved methodically from room to room, checking everywhere, on the off chance Zalinsky somehow sensed his coming and managed to hide before he caught up with him. He found nothing.

Vernhausen couldn't believe Zalinsky had eluded him. He was sure he'd seen the green Lincoln in the driveway and his surveillance told him Zalinsky never went anywhere without the car. Now the broken window on the back door would put Zalinsky on notice that someone had been in his house. From here on out, getting at Zalinsky would be more difficult. Worse yet, Vernhausen had no idea where to find him.

When Vernhausen returned to the kitchen, the blinking red light on the answering machine again caught his eye. He stared at it for a few seconds, watching the red light blink on and off, over and over again. Satisfied it was safe, he turned to make his exit. Then he paused and turned back. On a whim, he reached out and pushed the *play* button:

> Hello, Mr. Zalinsky? This is Sarah Stilwell, Steve Stilwell's wife. He's the attorney coming up to get you today. Would you please ask him to call me when he gets in? Tell him I got his message, but I don't understand it. I couldn't tell whether I'm supposed to pick you up at the airport in Williamsburg or whether you'll be driving back to Virginia. I'm looking forward to meeting you and have a safe trip. Goodbye.

Vernhausen couldn't believe his good fortune. Two minutes ago, he didn't have a clue where to look. Now he could locate Zalinsky with pinpoint accuracy. He played the message again and memorized the names. He'd write them down as soon as he got back to his car. After the message played for the second time, he retreated toward the back door. It was time to head to Williamsburg.

* * *

STEVE WAS EXHAUSTED. He'd been awake for nearly forty hours straight, with the exception of the flight to Cleveland Hopkins Airport. Tadeusz Zalinsky was exhausted too, because he rarely stayed awake past ten o'clock. It was already 2:00 a.m., and they were both ready to drop. Steve gave in first. Despite consuming enough coffee to jumpstart a marching band, he found himself staring aimlessly down the Pennsylvania Turnpike and occasionally even veering off the darkened road.

"I'm afraid we've got to stop, Mr. Zalinsky," Steve declared. "I'd hoped to make it all the way to Williamsburg tonight, but there's just no way. If I keep on going, we'll end up dead for sure."

"That would defeat the purpose of the trip, then, wouldn't it? Of course we can stop. I'm very tired myself."

"How about we exit at Breezewood and find a place to stay for the night? It's only about three miles away, and we have to pass through the town anyway."

"You're the driver, Mr. Stilwell. I go where you go."

Steve nodded and set his sights on Breezewood. He was glad Mr. Zalinsky was so accommodating, although he really hadn't planned on driving. He intended to catch a Sunday morning flight out of Cleveland for Williamsburg, but Mr. Zalinsky's fear of flying quashed that plan. Driving was the only alternative. When Steve arrived at Mr. Zalinsky's house at around 7:30 Saturday evening in a rental car, they'd decided it was best to drive as far as they could that night and stop when and if it became necessary.

Steve pulled up to a red light at the end of the turnpike exit. They drove down the main drag in Breezewood looking for a decent motel, but most had "no vacancy" signs. It wasn't until they spotted the Welcome Inn at the north end of town that they found a place to stay. Steve parked the car near the lobby and the two men went inside. The night desk manager was a scraggly kid with a goatee and a bad attitude. It was clear why he'd been relegated to the graveyard shift.

"Hi," Steve said as he walked in with Mr. Zalinsky.

The night desk manager looked up but didn't return the greeting. "May I help you?"

Steve didn't let the kid's attitude bother him. He was too tired to demand anything more than a bed to sleep in. "Yes, I'd like two rooms, adjacent, if possible."

"I've got one room left—two double beds. It'll cost you $69.99 plus tax."

Steve looked at Mr. Zalinsky but Mr. Zalinsky spoke first. "It's okay with me, Mr. Stilwell, if it's okay with you."

"Looks like you got a deal," Steve said to the kid. The kid said nothing. Instead, he began completing the paperwork for Steve to check in.

Steve handed over his credit card and waited for further instructions. He could hear a ringing in his ears that he attributed to a lack of sleep. All he could think about was plopping his head down on a pillow and getting a good night's rest.

Steve signed the charge slip and slid it back toward the kid. The kid took the receipt and tossed a key onto the counter. "Room 213. It's on the second floor in the back. Check out is 12:00 p.m. Enjoy your stay." The kid didn't even wait for a reply before returning to his desk. He had a late night TV show to finish watching.

Steve and Mr. Zalinsky drove the car around the motel and parked as close to the room as they could. They trudged up the stairs, each carrying a small overnight bag, and dragged themselves toward their room. After a quick bout with an uncooperative door, they entered an austere motel room.

"It's got two beds and a shower," Steve announced, feeling the need to say something positive about their accommodations, "and that's all I really care about right now."

In a matter of minutes, both men were in bed. As Steve reached to turn off the light, Mr. Zalinsky had one last comment. "Mr. Stilwell, I really appreciate what you are doing for me. You didn't have to do it."

"Yes I did, Mr. Zalinsky." Steve turned off the light and pulled the sheet up to his neck. "At least you'll be safe in Williamsburg until we can get this thing straightened out."

Mr. Zalinsky thought for a second before answering. He wasn't sure if he should ask the next question. He didn't want to seem ungrateful, but he also didn't want to remain in limbo forever. He'd gotten along well with Steve in the car and thought he was a nice young man, someone he could trust. He decided to go ahead and ask.

"How long do you think it will take to get this over with, Mr. Stilwell?"

Steve was already asleep. The rest of the conversation would have to wait until morning. Mr. Zalinsky rolled onto his back and stared up at the ceiling. He prayed to God this would be over soon. He really just wanted to get back to his wife and spend time with his grandchildren. Two days earlier, his life had been so uncomplicated, so free. Now those days seemed gone forever. He felt a fear he hadn't known for fifty years. He was losing control—control over even the simple things in life. He couldn't go when he wanted to go or be where he wanted to be. And if he strayed from the path set out for him, he'd be killed. He closed his eyes and prayed. He knew it would take inner strength to survive this ordeal. He had no idea what he would face, or how he would face it. But he did know one thing about himself that others would soon have to recognize: he was not yet ready to die.

25

Berlin, Germany

THE SETTING OFFERED a stark contrast to their meeting of a little more than a week ago. The colorful leaves were all but gone. In their place was a starkness made even starker by the dark branches above their heads running like veins across the somber gray sky. Last week's autumn breeze had given way to the beginning of the winter wind, sending a chill through the air that penetrated the skin wherever exposed. Even the ducks were gone, away seeking shelter in some more hospitable locale.

The two men who sat on the gray bench were unaffected by the cold. Their conversation began without the usual exchange of pleasantries.

"They've identified him," Werner said just loud enough to be heard over the wind.

"Who do they think they've identified?" Hermann retorted sarcastically.

"Strauss."

"There is no Strauss."

"They'll figure it out, Hermann. You know they will. They figured out Strauss. They'll figure out Vernhausen, too. We've got to shut him down."

"No, not yet." Hermann's defiance rang through the air like the cold wind.

"What do you mean, not *yet*, Hermann? You can't gamble here. There are others in the Five. Do you remember that?"

Hermann sat silently, unmoved by Werner's comments or the elements.

"Did you hear me, Hermann? I said, there are others in the Five."

Still, Hermann said nothing.

"For God's sake, Hermann, listen to what I'm saying. If we don't put an end to this now, they'll trace it to us. I'm certain of that. I cannot let that happen. No! I will *not* let that happen."

"It's too late, Werner. We're committed. We must see this through to the end."

"No, Hermann, that's where you're wrong. *You're* committed. We're getting out now."

Hermann laughed uncontrollably until his laughter grew loud and obvious, even to the point of absurdity. "You can't get out," Hermann said as he looked Werner straight in the eye. "You can never get out. Do you think you can turn back time? Do you think you can undo what's already been done in your name? No, Werner, you're in this until the end."

"How dare you threaten me? We've been your friends for forty years! Are you going to throw us away like rotting garbage? Besides, your father is an old man, Hermann. He'll be gone soon. You've avenged enough. Let this die with your father."

Hermann's eyes flared. Only *he* was permitted to invoke his father's name. How could Werner understand what it meant to him? Werner's father had survived the war, a hero to the Fatherland. For fifty years Hermann had been ashamed to even acknowledge his father was alive. Now that he had finally decided to act, he would not let some elitist bastard get in his way. Hermann's hate and anger burned white hot inside him; his face began to flush. He jerked his head back to looking out over the lake without replying to Werner's comment. Then, suddenly and unexpectedly, he relaxed. He spoke softly, his voice barely audible.

"One more Jew must die."

"What did you say, Hermann?"

"I said, one more Jew must die." Hermann turned his head slowly back toward Werner. "You may drop out if you wish, but don't try and stop this." Hermann paused for a second before continuing. Then, again looking deep into Werner's eyes, he added, "I will let nothing—no one—get in my way on this." He calmly returned to looking over the lake. "It looks like winter is here for good now, doesn't it, Werner?"

Werner had nothing more to say. He stood and looked down at Hermann, hoping for a last minute retraction of his ultimatum. There was none. Instead, Hermann continued to stare in the direction of the lake, blocking out any objectionable stimuli. Werner knew the situation was hopeless. He didn't bother to say goodbye. Adjusting his coat to better shield himself from the wind, he started walking back to his car. Hermann remained on the bench for more than an hour, impervious to his surroundings and the loss of his best friend.

* * *

Williamsburg, Virginia

THE CAR PULLED up the Stilwell's driveway in Williamsburg at just about suppertime. The sun sat low in the sky and the cool night air was already making its presence known. When the car shut down outside the garage, two exhausted men emerged and lumbered toward the trunk to retrieve their belongings. Steve stretched his arms over his head and yawned. They had stopped only once along the route from Breezewood and he was feeling the stiffness that comes with age settle in.

"This is a beautiful neighborhood," Mr. Zalinsky said as he stood with his back to the car. He perused the street up and down, admiring the remnants of a garden here or a particularly attractive home there.

Just as Steve began to close the trunk, his wife came out from around the back of the house. "How was your trip?" Sarah asked before either man saw her.

"Hi, honey," Steve replied. "It went just fine." He turned to Mr. Zalinsky.

"Mr. Zalinsky, this is my wife, Sarah."

Sarah continued to approach Mr. Zalinsky and offered him her hand. "I'm very pleased to meet you, Mr. Zalinsky. I'm so glad you're able to stay with us."

"Why thank you, Mrs. Stilwell," Mr. Zalinsky said graciously. "I'm sorry to have to bother you like this."

"Oh, it's no bother at all, and please, call me Sarah. Why don't we go inside where it's a little warmer? I've got supper ready. You two can freshen up and tell me all about your trip over dinner. I hope chicken is all right?"

"That sounds great," Steve chimed in.

"I know *you* like chicken," Sarah shrugged. "I hope you do, as well, Mr. Zalinsky."

"I do," Mr. Zalinsky answered as they all began to walk to the front door.

* * *

Once they were gone from sight, Karl Vernhausen smiled and started the rental car. He'd located his target again. He pulled out of his parking space along the street and began to drive slowly past Steve Stilwell's house. This job promised to be the most difficult of all because of the two individuals staying with the old man. Still, good planning and proper surveillance could overcome almost any obstacle. As he headed back to his room at the Colonial Inne, he saw this job as no exception.

Back in his room after stopping for dinner, Vernhausen sat down at his computer. He'd logged on earlier in the day, but had been unable to connect with his client's server. He clicked *refresh* to establish the required connection. He'd grown so accustomed to checking his client's Web page that he'd arranged for all of his passwords to be retrieved automatically whenever they were called for. Within a minute, the latest message from his client appeared: "Complete immediately. Payment doubled if within forty-eight hours."

Vernhausen had no idea why his client needed to get the job done so quickly, but $2 million was reason enough for him. In fact, for that kind of money, he was willing to take some chances. Of course, there might be incidental casualties, but that was unavoidable, given the necessity of doing things in a hurry. Anyway, casualties were his client's concern, not his.

Vernhausen stood up and walked to the window to check the weather. It was perfect for a little late-night surveillance. Darkness reigned supreme and it was only 8:00 p.m. Even the stars had retreated into the blackened sky and the moon was nowhere to be seen. He hoped for the same conditions tomorrow night, so he'd be able to finish the job and collect the bonus.

26

Monday, October 27
Williamsburg

STEVE WASTED NO time getting into his office. By 7:05 a.m., he was sitting at his desk preparing for a "normal" day. He'd been on the road so much recently that he really needed to get his work schedule back on track. More important, he wanted to call Detective Belmar to see if the German police had made any progress. He had spoken to Belmar only long enough on Saturday to relay his findings about the Nazi doctor. Belmar had heard him out, but clearly didn't put much stock in the theory. Steve knew he had little to base it on other than instinct. Truth to tell, his instincts were generally pretty good.

After thumbing through his index and finding Belmar's number, Steve called him, hoping to catch him in the office. It was early afternoon in Düsseldorf, so there was a chance the detective could be off investigating some other case. After three rings, someone answered the telephone.

"*Hallo, Polizei Düsseldorf. Belmar hier.*"

"Good afternoon, Detective Belmar," Steve said, forgetting

Belmar understood English as well as he did and over-enunciating each word. "This is Steve Stilwell."

"Why good afternoon, Mr. Stilwell," Belmar replied in perfect English. "How are you this afternoon? Errr, I guess it's morning there, isn't it?"

"It is and I'm doing quite well, thank you. Can you tell me, Detective, have you had any luck pursuing the doctor? You know, the one we discussed on Saturday."

"Dr. Borne?"

"Yes, that's the one," Steve said, excited a lead he generated could be the clue that would solve this international murder scheme. "What have you come up with?"

"Nothing," Belmar replied bluntly. "We were able to confirm he was released from prison last December and that he lives with his son, Hermann Borne. Are you familiar with him?"

"With whom?" Steve asked, lost in the pronouns.

"Hermann Borne. He's very rich. He made a fortune in computers, starting in the sixties. Now his father lives with him in Berlin. We've checked around as much as we can and we've come up with nothing, other than Hermann Borne's family situation, and that really has nothing to do with the murders."

"What's his family situation?" Steve wanted to judge the relevance for himself.

"Well, Hermann Borne and his wife lost their oldest son in a skiing accident back in February of 1996. Then Borne's father was released from prison in December." Belmar hesitated. "I guess those two events were too much for the family to handle, because Borne's wife left him earlier this year. Now Borne and his father live together in a flat in Berlin."

"Is that all you've got?" Steve asked.

"That's it, and obviously, we're not going to go bother one of the most successful businessmen in Germany unless we have hard evidence linking him to the killings."

"In other words, you're not going to pursue my lead any

further, are you?" Steve wanted to make sure he knew exactly where he stood.

"I'm afraid that's correct."

"So what does that mean for Michelle Siegel? You've got to be nearing the end of your custody deadline. Are you allowing her to leave the country?"

"We convinced her to stay for a few more days … at her expense, of course."

"Has she been cooperating?"

"Let's just say she hasn't been a problem. There really hasn't been anything for her to cooperate with. We're at a dead end."

"What about Emil Weisentrope's killer?"

"We've lost him. Your government said he left America on October 7. We traced him to Syria and then he vanished."

"I've got news for you," Steve proclaimed, realizing he was once again a step ahead of Belmar. "He was in Cleveland, Ohio, less than forty-eight hours ago."

"How do you know that? Did you see him?"

"I didn't, but Tadeusz Zalinsky did. The killer came right to his door, just like he did at Professor Siegel's house before the Professor was killed. I'm sure he's after Mr. Zalinsky now."

"Isn't Zalinsky the last beneficiary under Professor Siegel's will?"

"Yes, and that's precisely why Michelle Siegel is innocent. Why would she care about Mr. Zalinsky now that her father is dead? Mr. Zalinsky is already entitled to a share of her father's estate and there's nothing she can do about it."

"It could be a mistake on the killer's part, or something to throw us off track."

"Or it could be Dr. Borne killing off the last living witness from his war crimes trial," Steve concluded. Then, to drive his point home, he added, "You tell me which one makes more sense."

"I appreciate what you are saying, Mr. Stilwell, but Michelle Siegel is still our best suspect. Need I remind you that you are the one who told us she was involved? Anyway, did Zalinsky say what the killer's name was?"

"No, but you have that, don't you?"

"Apparently not. As I said before, your government said he left your country on October seventh and we lost him in Syria. He must have obtained a new identity and returned to the United States under a new name. You better make sure Zalinsky is safe, just in case."

"He's safe," Steve said. "When I heard he saw the killer, I went up and got him right away. Now, he's with me in Williamsburg. He'll be safe here until you get the American authorities to act on an extradition request."

"That's not going to be so easy," Belmar said. "First, we don't even know the suspect's name. Second, all we have right now is circumstantial evidence. I don't think your government will extradite him."

"What do you mean all you have is circumstantial evidence? I thought you had an eyewitness to Emil Weisentrope's murder." Steve stood up as if to make his objection over the phone more emphatic.

"All we can do is put him in the right place at the right time. The Americans will want more than that."

"But he was also in the right place at the right time for Professor Siegel's murder, and now he's after Tadeusz Zalinsky," Steve bristled. He perceived Belmar shifting away from the case now that he had Michelle Siegel in hand. It looked like Belmar wanted to take the easy way out.

"Mr. Stilwell, you, as an American lawyer, should be familiar with the probable cause requirement. Your courts would never extradite this man on what we have now, even if we knew his name and where to find him. I'm afraid that until we get some hard evidence linking him to the murders, there's little we can do."

Steve knew Belmar was right, but it didn't make it any easier. He was frustrated Belmar wouldn't consider what Steve saw so clearly. "So what am I supposed to do, keep Mr. Zalinsky with me until they find him and kill him too?"

"I'm sorry, Mr. Stilwell, but there's nothing we can do without more evidence. We'll tell the American authorities what's going on."

"Please, Detective Belmar, keep me informed. I've got a man who is very afraid for his life right now."

"I can assure you we're doing everything we can. Goodbye, Mr. Stilwell."

"Goodbye," Steve said halfheartedly. He slammed down the receiver, sat down, and spun around on his chair to look out the window. He'd been so engrossed in his conversation that he hadn't heard the outer office door open and someone come in.

"Good morning, Mr. Stilwell," Marjorie said as she poked her head into his office. Her voice startled him enough for Marjorie to notice. "Oh, I'm sorry, Mr. Stilwell, I didn't mean to scare you."

Steve turned around to greet her, but not with his usual early morning zest. Instead, his brow was furrowed with concern.

"Ah, good morning, Marjorie," Steve said, trying to regain his composure. He looked at his watch; it was 7:35. "You're a little early this morning, aren't you?"

"Just a bit. But I knew you'd be in today and I wanted to go through your schedule with you. You actually have some appointments."

"Well, why don't we get a couple of cups of coffee and then go through it," Steve said, fighting to summon some of his customary cheerfulness. Marjorie agreed and the two headed for the coffee pot.

Within a couple of minutes, Steve returned to his office with a steaming mug of freshly brewed coffee. He set the mug down on his desk and was just about to sit down himself when Marjorie came in, deftly balancing a hot cup of coffee in one hand and her office calendar in the other. She maneuvered over to the chairs in front of Steve's desk and set her cup down on a coaster on the table between the two chairs. She took a seat and transitioned to business.

"Are you ready, Mr. Stilwell?" she asked, waiting for him to get comfortable. He picked up a pen and prepared to copy the scheduling information into his day planner.

"Shoot."

"All right. You have a nine o'clock for initial estate planning. Then you've got will executions at ten-thirty and eleven. Finally, you've got a meeting at twelve with the Williamsburg Bar Association. It's a busy morning."

"Sounds like it," Steve agreed. "Are the wills ready for me to review?"

"They're in the folders at the top of your desk." They'd been ready and waiting since the end of last week.

"Great. I'm looking forward to practicing some law again. Did you say the Bar Association meeting is at twelve o'clock?"

"That's right," Marjorie confirmed. "I RSVP'd for you two weeks ago. Do you still want to attend?"

"I think I need to. I've got to make sure people start to recognize me." Steve leaned forward and reached into his inbox to signal the end of the scheduling session.

"Is that it then, Mr. Stilwell?"

"I think so. Oh, there is one more thing. Where did you say the Bar Association meeting will be?"

"The usual," Marjorie said as she headed for the door carrying her scheduling calendar and her still untasted cup of coffee. "The Colonial Inne."

BY TWELVE O'CLOCK, Steve was still going strong. The morning had reinvigorated him. He found the law truly refreshing and was at his best when he had the opportunity to interact with his clients. He also felt quite confident in his abilities now and had weaned himself from the close supervision of Mr. Smythe on all but the most complex estate matters. The Bar Association meeting proved interesting as well, with the guest speaker discussing some anticipated Federal Income Tax changes that seemed particularly relevant to his practice. Better yet, the meeting actually ended ahead of schedule and Steve found himself heading toward the lobby discussing an upcoming social function with two of his colleagues.

The group's intended path through the lobby took them past the mahogany check-in desk, under the crystal chandelier in the foyer, and out the main entrance. As they neared the check-in desk, a man wearing multi-colored runner's shorts, running shoes, and a bright yellow T-shirt caught Steve's eye because the outfit seemed out of place. Not that the runner was poorly dressed, but his running clothes stood out in the sea of blue blazers and red silk ties.

Steve couldn't help but notice what the man was doing. He appeared to be handing his magnetic room key to the front desk clerk to hold for him while he went for an early afternoon run. It was a beautiful day and the sight of the runner made Steve feel like he should be out running, too. He often ran during lunch, but today the Bar Association meeting was forcing him to skip his afternoon exercise option.

As Steve's feelings of guilt increased with each passing step, he continued to watch the runner until he stood within ten feet of him. It was then that the runner turned to head for the foyer and the warm Williamsburg sun waiting outside. For a split second, the runner and Steve made eye contact. The runner averted his eyes, apparently uncomfortable at having been detected looking directly into the eyes of another, even though the contact was inadvertent. He continued on his way and headed out the main entrance. Steve, on the other hand, wanted to get a better look, but turned his head to avoid being recognized. He had no way of knowing whether the runner remembered him, but there was no doubt in his mind who the runner was. It was Emil Weisentrope's killer!

Steve slowed as he walked toward the front entrance. He couldn't risk giving the killer another chance to identify him.

After all, as far as Steve knew, the killer had only seen him once before—the afternoon at Professor Siegel's house in Tappahannock. Steve tried to reassure himself. "Surely, he didn't recognize me," he said under his breath.

"I'm sorry Steve, did you say something?" one of the lawyers walking with Steve asked.

"Oh, no. I was just thinking out loud." Without missing a beat, he continued as if to finish the thought. "Would you gentlemen excuse me? I need to find a telephone. I forgot I told my wife I'd call her after the meeting."

"Of course," said the other attorney. "It was good seeing you again, Steve."

"I'll see you next time," Steve replied, now fully preoccupied. He peered out the front entrance as the killer did some stretching exercises on the lawn just outside the Inne. Steve walked out of the killer's field of vision to avoid detection. He had to find out the man's name. But how? And what was he doing in Williamsburg? He was supposed to be in Cleveland. How could he have discovered Mr. Zalinsky's whereabouts? Nobody knew that except for Belmar. Was there a leak on the German police force?

Steve took another look outside and saw the killer begin to run down the driveway leading away from the Inne. He had no idea how long the killer would be gone, so he quickly tried to assess what he needed. He definitely had to find out the killer's name. That would help Belmar work the extradition request. He also wanted to find out what room he was staying in. That might come in handy for tracking him in the event he changed his identity again. Steve decided to act first and let a plan evolve on its own. He walked up to the registration desk and hoped for the best. There was no one in line in front of him.

"Excuse me," Steve said as he put his hand on the counter. The young, red-haired check-in clerk looked up from the papers she was organizing on the ledge behind the counter. She looked barely twenty years old.

"May I help you, sir?" she said with the big smile of someone genuinely enthusiastic about her job or a college student who desperately needed the money.

"I hope you can," Steve answered. "I'm here with the Bar Association meeting, and I met a foreign man this morning and offered to show him around Williamsburg later today. I was supposed to meet him here in the lobby for a run after my meeting, but I got tied up and I'm afraid I've missed him. You haven't seen a rather tall blond-haired man who speaks with a German accent dressed in running clothes around here recently, have you?"

The hotel clerk beamed. "As a matter of fact, I have. There was a gentleman down here just about five minutes ago. He dropped off his room key and went for a run."

"Did you catch his name?"

"Let me see," she said as she picked up the magnetic room key the runner left with her. She studied the card briefly and then typed something into her computer. "Was it Mr. Vernhausen? Karl Vernhausen?"

"That's him!" The hotel clerk's smile told Steve what he needed to know. She wanted to help him; he just had to ask the next question in a way that would allow her to do so.

"Could you tell me how to get to his room? I want to be sure not to miss him again."

The front desk clerk hesitated. "I'm really not supposed to give out a guest's room number. It's hotel policy. But he has to come back here to get his room key. If you have a seat in the lobby, I'll be happy to refer him to you as soon as he comes back."

"Thanks, but that won't be necessary. I have to retrieve some material from my car, and then I've got to make a couple of phone calls. I thought if I could swing by his room right after I made the calls, I'd be sure to catch him." Then Steve laid it on as thick as he could. "I feel real bad about missing him, though. I think he was counting on me to show him around

Williamsburg this afternoon and I'm afraid I've let him down."
Steve could think of nothing else to say. He was out of ideas
and could only wait for the clerk's response.

"He's in Suite 191. It's all the way down that hall, over there,"
the clerk said, pointing. "When you get to the end of the hall,
turn right. It'll be at the very end of the hallway."

"I can't tell you how much I appreciate your help. You've
saved me a great deal of embarrassment."

"I'm glad I was able to help," the clerk said with a smile.

"Thanks again," Steve said as he turned and began to walk
toward the main entrance. He had the information he'd hoped
for. Now all he had to do was report it back to Detective Belmar.
Yet the information only served to whet his appetite. Now
he had a burning desire to actually see Suite 191. Wouldn't a
fox seize the opportunity to out-stalk the hound? Perhaps he
would also gain some satisfaction from knowing precisely
where the killer was staying. But something else told him this
might be his only chance to get the information he needed to
link Vernhausen to the Nazi doctor in Berlin. He realized all
he was likely to see was the locked door to Vernhausen's room.
Still, he felt strangely compelled to at least walk by. He knew
that not doing so would gain him nothing.

Steve looked at his watch as he walked outside into the
cool autumn air. It was 1:10 p.m.; Vernhausen had been gone
almost ten minutes. Steve didn't know how much longer he
had. For all he knew, Vernhausen could be on his way back
to the room right now. Steve guessed, though, that he wasn't.
If Vernhausen ran outbound for ten minutes, he would be at
most a mile and a half away. That gave Steve at least ten minutes
before Vernhausen returned, probably more. He rationalized
that Vernhausen had to be going farther than three miles, so
he believed he had more time. He decided to act.

Steve turned around and went back into the main lobby.
He avoided looking directly at the helpful check-in clerk, but,
out of the corner of his eye, he could see that she was busy

with another customer and not paying any attention to him. He veered down the hallway she had pointed out for him and walked briskly until it ended in an intersection. Turning right, he continued past room after room in search of Suite 191. Near the end of the hallway where he guessed the room must be, he saw two maids' carts loaded with towels and cleaning supplies waiting outside the rooms. He approached with caution.

Steve first passed the cart belonging to the maid cleaning Suite 186 on the right side of the hall. He casually looked in that suite as he strolled by. He could see the maid making one of two disheveled beds. The suite was large and had a big sliding glass door leading to the outside. He didn't stop to take in any more details, but instead continued down toward the second maid's cart on the left side of the hall. He slowly passed rooms 187 and 189 and came up on the cart parked just outside Suite 191—Vernhausen's room! He couldn't believe his good fortune; he could actually see inside the killer's room.

The layout appeared to be exactly the same as Suite 186. He could hear the maid cleaning the bathroom just inside the doorway. He could also see Vernhausen's laptop computer sitting open on the desk near the back of the room. He desperately wanted to get at it and search the rest of the room, but didn't know where to begin. He looked at his watch—1:15 p.m. Vernhausen could be inbound at this very moment. Steve estimated he had no more than fifteen minutes until Vernhausen reappeared.

Steve felt a cold sweat beading up under his arms. He'd been a conservative, law-abiding citizen all of his life. Sure, he'd taken risks in the military, but they were acceptable, allowable risks. He'd also played the stock market aggressively, but his investment strategies were within the box of permissible alternatives. He'd always been in the mainstream of American values, achieving controlled success by taking the acceptable, approved path. This situation presented an entirely different option. He could safely walk away and perhaps miss the opportunity to get the critical evidence Detective Belmar needed to link Vernhausen to the Nazi doctor. Or he could go into the room and get the evidence, and maybe even save Tadeusz Zalinsky's life, at the risk of being nailed for breaking and entering and losing his license to practice law, not to mention what would happen if Vernhausen came back while he was still in the room.

As Steve stood frozen in indecision for what seemed like an eternity, he tried to rationally weigh the positives and negatives of each alternative. Unfortunately, the pressure of the situation wouldn't let him think clearly. He simply couldn't focus. His mind dashed from point to point, erasing its mental calculus as it went. Strangely, though, one philosophical point kept overriding his attempts at reasoning. It wasn't the work of a classical philosopher, or the moral teachings of a distinguished clergyman, or even the words or deeds of some great historical figure of the twentieth century. Instead, it was a silly line from a movie he'd seen about ten years earlier. The harder he tried to analyze the situation logically, the louder the line beat in his brain. "Sometimes you just gotta say, 'what the hell,' " or something to that effect. Steve looked at his watch one last time. It was 1:16 p.m. It was now or never. He couldn't believe he was going to hang his life on a line from a movie, but he took one more look at the laptop and thought, *What the hell!*

Steve looked behind him to make sure no one was watching. He also peered into Vernhausen's suite to make sure the maid in the bathroom couldn't see him. He toyed with the idea of boldly walking into the room as if it were his own, but he had no way of knowing if the maid had already seen Vernhausen. He simply couldn't risk being challenged from the very start. Instead, he turned to an old fraternity trick that had gotten him into more than one supposedly locked room at the College of William & Mary twenty-five years ago. He reached into his wallet and removed a dollar bill. He folded it until it was just small enough to fit into the notch in the doorframe where the door latch engaged. He stuffed the bill into the notch so it filled the notch almost entirely, yet nothing was obvious to someone not looking closely at the notch itself. Then he turned around and started walking slowly back down the hall toward the lobby.

He hadn't traveled ten paces when the maid cleaning Vernhausen's room emerged into the hallway. She pulled the door closed behind her and moved to the next room, opening it with her passkey. Steve walked five more paces down the hall. By then the maid would be hard at work in the next room.

When Steve turned around, only the maid's cart was visible. He hurried back to Vernhausen's room, checking his watch as he went. It was 1:17; he had thirteen minutes tops. He grasped the doorknob, but before he pushed on the door to see if it would open, he thought about the line from the movie one last time. He had reached the point of no return.

* * *

VERNHAUSEN'S PACE WAS fast even for him. He attributed his newfound speed to the perfect Virginia fall afternoon. The temperature hovered at sixty-two degrees and the sky was solid blue with only a few light, puffy clouds wisping lazily from one horizon to the other. With no breeze to impede his performance, he found himself gliding effortlessly through Williamsburg's colonial landscape.

Although he liked to go out for 10k runs, today he was running a five-mile course mapped out by the Colonial Inne for its guests. Although the run started with a segment down the tourist-congested Duke of Gloucester Street, it soon took him winding toward the Colonial Parkway, where he could enjoy the dazzling fall colors in an area free of pedestrians and development. He planned on using the relative quiet of the run to finalize his plans for the work that lay ahead later that evening.

To his dismay, he had trouble concentrating. For the first

mile through the restored colonial section of town, he found himself watching the tourists and looking for attractive women. Not that he planned on stopping if he saw one, but the search gave him something to do to pass the time besides think. When he finally cleared the tourist section, he again tried to concentrate on his assignment, but instead found his thoughts being inexplicably drawn back to the hotel lobby. Something was out of place, but he couldn't put his finger on it.

At first his thoughts were random, going rapidly from image to image of things he had seen in the lobby with no apparent connection. The approach was so disjointed it confused him by blurring what his real memories were. By the time he passed the mile and a half marker, he had no plan for the night and no idea what it was about the lobby that bothered him.

Over the next quarter mile, he tried a different approach to solving the mystery. He decided to mentally reconstruct his path from the time he entered the lobby until the time he left. He remembered nothing unusual about the walk from his room to the front desk. He could picture the young, pretty, red-haired woman assisting him with his room key. He zoomed in on the room key, thinking it was a likely source of his uneasiness. He was sure, though, that the woman took the key and set it on the counter behind the check-in desk, so he hadn't left it out where someone could get it. Then he remembered turning and making momentary eye contact with a man in a suit. The eye contact made him uncomfortable because he felt as if the man had been staring at him. At the time, he attributed the feeling to the paranoia that goes hand-in-hand with being a hired gun. But the more he thought about it, the more he realized it was more than paranoia. It had something to do with the man himself.

Vernhausen began to slow slightly as he focused his energy on developing an accurate mental image of the man in the suit. His mind worked with computer-like efficiency, in effect, digitizing the man's image, enlarging it, and adding needed clarity. He no longer noticed the beauty of the Williamsburg afternoon or the tranquility of the running trail. He didn't even realize that his pace had slowed to almost eight minutes per mile. Then, recognition came.

It was not a face he knew well, but one he knew all the same. Now he had to determine why he recognized it. He had so few contacts in the United States that the list of possibilities was not long. Still, he had no idea whether the man was someone he had actually met or just seen before. The memory, though, seemed recent. In fact, instinct told him the man posed a threat, but his instinct did not tell him why.

With danger bells ringing and adrenaline pumping, Vernhausen reversed directions, picked up his pace, and headed for home. He pushed the display button on his watch to switch from stopwatch to time. It was 1:17 and he had about two miles to go. He had to get back, for what, he wasn't sure. But he was certain the answer would be waiting for him.

* * *

STEVE TOOK A deep breath, pushed on the door and stepped forward. The door tried to resist, but the dollar bill wouldn't let it. With a small click and a lot of luck, the door to Vernhausen's room swung open.

Steve paused before going in. He knew once he broke the door plane, there was no turning back. He took another deep breath, glanced behind him one last time, and walked into the room, pulling the door closed as he went. He looked at his watch; it was 1:18. Still in the foyer and with his feet feeling glued to the floor, he scanned the suite thoroughly for the first time. It suddenly occurred to him he had no idea what he was looking for. The laptop sat invitingly on the desk at the back of the room, but other than that, there was nothing obvious lying about. Steve wished he'd realized that just a few seconds earlier. Now it was too late.

Steve started walking toward the laptop, then remembered

the dollar still in the door. He stepped back to the door, opened it just enough to extract the bill, and closed it again with a nudge. As a final precaution, he latched the door chain just in case Vernhausen returned while he was still in the room, although he had no intention of allowing that to happen.

Steve again directed his attention to the laptop. The dark gray computer presented a bold silhouette against the sunshine streaming through the sliding glass doors behind the desk. He maneuvered up close to get a better look. The display was blank, but the tiny green power-saver light blinking on and off told him that the killer had left his computer on. He reached down and pushed the space bar. The green light stopped blinking and the laptop's disk drive whirred into action. A few seconds later, the screen popped back to life.

At first, Steve didn't realize what he was looking at. He recognized the screen as an Internet Web page, but all the text was in German. He guessed it was the last screen Vernhausen viewed, but it did him little good because he couldn't read or write the language. And without an attached printer, he couldn't even print the page to have it analyzed later.

Just as he was about to give up, he noticed that the scroll bar on the right side of the screen sat about dead center in the display. This meant there was more material hidden from view both above and below what was currently visible on the screen. Not overly concerned with leaving fingerprints, he scrolled to the bottom of the screen, only to find more of the same incomprehensible German text. He tried to decipher the writing, but it was hopeless.

More out of habit than rational choice, Steve scrolled to the top of the document. Then he saw it. There, as plain as day, was a color picture of Tadeusz Zalinsky and what appeared to be biographical data in the caption below the photograph. He presumed it was biographical data because the information appeared in bullet format with one of the bullets containing Tadeusz Zalinsky's name. He wanted to print the page, but had no way to do so. He thought he might be able to download the screen to a disk, but he didn't see any disks sitting around. He rifled through the desk drawers in vain, turning up only hotel stationery. He thought about emailing the page to his home computer, but didn't know how to do it from Vernhausen's machine. "Shit!" he uttered in frustration, believing he had the key to the case in front of him and no way to use it.

Steve gazed at the screen and tried to maintain control. He had to figure out some way to preserve the information so he could access it later. His eyes drifted to the Internet address in the toolbar section of the screen, and then to his watch without noticing the time. His face started getting hot and he could feel panic setting in, so much so that he actually contemplated taking the entire laptop with him. He stood up to leave and then sat back down again. Finally, he looked back at the Internet address in the toolbar section.

It was so damned simple! Why hadn't he recognized it earlier? He opened the drawer again and pulled out a piece of stationery. All he had to do was write down the Internet address for the Web page. Then he, or more likely Detective Belmar, could access the Web page and get all the information they needed. He'd wasted valuable time by overlooking such a simple solution. Now he really had to get going.

Steve shuffled through the remaining stationery in the drawer in search of something to write with. He knew time was running out, but he was too afraid to look at his watch. "Tell me this isn't happening," he said frantically. He started tearing through every drawer to find a pen. Then he remembered he had one in his breast pocket and reached inside his suit to pull it out. He began writing down the Web address as quickly as he could. It was incredibly long and difficult to copy because it had no pattern. He wrote carefully, making sure to duplicate case and character exactly as they appeared on the screen. Then, to make sure he copied down the material correctly, he verified each character one last time.

"Finished," he said out loud as if someone else were listening. He sprang up from the chair and grabbed the annotated piece of stationery. He folded it twice until it fit neatly in his breast pocket with the pen that had saved the day. An air of relief settled in and he was actually composed enough to pause and check his watch.

"Holy shit!" His digital watch displayed 1:35—five minutes beyond his safe departure time. He had to get out of there, and fast.

Steve headed for the door, but then turned back to make sure he'd left things the way he'd found them. Not satisfied with what he saw, he adjusted the chair in front of the computer. He also pushed in each of the drawers to make sure it was fully closed. Then he noticed the Web page on the computer screen. The computer had been in power saver mode when he arrived. Now, the only way the screen would go blank again was if the computer reverted to power saver mode automatically, which would take time. Steve couldn't turn off the computer because Vernhausen would surely remember leaving it on. He decided to take the chance that power saver mode would kick in before Vernhausen returned. Recognizing he had done all he could, he again made his way to the door.

* * *

VERNHAUSEN DIDN'T BOTHER slowing as he neared the main entrance to the Colonial Inne. Normally, he would have walked around for a while to cool down after reaching some imaginary finish line. Today he ran right to the entrance of the hotel and walked into the lobby, sweat dripping from his face. He was still panting when he approached the front desk to claim his room key.

"Excuse me, miss," he said hurriedly to the red-haired hotel clerk. "I dropped off my room key earlier. I'd like it back now, please."

"Of course, Mr. Vernhausen," the clerk said with a smile.

Vernhausen was shocked that she remembered his name. In his business, that generally wasn't a good sign. The clerk retrieved the key and handed it to him.

"Oh, by the way, Mr. Vernhausen. The man you met earlier today came by to see you."

Vernhausen shuddered. He hadn't met anyone earlier in the day. Someone there knew him, but who?

"I'm sorry, miss," he replied, trying not to look surprised. "I've met a number of gentlemen today. Could you be more specific?"

"Oh, of course," the clerk said with the same energetic smile she'd worn all afternoon. "The man who promised to show you around Williamsburg."

"Oh, yes," Vernhausen said, feigning a smile of recognition. "You didn't happen to get his name, did you? I seem to have forgotten it."

"He couldn't remember your name either, Mr. Vernhausen, so don't feel so bad. I'm sorry, too, though, because I didn't get his name either. I do remember he said he was here with the Bar Association."

As soon as he heard the words "Bar Association," he knew who the mystery man was. It was the lawyer he'd met at the professor's house and who had brought Tadeusz Zalinsky to Williamsburg. The fact that the lawyer was looking for him could only mean trouble. He needed to get back to his room right away to look up the attorney on the Web. Then he'd know who he was dealing with.

Vernhausen bolted from the check-in area without so much as a thank you. His rude departure didn't go unnoticed; the check-in clerk branded him as ungrateful and watched him scurry off toward his room. His behavior made her glad he'd left before she could tell him that she'd given the lawyer his room number. "Now," she thought, "he'll just have to figure that out for himself." And with that, the big smile returned to her face and she began to help the next customer.

* * *

STEVE COULDN'T WAIT to get out of the room. He rushed to the door and looked back one last time. The computer screen was still on, but there was nothing he could do about it. He reached out and turned the doorknob and began to pull on the door. As he did, the door jerked open toward him. The chain lock strained and stretched taut just in time to keep the door from slamming into his face. "Ahhhh!" he yelled as he let go of the door and jumped back to assess what was happening. As he did, someone tugged the door back and tried to open it more forcefully, only to again be repulsed by the chain. He couldn't believe it. Vernhausen was back!

Steve panicked. He knew the chain wouldn't hold much longer, especially if Vernhausen threw his weight into it. Then a hand reached inside the door to unfasten the chain. Steve kicked the door with all his might and smashed the hand against the doorframe. Vernhausen screamed in pain and pulled his hand back outside the door. Steve tried to close it all the way again, but Vernhausen lodged his foot against the bottom edge of the door to keep it from closing.

Steve knew in a minute that either Vernhausen or the police would come bursting in and he'd be dead or in jail. He thought about yanking the door open and forcing his way down the hall, but he knew that offered little chance of success. Again the door slammed against the chain and a screw flew from the lock's mounting bracket and bounced on the floor at his feet. He turned to grab something to use as a weapon when Vernhausen broke through. Then he noticed the sliding glass door. He ran for it as fast as he could, hitting his left shinbone on the bedpost but not even feeling the pain. As he unlocked the sliding glass door, he heard the main door slam again and

again against the chain. Finally, he opened the sliding door
and in a flash was out on the terrace and running to his car.
He never looked back. He literally ran for his life, fearing
Vernhausen was close behind.

* * *

FOUR SLAMS LATER, the chain's mounting bracket broke and
Vernhausen charged into his room. He immediately saw the
open sliding glass door but thought it was a ploy. If it was, as
soon as he ran out the sliding glass door, the intruder would
slip out of hiding and leave by the room's main entrance. To
keep that from happening, he checked the bathroom and
under the beds, and searched the closet in the main room. The
room was clear.

Vernhausen walked to the back of the room and stepped
outside through the still-open sliding glass door. All he could
see was the peaceful fall afternoon and the fiery Williamsburg
sun. With no one in sight, he went back into his room and
locked the sliding glass door. Only then did he notice the blood
on the back of his hand. The cut from the door wasn't deep,
but his entire hand throbbed. He went into the bathroom and
grabbed a white towel and wrapped it around his injured hand.
As he came out of the bathroom, he heard a knock at his door.

"Who is it?" he asked without moving any closer to the door.
After what he had just been through, he was suspicious when
yet another uninvited visitor came calling.

"Hotel security."

Vernhausen walked to the door and slowly opened it with
his good hand. He kept his injured hand behind the door,
hidden from view.

"May I help you?" Vernhausen asked as if nothing had
happened. He found himself standing face to face with a stocky
man in his mid-forties, sporting a crew cut. Although the man
wore a gray business suit, he was obviously better equipped to
quell disturbances than close deals on Wall Street.

"Excuse me, sir, but we had a report of a problem at your room. Is everything okay here?"

"Oh, yes," Vernhausen replied with a smile reminiscent of the red-haired front desk clerk's. "I did have a little trouble getting into my room. Something must have fallen in front of the door and caused it to jam." Vernhausen hoped the man bought the story. It was the best he could come up with.

"May I ask your name, sir?" the security guard asked, apparently unconvinced.

"Of course. My name is Vernhausen, Karl Vernhausen."

"Do you have a picture identification card, Mr. Vernhausen?"

"Yes, of course. Let me get it for you." Vernhausen left the door open at a forty-five degree angle while he retrieved his passport. He tried to ease away and keep his injured hand shielded from view. By now, a small amount of blood had soaked through and was visible to anyone who could see the towel.

Vernhausen retreated to the closet where he kept his computer case. He retrieved his passport from the case and returned to the door to hand it to the security guard. Although the task took no more than a minute, it gave him time to come up with a plausible explanation for his hand. As he passed the passport to the security guard, the screensaver on his computer kicked in.

The security guard took the passport and thumbed through it until he came to Vernhausen's picture. He studied it for a moment and then looked up to compare it to Vernhausen's face. Unexpectedly and quite abruptly, the security guard's expression softened. He closed the passport and handed it back to Vernhausen.

"I'm sorry to have bothered you, Mr. Vernhausen. Next time, if you have any trouble getting into your room, just come to the front desk and we'll take care of it for you." Then he added, as if to catch Vernhausen letting down his guard, "What did you do to your hand?"

"Oh, this ...." Vernhausen replied nonchalantly, displaying his towel-wrapped hand in full view so the security guard wouldn't think he was trying to hide anything, even though he was. "I just got back from running. I think I banged it on a wire fence or something, but I really don't remember it happening. I didn't even notice it was bleeding until I got back to my room."

"Well, we have a doctor available if you'd like someone to take a look at it," the security guard offered, convinced by the explanation.

"Thanks, but I don't think that will be necessary. It's just a small cut."

"Okay, then, Mr. Vernhausen. I'm sorry I bothered you."

"Good day," Vernhausen said. He closed the door and turned around to go through his room more carefully. He had no idea what the intruder was after. He checked his cash, but all of it was just where he'd left it. In fact, he'd left his wallet out on the nightstand next to his bed and it appeared untouched. That told him the intruder wasn't a thief; it was someone on a mission. He had three possible explanations. The one he believed most plausible was that his client sent someone to either check up on him or kill him. Second, it could have been the police, but he didn't think he'd blown his cover yet, so that possibility was remote. Finally, it could have been the lawyer he'd seen staring at him in the lobby. Because he couldn't fathom why the attorney would break into his room, he discounted that alternative as well. As far as he was concerned, his client was watching him. But what had the intruder come into the room for? Everything seemed undisturbed. Then he noticed his computer screen.

And he knew.

27

STEVE DROVE BACK to his office like a wild man. His heart was pounding so hard he swore he could actually hear it beating. He intentionally took a roundabout way in case he was being followed, and his eyes bounced back and forth between the rear and side-view mirrors, watching for anything and everything suspicious. When he finally convinced himself no one was on his tail, he headed for North Henry Street and turned into his office parking lot. His adrenaline was still pumping when his aging Toyota Celica skidded to a stop close alongside the building.

Marjorie was on her feet and already heading for the door when Steve entered. "Mr. Stilwell, was that you?" she asked, not attempting to hide her astonishment. Steve ignored the question and walked straight back to his office, simply saying hello as he passed.

Marjorie didn't know what to do. She was upset because she could see Steve was upset. She vacillated between staying out of his way and poking her head into his office to see what was wrong. She started to head for her desk, but her curiosity and her concern got the better of her. She reached for her desk and grabbed her scheduling calendar. She could use it as an excuse to find out what was going on. With the calendar and a sharp pencil in hand, she inched her way into Steve's office. He was already on the phone. She started to leave, but Steve motioned to her with his free hand to remain. She listened intently to every word of his conversation.

"I don't have time to explain," Steve said firmly. "You've got to get your things together and get out of the house right away." There was a moment of silence as he listened to the response. Steve began speaking again.

"I know it's a change in plans, but we really don't have a choice. I need you to drop Mr. Zalinsky off at the new post office at 2:30 and then you go on from there." After Steve listened for another short period, he concluded the conversation.

"I love you too, honey. And I promise, this will all be over soon." He was absolutely certain his last statement was true. What he wasn't certain about was exactly how it would end. He hung up the receiver and looked up at Marjorie.

"Marjorie, I'm afraid I'm in a bit of a jam." He tried to muster some semblance of a smile but couldn't bring himself to do it.

"What's the matter, Mr. Stilwell? You have me worried."

Steve stared down at the telephone trying to figure out what he should tell Marjorie and what his next step should be. He wanted to contact the Williamsburg police, but he knew he couldn't after having explored Vernhausen's room at the Colonial Inne. His only option was to work through Detective Belmar. Belmar could contact the authorities in the United States. He wanted to call Belmar right away, but first he needed to deal with Marjorie. He looked up and saw the genuine concern deepening on her face. She had to be told, and now.

"Marjorie," he began. "I need you to promise you'll keep what I am about to tell you in the strictest confidence." Steve waited for Marjorie to concur. She said nothing and offered only a single affirmative nod to signal her begrudging acceptance of his terms.

"What I'm about to say is going to sound unbelievable, but here goes. I don't think Michelle Siegel had anything to do with the murders. There's someone behind them in Germany, and he hired a hitman to kill all the men named as beneficiaries under Professor Siegel's will. The good news is one of the beneficiaries is still alive—Tadeusz Zalinsky. In fact, he's staying with me. I brought him to Williamsburg so he'd be safe. The bad news is, I just saw the hitman at the Colonial Inne, so he must know that Mr. Zalinsky's here. I'm afraid it might be dangerous to stay around here any longer. I need you to go home and keep away from the office for a while."

Marjorie stood motionless during Steve's announcement; that is, until her left hand began to quiver and her knees started to shake. She gripped the back of the chair in front of her to steady herself. Steve could tell she was scared, so he tried to lead her to a more familiar topic to help her calm down.

"What's my schedule look like for the rest of the afternoon?"

Marjorie froze while her mind digested that she was being asked something non-threatening.

"Marjorie?"

"I'm sorry, Mr. Stilwell." She held up her calendar and checked his afternoon. "You've got nothing scheduled for the rest of the day." Then she paused while she flipped to the next page. "You've got nothing scheduled tomorrow morning, either, but you do have two new client intakes tomorrow afternoon."

"Good. What about Mr. Smythe?"

Talking about the office schedule had helped Marjorie settle down. "Mr. Smythe has a deposition later today in Newport News and two appointments tomorrow morning."

"That's what I needed to know. Go ahead and call it a day. I can handle it here for the rest of the afternoon, especially with Mr. Smythe out. I'll tell him what's going on."

"What about the police, Mr. Stilwell?"

"I can't involve them yet, Marjorie." Steve looked directly into Marjorie's downcast eyes. "I wish I could, but I just can't …

not just yet. You've got to trust me on that."

Marjorie nodded, her eyes unable to mask her fear.

"Look, I promise to call you tonight to let you know how things are going," Steve continued. He picked up the telephone receiver to signal he was ready to move on. "Oh, and I'm counting on you not to tell anyone about this. You've got to promise me that."

Marjorie didn't say anything.

"Marjoreeee?"

"Okay, Mr. Stilwell," she answered reluctantly.

"Thanks. And plan on taking tomorrow off, too. I'll let you know for sure when I call tonight." Then Steve began to thumb through his phone list to find Detective Belmar's number.

Marjorie could see Steve was preoccupied, so she retreated out of the office and gathered her things. Before she left, she switched the office phones to voicemail mode. She knew it would be a disaster if Steve tried to answer the phones all afternoon by himself. He obviously had bigger things on his mind. She looked back into his office as she walked toward the door. He was already on the telephone with someone. She wondered who he was talking to and if it had anything to do with Professor Siegel. More important, she wondered if she would ever see her boss alive again.

* * *

DETECTIVE BELMAR'S TELEPHONE started ringing just as he began putting on his coat to go home. It seemed to happen that way every night. He told his wife he thought the detectives in the pit watched until they saw him getting ready to leave and then rang his office just for fun. He debated whether to answer it. If he let it go, after five rings it would roll to the Duty Detective's desk, so it wasn't like the call would be lost. Still, a ringing telephone was like the Sirens' song, beckoning Belmar back to his phone to see what hot new case might roll in. More realistically, the call could be his wife letting him know she'd be working late, which meant he could grab a sandwich at the office and catch up on some paperwork. No, he couldn't walk away from a ringing telephone tonight. He never could and he never did.

"*Hallo, hier ist Belmar.*"

"Ah, hello, Detective Belmar, this is Steve Stilwell. How are you tonight?"

Belmar rolled his eyes when he heard who it was. Now he wished he hadn't picked up the phone. He could see the pattern developing. This American attorney would keep bothering him and pushing his Nazi conspiracy theory without offering any evidence. Every difficult case seemed to generate one or two persistent callers who thought they were being helpful, but actually served only to distract his investigators. This was particularly so when they became dissatisfied with the investigative efforts. They'd write his superiors and demand an accounting of why the investigators weren't pursuing their leads. Then his detectives would have to devote their valuable time running down a bunch of half-baked theories just to satisfy some politician that the police force was being responsive to the citizenry. He decided to dispose of the call quickly.

"I'm fine, Mr. Stilwell. You caught me just as I was leaving my office. Is there something I can do for you?"

"Yes, there is," Steve said hurriedly. "Do you have a sheet of paper you can copy something down on?"

"Yes. What is it you want to give me?" Belmar wanted control of the call. He had no intention of blindly writing down everything the American said. He insisted on relevance first.

"I'm going to give you a World Wide Web address. If you can access it, you'll know who hired Emil Weisentrope's killer."

Belmar was skeptical. He'd been down this road enough times before not to get his hopes up. Nevertheless, he sat down at his desk, still wearing his coat, and grabbed a yellow legal pad and a dull pencil. He began to probe Steve to see if the information was worth working.

"How do you know that?"

Steve spoke rapidly, making it difficult, even for Belmar, to understand. "The man you showed me a picture of, the killer … he's in Williamsburg, Virginia, and he's staying at the Colonial Inne. His name is Karl Vernhausen and I saw him there today, just after I brought Tadeusz Zalinsky to Williamsburg to keep him safe. You've got to get in touch with the American authorities and have him arrested, or Mr. Zalinsky is as good as dead."

"Slow down, Mr. Stilwell, slow down. I understand that, but what does that have to do with the Web page and why should I check it out?"

Steve regrouped and tried to slow down, although his heart was racing just as it had in the car on the way back from the Colonial Inne. He started again, this time trying to set the facts out more logically so their importance would be clear.

"Let's just say that this afternoon I got a look at the killer's computer. He had been accessing a Web page with a picture of Tadeusz Zalinsky on it. I'm guessing the page originates somewhere in Germany, because the whole thing was in German."

"So that's all it was, a picture of Zalinsky?"

"Don't you see, Detective?" Steve asked, beginning to sound a little irritated with what he perceived as a lack of understanding on Belmar's part. "Two days ago, Mr. Zalinsky was in Cleveland, Ohio, and the killer knocked on his door looking for information. Then I got Mr. Zalinsky out of Cleveland and brought him to Williamsburg to hide him. The only people that knew I brought him here were you and me. Then today, the killer shows up in Williamsburg and Mr. Zalinsky's picture is on his computer screen. My God, Detective Belmar, if you don't do something soon, Mr. Zalinsky will be a dead man!"

Belmar could see it all right. If the principal had been

careless or conceited enough to leave everything accessible on a Web page, this might break the case wide open. It was worth a chance, but they'd have to act fast, before the killer got to Zalinsky. The Web page might give them what they needed to have the American authorities arrest the killer pending extradition. But if the killer got to Zalinsky first, Zalinsky would be dead and the killer gone. Not only that, if Steve kept trying to protect Zalinsky, he'd be dead too.

"Okay, Mr. Stilwell, give me the address."

"Are you ready to copy?"

"Go ahead."

Steve dictated the lengthy alphanumeric string. "Did you get it all?"

"I believe so." Belmar repeated the Web address so both could confirm he copied it correctly.

"You've got it."

"Are there any passwords?"

"I'm sure there are, but the Web address was the best I could do. You're going to have to crack that yourself."

"Tell me, Mr. Stilwell, just how did you get to look at the killer's computer?"

"Don't ask. Just promise me you'll run this down. Mr. Zalinsky's life depends on it."

"You have my word. I'll get back in touch with you. Be careful, Mr. Stilwell."

"Thank you, Detective Belmar." Steve hung up the phone, flopped back into his leather chair, and stared out into his outer office. He finally felt as though he had gotten his point across. All he had left to do was keep himself and Mr. Zalinsky safe until Belmar put Vernhausen permanently behind bars.

There was only one problem: failure now meant certain death.

28

Today was a day Steve could have done without. What started out so promising had devolved into a nightmare. When he'd driven into work that morning, he'd believed Vernhausen had been left clueless in Cleveland, which had bought Mr. Zalinsky some time. Now Vernhausen was lurking in Williamsburg, ready to strike without notice. Worse yet, Steve felt like he couldn't go to the Williamsburg police for help. The only bright spot was that Detective Belmar finally seemed convinced he had a legitimate case against Vernhausen. All Steve could hope for was that Belmar arranged for Vernhausen's arrest before the hitman arranged for Mr. Zalinsky's death.

After Steve spoke with Belmar, the day seemed to settle down. Sarah dropped off Mr. Zalinsky at the rendezvous point as planned and continued on to her mother's house in Charlottesville. Steve brought Mr. Zalinsky to his office and the two men spent the rest of the afternoon discussing their options. They spoke for almost three hours, covering every aspect of the situation and stopping only to take delivery of a pizza at 6:30 p.m. In the end, both agreed Mr. Zalinsky needed to remain at the office until either Steve found a safer location or the situation resolved itself.

The office was an ideal place for Mr. Zalinsky's secret hideout. Steve worked there all day, making it easy for him to monitor his charge, and the place would look deserted after hours. Even better, no one used the upstairs; it was a dusty, grimy graveyard for old furniture, archived files and scrap building supplies never discarded after the first floor renovation. There was plenty of room to camp out for a few days, and that was exactly what the two men intended to do. All they needed were a few camping supplies to make the place livable. Unfortunately, Steve hadn't thought far enough ahead to tell Sarah to bring the supplies with her when she dropped off Mr. Zalinsky. At the time, his main concern was getting Sarah safely out of Williamsburg. Now he had to retrieve the supplies himself.

Steve didn't tell Mr. Zalinsky or Sarah about the other item he intended to retrieve—his Colt M1911A1 .45 caliber service pistol. He kept it locked in a case in the attic above the master bedroom and wasn't even sure if Sarah remembered he had it. The gun wasn't for protection; it was more of a family heirloom. It had been his father's from his days in the Air Force. His father gave it to him when he joined the Navy, saying every military officer needed to have and know how to use a personal sidearm. Steve did learn how to shoot in the Navy, but JAGs rarely carried pistols, and when they did, the Navy issued them their weapons. So Steve relegated the weapon to the attic, bringing it down once a year to clean it when Sarah was not at home. He didn't know if he could actually fire the weapon at another human being, but his sense of duty to protect Mr. Zalinsky told him he better be ready to do so.

Steve waited until just after midnight to make the one-mile trek to his house. He wanted to eliminate any possibility Vernhausen might see and recognize him during another chance encounter. Besides, midnight in Williamsburg seemed to evoke safety. Just in case, though, as he prepared to leave the office, he established some ground rules with Mr. Zalinsky.

"I should be back in about an hour," Steve said as the two men stood by the front door to the law office. "Don't open the door for anyone—even someone who says he's with the police. I've got a key, so I can get in. Also, we always keep these two lights on for security," he added, pointing to the lamp on Marjorie's desk and the light just inside the front door. "Don't turn on any other lights or the police will get suspicious when they drive by and don't see my car here."

"May I go upstairs?" Mr. Zalinsky asked, now quite tired from the long, worrisome afternoon.

Steve paused before answering. He noticed for the first time the weariness in Mr. Zalinsky's eyes. Still, he was concerned about having the man upstairs while he was gone. But with Mr. Zalinsky staying there for the next few days anyway, he decided to give the okay.

"I don't see why not. Remember that old leather sofa up there in the back room? That might be a place for you to lie down and get a little sleep."

"I think I'll do that."

"Remember, stay away from the windows and don't turn on any lights up there." They had explored the upstairs earlier in the evening and found sufficient light from a nearby streetlight to navigate most of the floor. Turning on an upstairs light after midnight would surely attract a visit by the Williamsburg police. Not that having Mr. Zalinsky upstairs violated any laws; the real concern lay with anyone learning he was there. Steve feared the information would eventually work its way back to the apparently well-connected hitman. After all, he had tracked Mr. Zalinsky all the way to Williamsburg. It was only a matter of time before Vernhausen located Mr. Zalinsky again. Steve hoped, though, that before it was too late he would either be able to arrange another safe haven or Belmar would solve the case.

Steve said goodnight to Mr. Zalinsky and left the office

carrying his briefcase. The plan was for his exit to look like a routine late-night departure from work. He locked the front door as he always did and headed for his car. It was a beautiful, clear evening, with the fall air showing the telltale signs of the coming winter cold. Leaves crackled beneath his feet as he walked across the parking lot and stopped to unlock his car. He had been so preoccupied since Professor Siegel first appeared that he had actually forgotten to stop to appreciate Virginia's glorious change of seasons. He stood motionless, breathing the crisp night air. The night was so still—no breeze; no dogs barking; no sounds. Under any other circumstances he would coerce Sarah into going for a late night walk. Then the whoosh of a passing car on North Henry Street snapped him out of his moment of peace. He looked at the car with disdain until it disappeared from view.

The drive to his house was a short one. Except for the college campus, Williamsburg generally closed its shutters by 10:00 p.m. He saw no one as he cruised by the three-hundred-year-old three-story Christopher Wren building on the grounds of the College of William & Mary or on the residential side street where his house was located. He drove past the cars parked neatly on both sides of the tree-lined street and pulled into his driveway, stopping only long enough for the automatic garage door opener to clear the way into his garage.

Steve hated coming home late at night when Sarah wasn't there. Here he was, almost forty-nine years old, and he still felt uneasy about entering a dark house by himself. He signaled the garage door again and waited for it to close completely before getting out of his car. Then he grabbed his briefcase and headed for the door.

Steve fumbled with his keys, trying to find the right one to unlock the door. After jumbling them a couple of times in an attempt to move the door key into a usable position, he simply tried the door and it opened. He reached around into the pitch-black kitchen and flipped on the light before he entered.

With everything in the kitchen now fully visible, he walked inside and closed the door behind him. As he started toward the hallway, he noticed the back door leading to the deck was ever-so-slightly ajar.

"Dammit, Sarah," he said aloud. He couldn't believe she'd left the door open, given what was going on. She'd done it before and he'd warned her about it. He went over to the door, pushed it all the way closed, and locked the deadbolt. As an added precaution, he turned on the backyard security light and lit up the whole backyard. With most of the leaves off the trees, the light illuminated a large part of yard belonging to the house behind him, but he figured it was better to play it safe now and deal with any complaints later. Plus, it was after midnight and none of the houses around his had any lights on; everyone was already asleep.

Steve walked across the kitchen and turned on the hallway light. He made it a point to turn on every light in his path; he would reverse the process on his way out. When he was home alone at night he liked a well-lit house. He walked past the darkened living room, shifted his briefcase to his right hand and turned to go up the stairs. At the bottom of the stairwell he switched on the light at the top of the stairs and started thudding his way up, still preoccupied with Sarah's leaving the backdoor open. When his head rose above floor-level on the second floor, he glanced to his right and saw something that stopped him dead in his tracks. All the way at the end of the master bedroom, a light shined brightly under the closed door to the master bath. The only time he or Sarah ever closed that door was if one of them was in the bathroom. Plus, the room had plenty of light during the day. Sarah wouldn't have turned on that light before she left; it simply wouldn't have been necessary. Now the entire house was dark except for that one room, and its door was inexplicably closed.

Suddenly it occurred to Steve that Sarah might not have left the backdoor open. Maybe the killer found out he was the one hiding Mr. Zalinsky, and he'd come to the house to kill them. For the first time in his life he felt a fear that ran bone deep. He tried to get a grip but couldn't formulate a focused thought. Then, out of nowhere, a random memory surfaced. He pictured himself giving training lectures to fleet sailors on the Navy Code of Conduct. "I am an American fighting man," he thought. Never mind that he had been a Navy lawyer and not someone at the pointy end of the spear. The heritage alone gave him strength.

The brief break in panic was all he needed to begin an orderly retreat. Slowly and silently, he started backing down the stairs, keeping his eyes fixed on the light beneath the master bathroom door. At the first sign of movement he was prepared to jump down the stairs and fly out the front door, provided he could get it unlocked before whoever was upstairs got to him. He eased down the stairs, one step after another, clutching the railing with his left hand and his briefcase with his right. With three steps left to go he started to turn to make his exit.

"AHHHHhhhhhh!" Steve shrieked, as he saw the killer waiting for him at the bottom of the stairs. He didn't hear Vernhausen call his name, nor did he see the gun Vernhausen held at his side—Steve moved too quickly for that. For the next fifteen seconds, he acted on instinct, made possible only by the resolution of his panic at the top of the stairs. As he completed his turn, he continued swinging his briefcase and aimed it directly at Vernhausen's head.

Steve's maneuver caught Vernhausen completely off guard. He started to raise the gun toward Steve but was a split second too late. The corner of Steve's briefcase struck him squarely on the left side of the head. Vernhausen fired his weapon as he fell and the bullet grazed Steve's left calf. Steve didn't feel it, though, nor did he stick around to survey the damage. As Vernhausen fell, Steve jumped down the last three stairs and threw his briefcase at Vernhausen's head. This time, though, the briefcase only glanced off its target. It was the first blow that left Vernhausen stunned on the floor, still clutching his gun.

Steve raced around the stairwell and headed for the backdoor. He flicked off the hallway light as he ran into the kitchen and tossed a chair behind him to slow down the inevitable pursuit. At the backdoor, he grabbed the doorknob with both hands. First he tried to open the door without unlocking it, but of course that didn't work. He wished to God he hadn't locked it on his way in and started to shake it out of frustration. "Open up, you bastard!" he shouted in defiance, but the door didn't listen. He heard shuffling coming down the hall. "Holy shit!" he screamed. Finally, he realized he had to unlock the deadbolt before it would open. He twisted the lock and pulled the door open just as Vernhausen appeared in the hallway. Vernhausen paused to point the pistol at him and pulled the trigger. The bullet slammed into the doorframe just next to Steve's head but didn't injure him. He flew out onto the deck, pushing the backdoor closed as he left, and took off running through his brightly lit backyard.

As soon as he hit the grass, Steve jettisoned his suit coat. He couldn't risk turning around yet to see if Vernhausen was following because the light that made it easier for him to run also made it easier for Vernhausen to shoot. When he hit the now barren stand of oaks between his property and the house behind him, he turned for just a second to see if Vernhausen was after him. He was! Vernhausen was just coming out the door and onto the deck. The hitman saw Steve pause and stopped to take aim. Steve started running again and veered to the left, causing Vernhausen's shot to miss wide. Jumping off the deck, the hitman began his pursuit.

Steve ran for all he was worth. His weekly running regimen made him a good runner for a forty-eight-year-old, but he knew he wouldn't be able to stay ahead of the younger hitman forever. He crossed Jamestown Road and ran onto the William & Mary campus, hoping to see a police car, but there was none.

Looking over his shoulder, he saw Vernhausen hot on his trail and no more than fifty yards behind. He couldn't run to a house to ask for help because he feared Vernhausen would kill him, along with whoever answered the door. With no other options available, he kept running toward the historic Wren building and Colonial Williamsburg, praying for something to save him. He wasn't slowing yet; right now he was betting his life he could maintain the pace for a little while longer.

Steve rounded the corner of the Wren building and started running along the red brick sidewalk to the main entrance. He could see the stairway leading up to the Wren building's front doors and the stairwell below leading to the building's basement. That was it … the catacombs. They were his only chance. He darted down the stairwell, and without hesitation made a fist with his right hand and punched through the rectangular pane of glass closest to the doorknob. He reached through with his bloody but numb knuckles, opened the door, and dashed inside just as Vernhausen rounded the building's corner.

Steve pinned his survival on an old William & Mary fraternity tradition. When he'd attended the college thirty years earlier, the fraternity he pledged told him that catacombs below the Wren building contained the rotting remains of the college's founding fathers. Throughout the year, various gullible pledges were sent down into the basement to bring back a snapshot of the tombs. During one of those excursions, Steve had learned firsthand that the catacombs were really antiquated steam tunnels connecting the Wren building and three of the college's oldest academic structures bordering the Sunken Gardens—a large recessed football field-sized grassy area accessible by stairs and crossed by several evenly spaced red brick sidewalks. At the start of every school year, the college sealed off the tunnels with plywood to keep would-be thrill seekers from getting hurt. With similar regularity, the fraternities broke through the seals, leaving them accessible for the heartiest of their pledges. Now Steve hoped the tradition lived on as he bumped and banged his way through the basement in search of his only hope of escape.

Steve found the entrance to the catacombs just as it had been thirty years before. Although the plywood seal appeared new, he was able to grab it with both hands and yank one side out far enough to allow him to slip past the nails and into the tunnel. He eased one leg inside but hesitated before climbing in the rest of the way. The interior of the tunnel was pitch black. Once he pulled the plywood closed behind him, he would see nothing. He remembered all too well his first trip into the rat-infested tunnel with a flashlight and a Polaroid camera. It oozed giant roaches and big black spiders hanging from webs stretching from one side of the tunnel to the other. This time he could not avoid what he could not see. Even worse, he had no way of knowing if the tunnels went through anymore or if they were blocked somewhere down the line.

He had no more time to ponder his choices. As he looked back into the basement, he could see Vernhausen's shadow coming down the basement stairs. He ducked inside the tunnel and pulled the plywood closed behind him.

As the plywood creaked back into position, Vernhausen entered the basement.

29

Düsseldorf

BELMAR SAT SILENTLY, seething with frustration. Hackers from the Computer Crimes Division had worked through the night but had not yet been able to gain access to the killer's Web page. Try as they might, they couldn't circumvent the password. With millions of combinations possible, breaking into the host computer was fast becoming a pipe dream.

"Any progress yet?" Detective Schueller asked as he strolled into Belmar's office without knocking. The look on Belmar's face was all the answer he needed.

"We're losing the window, Hans."

"What do you mean?"

"When the killer sees we've been trying to access his computer, he'll shut down for good."

"Can we call the American and ask him to get the password?"

"There's no time, Hans. Plus, it's the middle of the night in America."

Belmar opened the Weisentrope file and stared at Vernhausen's picture. He could feel the case slipping away.

"Dammit, Hans! There must be something we can do!"

"You know," Hans began, hoping his boss wouldn't find the suggestion he was about to make stupid. "If we ask the Americans to arrest Vernhausen, they could search him for us. I'm sure he must have the password written down somewhere, in case he forgets it."

"Even if there was enough time, the Americans would never arrest him on what we've got, let alone search him."

"I'm sorry, Detective, it was the best—"

"Wait a minute, Hans," Belmar exclaimed. "I think you've done it!"

"Done what?"

"The customs search, Hans. Remember the customs search?" Belmar began flipping through the pages in the Weisentrope file, stopping only when he came to the cover sheet that came with the pictures of Vernhausen from America. His eyes moved quickly to the bottom of the page. "Here it is!" he said, circling something with a pencil.

"Here's what?"

Belmar grabbed the bottom of the cover sheet, tore it from the folder, and ran out of the office without answering. Finally, he had what he what he needed to solve the case. He just hoped it wasn't too late.

30

Williamsburg

To make forward progress possible, Steve placed the palm of his right hand on the tunnel wall and held his left hand out in front of his face. He started moving through the dank blackness, sliding his right hand on the tunnel wall as a guide. His outstretched hand soon severed a plethora of invisible webs, causing their sticky silk threads to flow back and cling to his face and hair. He swatted them away and continued on. Two paces later it happened again. This time, though, Steve's shaking knees reminded him Vernhausen could burst into the tunnel at any moment and gun him down like a stray dog. The thought of lying wounded and conscious and waiting for death in this God-forsaken hellhole provided all the incentive he needed to press forward. So he moved deeper and deeper into the tunnel, ignoring the crunches below his feet and all the things he couldn't see landing or brushing up against his eyes and ears. With the fear of death urging him on, he stopped for nothing.

Back in the basement, Vernhausen moved with similar

caution. He had underestimated Steve before and had a handy gash on the side of his head to show for it. Now he kept his gun at the ready and moved deliberately through the basement, checking under every dust-covered table and around every red brick wall with the precision of a crackerjack swat team. With only the dim light of a few streetlights filtering through the basement's ancient windows, every object created a dark, shadowy hiding place that had to be explored. By methodically searching each sector of the basement and keeping the only exit behind him, Vernhausen was confident he would find Steve; it was only a matter of time.

Steve counted his steps as he shuffled along, periodically looking over his shoulder to see if Vernhausen had found the entrance to the tunnel. Then, after nearly seventy paces, a dim trickle of light appeared on the side of the tunnel up in front of him. He didn't know what the source of the light was, but it drew him on, closer and closer. He saw the light as his only chance of salvation and worked toward it like a man possessed. Twenty more feet and he'd be there.

As Vernhausen neared the back of the basement, he discovered the boarded-up section of the back wall. He guessed that the boards blocked access to some subterranean chamber and maneuvered over to it as quickly as he could. He ran his free hand along the edge of the plywood seal to see how it was fastened to the wall. The one-inch gap between the seal and the wall told him the plywood had been pulled back and the nails that normally held the plywood in place now prevented it from sitting flush against the wall.

Vernhausen pressed his right eye into the gap but could see nothing. He tucked his pistol under his belt at the small of his back, grabbed the exposed edge of the plywood and pulled with all of his might. The plywood bowed and then, one by one, the remaining nails popped out of the wall until the plywood peeled back like the skin of a giant orange. When the plywood was about two-thirds of the way free, Vernhausen drew his gun and forced his way behind the seal. He stood inside the entrance to the pitch-black tunnel and debated his next move.

"*Scheisse!*" he said loud enough for Steve to hear. The sound of Vernhausen ripping away at the plywood warned Steve that Vernhausen had found the tunnel. But when he heard Vernhausen swear, the acoustics of the tunnel made it sound like Vernhausen was already right behind him. Fearing he was about to be killed, he darted for the light just up ahead. The light turned out to be coming from yet another steam tunnel intersecting his tunnel from the right. He flew around the corner and whacked his head on something suspended from the ceiling. The blow was hard enough to make him see stars, but he dared not make a sound. He rubbed his head to lessen the pain and looked toward the source of the light. Up ahead about fifteen or twenty yards, light was pouring in through the roof of the tunnel. With a beacon to follow and the prospect of freedom not far off, he ran to the source of the light as fast as the tunnel allowed. He knew Vernhausen could not be far behind.

Vernhausen stared into the tunnel's blackness. His instincts told him not to follow Steve inside. He had no light, no idea where the tunnel led, and no clue how to get out if he got lost. Something else told him to ignore his instincts and follow Steve or lose the perfect opportunity. If he didn't kill Steve now, Steve would certainly involve the police and then he'd be lucky just to get out of town. Still, getting ambushed in the tunnel was worse, so Vernhausen pushed open the plywood seal and retreated into the basement.

Before giving up entirely, Vernhausen decided to do one quick search around the building's perimeter in case Steve surfaced nearby. If he found nothing, he'd abort the mission and leave Williamsburg. He knew his client wouldn't want him getting caught because he had too much information. Plus, he'd been paid enough money already to allow him to disappear and live comfortably in obscurity for a long time to come. He worked his way back through the basement with gun drawn. His senses remained on the alert; something told him he would find what he was looking for.

The closer Steve got to the light, the faster he moved, until he found himself standing below a metal grating leading to the outside world. He grasped a ladder on the side of the tunnel and worked his way to the top. Although the grating's iron bars were extremely heavy, they were no match for his adrenaline-fueled legs and shoulders. He forced up one end of the grating far enough to wriggle his way completely outside. When he emerged, he saw that a tall green hedge surrounded him on all four sides, making him invisible to the outside world. He thought about remaining there until morning, when he could finally get to the police, but he was afraid Vernhausen would find his office before then. He had to move now; hesitating could cost Mr. Zalinsky his life.

Steve tried to let the grating down gradually to prevent it from slamming onto its concrete base. But when it reached a thirty-degree angle, gravity prevailed and he had to let go. The ensuing crash resonated across the nearby Sunken Gardens and bounced off the back of the Wren building. He hoped the hitman had not heard, but he had no intention of sticking around to find out. He poked his head through one side of the hedge to get his bearings. He could see the back of the Wren building to his right and the College's Sunken Gardens to his left. In fact, his hiding place formed part of the hedge barrier surrounding the Sunken Gardens. He pulled his head back and poked it out again through the opposite side. Everything looked clear.

Steve broke through the hedge and ran to the first brick path crossing the Sunken Gardens. He made no effort to hide that he was fleeing from trouble; he wanted the campus police to stop him so he could get help for himself and Mr. Zalinsky. But he couldn't afford to stop and look for a telephone or wait for the police to come to him. He sensed danger for Mr. Zalinsky and had to do something about it. He had to get back to his office right away.

Steve ran to the edge of the Sunken Gardens and climbed the brick stairs to ground level. There he paused, carefully surveying his surroundings before venturing away from the gardens' protective cover. With no one in sight, he started jogging along the path to a brick fence bordering Richmond Road. He made it to the fence and looked around before going any farther. There were no signs of life. No police, no people, no cars, and no Vernhausen.

Steve again started jogging back to his office, now no more than half a mile away. Confident he'd lost Vernhausen in the tunnels, he began to relax for the first time since seeing the light under the bathroom door. He also felt a dull throbbing sensation from several deep lacerations in his right hand as the morphine-like effects of fear began to wear off. He was regaining control. Four minutes more and he could call the police from his own office. *My God, that would feel good!*

* * *

VERNHAUSEN CREPT UP the stairs from the basement, stopping at the top to make sure no one was around. He scanned the grounds in front of the Wren building for signs of Steve. Although he wanted to move quickly to catch up, he refused to risk a run-in with the local police. When he was sure it was safe, he returned his gun to its hold position at the small of his back and set out to circle the Wren building one last time.

Vernhausen didn't waste time searching in front of the building. The back wall entrance to the basement tunnel convinced him that any vent to the surface would rise somewhere behind the Wren. So he left the stairwell and started making his way around to the back of the building. Suddenly, he heard the echo of a loud metallic crash coming from somewhere close by. He ran to the side of the building and scrutinized the landscape for the slightest signs of movement. Seeing nothing, he pressed on.

Vernhausen made a wide turn around the back corner of the Wren building just in case someone was waiting there to ambush him. When no one did, his eyes focused on the large grassy area leading out to the Sunken Gardens. Then, out of the corner of his eye, he detected movement off in the distance near a brick fence along Richmond Road. His senses locked onto the contact jogging on the other side of the fence about two hundred fifty yards away. Although the man was too far away to identify, Vernhausen was confident he'd found Steve. He commenced pursuit, this time maintaining a safe distance to avoid detection but remaining close enough to strike when the opportunity presented itself. He knew this was the last chance he would ever have.

* * *

FATIGUE TUGGED HARDER at Steve with every passing step. Although a decent athlete all his life, he'd never outrun death before and his muscles screamed for relief. By the time he hit North Henry Street, both his feet felt like bricks. Still, he trudged on until he reached the sidewalk leading up to his office. With safety in sight, every last ounce of energy left him and he nearly collapsed in place. He bent down, put his hands on his knees and breathed deeply, watching the steam blow from his mouth as he sucked in more and more fresh air. Finally, he mustered enough strength to drag himself to the front door. He jumbled through his keys until he found the right one and unlocked the door.

"Mr. Zalinsky," he yelled as he shut and locked the door behind him. "I'm back."

Mr. Zalinsky could barely hear Steve yelling to him from the first floor, but it was loud enough to wake him. These days, he wasn't sleeping very soundly anyway. He sat upright on the couch and looked at his watch. It was almost 1:45 a.m. He rubbed his eyes and wondered why Steve had called out. Surely, if all had gone as planned, Steve would have come in quietly and let him sleep. Mr. Zalinsky reached down in front of the couch and felt around on the floor until his hand stumbled across the two-by-four he'd put there just in case. He wasn't sure what he'd do if he actually had to use it on someone, but it made him feel more secure just having it in hand. He made his way over to the stairs and started to go down just as the door at the bottom of the stairwell flew open.

"Mr. Zalinsky, I'm back," Steve yelled again, not seeing Mr. Zalinsky at the top of the stairs. Steve's sudden appearance startled Mr. Zalinsky, and he froze until he was sure he recognized the voice as Steve's. He yelled back down to Steve, half out of irritation and half out of fear.

"Why are you yelling, Mr. Stilwell?"

"There's been a change in plans," Steve said as he stepped into the stairwell where Mr. Zalinsky could see him. Steve's silhouette was too dark for Mr. Zalinsky to make out any details.

"Oh?" Mr. Zalinsky said as he started down the stairs.

"I'm calling the police," Steve announced. "I've had a pretty rough night."

When Mr. Zalinsky reached the bottom of the stairs, he couldn't believe what he saw. Steve's shirt was covered with blood from the cuts on his hand and he had a gash on his head from the hit he'd taken in the tunnel. His clothes were filthy and torn, and the back of his left pants leg covering his calf was soaked with blood.

"What happened to you?" he asked, genuinely concerned at the state of his would-be guardian.

"I'll fill you in on the details later," Steve said as he backed away from the stairwell and started to head toward Marjorie's desk in the reception area. "First, though, I've got to call the police. Why don't you put that war club down and make us a pot of coffee? I'm afraid it's going to be a long night."

Mr. Zalinsky could tell it wasn't the time to ask questions. Something had obviously gone very wrong and Steve couldn't tell him what it was just yet, so he closed the door to the stairwell and walked around the corner to the coffeepot in the kitchen. He rested the two-by-four up against the wall and started looking at the coffee machine to see what was needed to make the thing work.

Back in the reception area, Steve walked up to Marjorie's desk and reached for the telephone. He adjusted the phone so he could read the buttons and picked up the receiver to place his call. Just as he pressed the 9 button to get an outside line, the front door burst open with a huge crash and the sound of splintering wood. Steve jumped and clutched the receiver as he looked up to see what was happening. To his horror, he saw Vernhausen charging into the office through the shattered remnants of the law office's front door.

Steve had no time to react. Vernhausen turned to face him and prepared to fire. Steve was too far away to lunge at his attacker but close enough to be shot at point blank range. In the split second he had to act, he tried to finish dialing "911" in a last ditch effort to save Mr. Zalinsky. But as he pushed the 9 button a second time, Vernhausen pulled the trigger.

The bullet tore through Steve's left shoulder, shattering bones and searing flesh as it went. The force of the impact knocked him backward and sent him reeling to the floor just inside the door to his office. Mr. Zalinsky looked on in horror as Steve suddenly fell not ten feet from where he was standing. All he could see, though, were Steve's legs protruding outside the office door. Although he didn't know what had happened, the crash at the front door and the silencer's ping told him that Vernhausen was near. He grabbed his two-by-four and moved closer to the corner to see what was coming. Fifty years ago he'd successfully confronted mass terror with his strength of character and his faith in God. Now, a little older but no less determined, he vowed not to go down without waging a considerable fight.

Steve lay on the floor in excruciating pain. He pressed his right hand over the hole in his shoulder and looked up to see Vernhausen walking toward him with the gun still drawn. Steve fought to remain conscious and prepared to die. He couldn't see Mr. Zalinsky, but he knew Vernhausen would find him and kill him, too. His vision began to blur and time seemed to slow as Vernhausen moved in for the kill.

"Our Father, who art in heaven," Steve yelled, trying both to shout away the pain and make ready for his death. "Hallowed be thy name."

Vernhausen was only a few steps away. As he neared the corner shielding Mr. Zalinsky, he aimed the pistol directly at Steve's head and prepared to pull the trigger as soon as he was positive he wouldn't miss.

"Thy kingdom come," Steve continued, as fear and pain began to overtake him. The room started spinning and everything looked black.

Vernhausen stopped just as the gun and his right arm stuck out past the corner where Mr. Zalinsky waited. He grasped the weapon with both hands and dispassionately lined up the pistol's sight with the center of Steve's face.

Mr. Zalinsky knew he had to act now or both he and Steve would die. He swung the two-by-four with all his might around the corner at where he guessed Vernhausen's head would be. The narrow edge of the board struck the unsuspecting assailant across the mouth and lower part of the nose. The bone-splintering blow lifted Vernhausen off his feet before he fell backward to the floor, unconscious, landing only inches from Marjorie's desk. His gun discharged harmlessly into the ceiling as he fell.

Mr. Zalinsky raised the board again to strike one more blow to Vernhausen's head, but he couldn't bring himself to do it. With a large pool of blood already forming on the floor, Mr. Zalinsky figured he'd done sufficient damage to keep Vernhausen at bay. He did have the presence of mind to wrench the pistol from Vernhausen's clenched fist just in case Vernhausen regained consciousness and tried to get up. If that happened, Mr. Zalinsky was prepared to be less merciful.

Mr. Zalinsky stepped over Vernhausen and up to Steve to see how he was. Steve could see Mr. Zalinsky looking at him, but he was in too much pain to speak. He tried to tell Mr. Zalinsky to call "911," but before he could get any words to come out, the room went dark.

Mr. Zalinsky hopped over Steve and went into the office to use the phone. He had to get the police there before Vernhausen revived. He set the gun down on Steve's desk and picked up the telephone. Then he dialed 911.

31

Tuesday, October 28
Düsseldorf

BELMAR RUSHED INTO the computer lab, still out of breath from the run down four flights of stairs. The crinkled sheet of paper he carried had not stood up well during the trip to the basement.

"Have you got anything yet?" he asked, half hoping the answer was no, so he could put his discovery to the test.

A young, orange-haired analyst in a peasant dress and combat boots looked up from behind her computer screen. "Are you serious?"

"Of course I'm serious," Belmar replied, a little taken aback by the woman's attitude. "Why wouldn't I be?"

"If you'd been here for the last twelve hours banging your head against this computer, you'd understand." The other analyst in the room, a pimply-faced longhair in his early twenties, nodded in agreement.

"I'm sorry," Belmar said mechanically. "I didn't realize it had been that long."

The orange-haired analyst returned to typing on her computer, apparently satisfied her point had been made.

Belmar couldn't believe the department had hired the likes of these two. No manners, enough piercings between them to set off a metal detector, and an obvious disdain for authority. But he knew they were good—the best, in fact, the department had to offer. If they got him into the Web page, he'd forget all about their peculiarities.

"I've got something I want you to try," Belmar announced.

The orange-haired analyst adjusted her 1950s vintage horn-rimmed glasses, let out a little huff, and looked in Belmar's direction. "Every time you interrupt me, it means it will take longer to get through this password protection."

"I understand," Belmar replied, struggling to remain calm. "Just try this for the password, and if it doesn't work, I'll leave you alone." Belmar held out the cover sheet that came with the pictures of Vernhausen taken by the American customs inspector weeks before in Washington, D.C.

The analyst flopped out her hand to take the paper. "Detective Belmar, you are wasting valuable time."

"Look, it will just take a second. Do you see the word I circled? The killer had that word in his wallet when he was searched just after the Weisentrope murder. It's just a hunch, but maybe he wrote the password down so he wouldn't forget it. What do you have to lose?"

"JINENIGHEILEN?"

"That's it, just type it in." Belmar walked behind the analyst to watch over her shoulder.

The analyst huffed again, set the paper next to her keyboard, and typed in "jinenigheilen." When she hit enter, nothing happened.

"I told you, detective. Now can I get back to work?"

"Give me the paper and I'll call off the letters to make sure you typed them in correctly," Belmar instructed. The analyst complied under protest.

"Wait a minute," Belmar said as he looked more closely at the word on the paper. "This is all in capital letters. Did you use all capital letters?"

"No, but it probably doesn't matter, anyway."

"Just do it, dammit!" Belmar snapped, finally losing his temper. He handed the paper back to the analyst and watched her do as directed, hitting the keys more deliberately than before. After entering the last letter, she hit enter, and then sat back in amazement as the Web page began to unfold on her screen.

"We're in!" she exclaimed. Then she stood on her chair and let loose a primeval scream that took even Belmar by surprise. Workers in nearby offices dropped what they were doing and either looked for shelter or ran to the common area to see who'd been stabbed. The pimply-faced analyst jumped up and gave his partner a high-five.

"That's fabulous!" Belmar found himself giving both analysts high-fives.

"What do you need us to get for you, Detective Belmar?" the now-smiling orange-haired analyst asked with a newfound measure of respect. Then she added in a more serious tone, "We need to move quickly before they detect we're in. When they do, they'll shut us out for good."

"Get everything," Belmar said as he grabbed the paper and started for the door. "And call me as soon as you know whose Web page it is."

* * *

Berlin, Germany

HERMANN BORNE'S WEARINESS touched the very core of his soul. He'd tried going to bed early the night before to combat the fatigue, but ended up lying awake for hours thinking of the four men he hated but never knew. Eventually, a strong dose of the prescription sleeping pills he'd been using to battle his incessant insomnia prevailed and he drifted off into a shallow sleep. But when morning came, his worries and the weariness returned, despite the meager sleep he'd been able to manage.

Hermann showered and hastily got dressed. He wanted to eat breakfast quickly and check his email to see what new developments had been reported from America. He preferred checking it as soon as he got up in the morning, but he'd learned through experience that the six-hour time difference meant he'd have no report until lunch. "Today will be different," he thought in an uncharacteristic display of optimism. "Perhaps having gone to bed early will not prove a waste after all."

Hermann emerged from his bedroom just after 9:00 a.m. His father's attendant had already deposited his father in the usual position in front of the window. The attendant arrived every morning around 7:30 and bathed the old man, dressed him, fed him, and then pushed him in his wheelchair to his favorite place in the living room looking out over the river. Often the attendant was gone before Hermann came out, but today he was just leaving. Hermann thanked the man for his assistance, ate the breakfast the attendant had left for him, and went to speak with his father. There was no change. His father sat boulder faced, refusing to acknowledge his presence. He walked around to the front of his father's wheelchair so the old man could not help but see him.

"Good morning, Father," Hermann said as he did every morning. "It looks like a beautiful day." Hermann made the announcement without bothering to look outside to see if it was true. Instead, he looked intently at his father and waited, just in case his father chose to speak. When the silence continued, Hermann felt the muscles in his lower back grow tense with anger. The longer the silence went on, the angrier he became. He couldn't stand it any longer. He needed this all to be over.

Hermann excused himself and retired to his study. He grabbed the back of his chair and yanked it into position as if to make a statement to the four corners of the room that he was in control. He sat down and initiated the logon process. After a minute, the computer screen displayed its standard desktop configuration and he clicked on email to see if there was any news. There was. He was sure this was the announcement he'd been waiting for. If it reported Tadeusz Zalinsky's death, he would tell his father immediately. This email would finally change both their lives. He double-clicked on the message and the text appeared:

> believe Web page compromised—will report completion by phone signal—end

Hermann was stunned. What did it mean? Did someone else actually see the Web page or did Vernhausen simply leave his computer on when the maids cleaned his room? What if someone got ahold of the password? Panic began tugging at Hermann. He looked at the time on Vernhausen's message. It showed Vernhausen transmitted the message from the United States at 7:23 p.m.—1:23 a.m. in Germany. It was now almost 9:30. That meant the outside world possibly had access to the Web page for at least eight hours. He had to find out what the world saw.

Hermann logged in to the server's access control. When the data came up on the screen, he fell back in his chair in disbelief. Someone using Vernhausen's password had logged in to the system at 8:22 a.m. and gained unrestricted access for fifty-seven minutes. He leaned forward and called up the user logon report. The list of files accessed filled screen after screen. He couldn't believe what he was seeing. Getting through his sophisticated password protection required a level of skill well beyond that of the typical street hacker. He knew no system was foolproof, but he thought his architecture was more than adequate to protect the obscure communications of the participants involved in the enterprise.

Hermann stood up and let go a string of profanities. He had planned every other aspect of the enterprise in minute detail, but he, of all people, had taken computer security for granted. He pounded his fist on the desk over and over. How could he have been so careless? He walked to the door and looked out at his father. He had to come up with a plan before it was too late.

Hermann paused for a moment to gather his thoughts. There was no escaping it; Werner Klecken had to be told. Werner would need to tell his worldwide network of operatives that the operation was compromised. Werner would be furious, but Hermann believed only the victims were actually identified by name in his computer files. The problem was that the Five's computer addresses were traceable, and it was his fault. He felt intensely embarrassed and ashamed.

Hermann walked out into the living room and picked up the telephone sitting on the glass table to the left of his father. He dialed Werner's number and waited for Werner to answer. He hadn't spoken to Werner since their last meeting in the park when he told Werner he would let nothing stop the operation. Now he was calling Werner to tell him everything had to stop, at least for now. After the fourth ring, Werner answered.

"Hello."

"Werner, this is Hermann. I have something I must tell you."

"Is the telephone the place for this conversation, Hermann?"

"Someone's gained access to my computer," Hermann responded, ignoring Werner's admonition.

"What do you mean?"

"You know what it means, Werner. They've got everything."

Werner didn't wait for anything more. He hung up and initiated call blocking for Hermann's number. Then he stood motionless as he glared at the telephone. He knew what he had to do; Hermann had left him no choice. There were others in the Five he had to think about and protect. Werner dialed the number slowly, listening to each tone as it echoed in the receiver. After two rings, he could tell someone on the other end of the line had picked up although they said nothing. Werner knew he'd reached the right number.

"Terminate." Werner had laid the groundwork for this call after his last meeting with Hermann. Now he'd given the execute order. Soon, every trace of Hermann's assassination campaign would disappear. Werner's only concern was whether it would happen soon enough.

* * *

It was 3:08 p.m. when the door to Hermann Borne's flat opened without a sound. Every step was slow, deliberate, silent. Through the foyer and into the living room the somber figure continued, pausing only to look at the old man in the wheelchair gazing out at the Spree. For a moment, it seemed as though the figure desired to go to the old man, but then it turned and resumed its steady course to the inner rooms. Step by step, the figure made its way toward Hermann's study, until it quietly slipped through the open door. Moments later, a single gunshot resonated throughout the flat, and a soon to be lifeless body slumped over in a chair.

* * *

BELMAR AND DETECTIVE Schueller spent the better part of two hours sifting through the documents the analysts had magically downloaded from the host computer. They were thrilled to discover that the files contained direct evidence linking together all three of the international hits. But it took another full hour before the analysts gave them the lead they both had been hoping for: the server and some of its resident software belonged to computer magnate Hermann Borne.

Belmar knew they needed to strike before Borne had the opportunity to assess the situation and decide not to cooperate. That meant surprising him without further delay. To effect the surprise, Belmar had Detective Schueller make arrangements with their counterparts in Berlin to pay a joint visit to Borne later that afternoon at his apartment. Then he and Detective Schueller crossed their fingers and hopped on the next flight to Berlin.

At 3:30 p.m., Belmar, Detective Schueller, and two detectives from Berlin were en route to Borne's flat when a call came over the radio reporting gunshots in the posh apartments of their prime suspect. The Berlin detectives responded that they were only minutes from the scene and would provide the initial police response until the uniformed units arrived.

"Two-to-one odds says the gunshots involve your suspect," the Berlin detective driving the car said as they pulled into the underground parking garage. Neither Belmar nor Detective Schueller took the offer, but the other Berlin detective gave a thumbs-up indicating his agreement with the driver. They stopped momentarily at the garage's security gate until the parking attendant waved them through after the driver flashed his police credentials. They parked in a visitor's area near an elevator and tried to radio back that they had arrived, but the radio didn't work inside the underground garage. They decided to call in later after they figured out what was going on.

The detectives rode to the lobby with the best of elevator etiquette; all four men stared at the floor indicator above the door and no one made a sound. When the elevator doors finally opened into the lobby, the men were met by a gray-haired security guard with a portly physique. The parking attendant had alerted him to their arrival and he began telling them what he knew before they even had an opportunity to identify themselves.

"Some residents reported hearing a gunshot coming from Suite 703," he declared. "I went up and cleared the floor right away and then I called you guys."

"Very good, Herr, eh?" the senior Berlin detective inquired. Belmar and Detective Schueller deferred to their counterparts while they were on the Berliners' home turf.

"Hinden. Peter Hinden," the security guard replied. "You

know, this is the first time we've ever had anything like this here. This is normally such a safe place."

"I'm sure it still is, Herr Hinden," the Berlin detective continued. "Did anyone see what happened?"

"If they did, they didn't tell me."

"By the way," the junior Berlin detective interjected. "Who lives in that suite?"

"Hermann Borne," the security guard answered, quite proud that he had checked that detail already and was able to answer the detective's question. As soon as the name "Borne" left his lips, the two Düsseldorf detectives and their junior Berlin counterpart made eye contact with their apparently psychic senior fellow. The senior Berliner, Detective Dierden, responded with a barely perceptible smile. Then the security guard added, "I think his father lives with him too. The father is a real old man. Confined to a wheelchair, I believe."

"That's all I needed to hear," Belmar said as he entered the conversation for the first time. "We need to get up there right away."

"Right," Detective Dierden confirmed. "How many ways are there up to Suite 703?"

"Just two," the security guard responded. "You can take the elevator up to the seventh floor and you'll be right there. Or you can take the stairs over there." The guard turned slightly and pointed to a doorway across a plush lobby richly furnished with mahogany, polished brass, crystal chandeliers, and deep burgundy Persian carpets. It was not your typical crime scene in Berlin.

"All right," Detective Dierden announced. "Detective Belmar and I will use the elevator; you two take the stairs. We'll meet on the seventh floor. Nobody goes in until I say so. Oh, and I suggest we prepare to defend ourselves. Any questions?"

"Let's go," Belmar said, growing more and more impatient. The junior Berlin detective motioned to Detective Schueller and the two headed for the stairs.

"Thank you, Herr Hindel," Detective Dierden said.

"That's Hinden, sir," the security guard corrected politely. "Do you need me to spell it out for your report?"

"Oh, I'm sorry, Herr Hinden. That won't be necessary. Right now, we need you to wait here until the uniformed officers arrive. Send the first two up by the stairs and hold the rest down here until we ask for them. Do you have that?"

"Yes, sir," the security guard barked with the enthusiasm of a new recruit.

With that, Belmar and Detective Dierden boarded the elevator for the ride to the seventh floor. "Whaddya think we'll find?" Detective Dierden asked Belmar as the elevator began its climb.

"Your guess is as good as mine." Belmar knew there were a number of possibilities, none of which were attractive. He believed they'd find themselves in a standoff with Borne, but he had nothing to base his opinion on. It was little more than idle speculation as he tried to mentally prepare himself for a situation where at least one shot had already been fired.

Neither man said anything else as the elevator arrived on the seventh floor. They drew their weapons just before the elevator settled to a complete stop and stood on opposite sides of the platform to minimize their exposure. As soon as the doors opened, Belmar disabled the elevator so they'd be guaranteed an escape route in the event that the situation went south.

Belmar poked his head out of the elevator to establish their position. He had a clear view of Suite 703 just down the hall with its door left wide open. Unfortunately, due to the angle of approach, he couldn't see inside the suite. They would have to maneuver to just outside the door before being able to see anything inside. They exited the elevator one at a time, each one covering the other, until they were certain the area was clear.

As Belmar and his new partner neared Suite 703, Detective Dierden saw a door at the other end of the hallway slowly begin to open and grabbed Belmar's coat to get him to freeze. They took a position on the opposite side of the hallway with their weapons ready in case someone other than their colleagues came bursting out upon them. Instead of a burst, they saw a familiar face peer cautiously around the door. Detective Dierden recognized his partner and gave Belmar the okay sign. He also motioned for the younger detectives to join them in the hall.

All four men converged on the door. Detective Dierden signaled that he and his partner would go in first, followed by Belmar. Detective Schueller would remain at the door to provide cover. The detectives nodded in agreement. Then, without giving time for second thoughts, Detective Dierden raised his weapon and gave the others a thumbs-up. It was time to go in.

Detective Dierden popped around the corner first and began to move through the foyer. His junior partner and Belmar followed right behind but shifted to the other side of the hall. The trio crept forward until they reached the entrance to the living room with its panoramic view of Berlin. Suddenly Detective Dierden motioned for all to stop and pointed to an empty wheelchair in front of the window. Its occupant was nowhere to be seen. With a few more motions of his hand, Detective Dierden directed the men to split up to cover the other hallways leading from the room. The junior Berlin detective veered to the right to cover the dining room and kitchen area, while Detective Dierden moved to the left. Belmar headed straight for the wheelchair.

Belmar walked up to the wheelchair and began to study its position. He remembered the security guard saying Borne's father was confined to a wheelchair, so he thought it unusual the old man wasn't there. He also noticed the wheelchair wasn't facing the window, as one would expect, but was turned to the left with its left front wheel butting up against an end table. He was just bending over to look more closely when he heard

Detective Dierden yell from the back of the flat.

"Back here!" came the excited announcement. "I've found him!" The junior Berlin detective hurried back to see just who his partner had found, while Belmar moved more deliberately to make sure no one tried to slip out behind them. Belmar also called to Detective Schueller to let him know they'd found something.

When Belmar walked into the study, the sight nauseated him. There, scrunched back in a swivel-type office chair, was a lifeless form with its chin resting on a blood-soaked chest. The visible brain matter on the top of the head and the blood-spattered wall and ceiling indicated a probable self-inflicted gunshot wound from a pistol pointed upward through the roof of the mouth. A 9mm pistol lying on the floor just off to the right of the body's dangling right hand supported the theory.

"Looks like suicide," Belmar said, declaring the obvious.

"Why don't you ask the witness?" Detective Dierden motioned to the left of the door where Belmar walked in. Belmar jerked his head to the left to see what he'd missed. There, in a black leather recliner in the corner of the room, just beyond a brass floor lamp, sat a wisp of a man. The large chair engulfed him and made him appear insignificant until his piercing black eyes made contact with Belmar's. Belmar averted his gaze to avoid the temptation to stare. The old man had no such inhibitions and continued to watch Belmar closely.

"He was sitting in here just like that when I came in," Detective Dierden said. Then the Berlin detective abruptly changed subjects to get the investigation underway. "Victor," he said to the younger Berliner. "Get on the phone and call the office. Tell them what we've found. We're going to need the evidence techs, an ambulance, and a photographer."

"Yes, sir," Victor responded. He started to make his way past Belmar to leave the study when Belmar added another instruction.

"Do me a favor, would you?" Belmar continued without

waiting to see if the answer was yes. "Give Hans a heads-up on what's going on. He probably thinks we're under siege back here."

Victor looked to his mentor for guidance. Detective Dierden nodded. It was all his protégé needed. He left the room to work on his assignments.

As Victor left, Belmar scanned the room more attentively to see what else he'd overlooked. Now other details caught his attention. He noticed for the first time the vast array of computer equipment on and around the desk immediately behind the body. If the computer files were intact, he hoped to put together a clear picture of all that had transpired. He already had a lot from what the technicians had been able to glean earlier in the day, but now he had access to the mother lode itself. Still, all that paled in comparison to what the old man might know.

"Has he said anything?" Belmar asked Detective Dierden, who, like Belmar, was looking around the room for clues.

"Not a word. But then, no one's asked him anything."

"Why don't we give it a try?" Belmar approached the old man and stood between him and the body to remove the grotesque distraction from the old man's view. He leaned down and spoke in a compassionate but firm voice. "My name is Detective Belmar. We came when we heard someone fired a shot. Can you tell me your name?"

The old man stared in silence at Belmar with his riveting, jet black eyes. Unsure whether the old man could hear him, Belmar repeated himself, this time speaking much louder. Still the old man stared, his eyes following Belmar's every move. Belmar recalled the information Steve Stilwell had given him concerning the old man's Nazi past and recent release from prison. The old man's withered frame seemed incapable of inflicting physical pain, but Belmar could sense from his eyes an evil that still burned deep from within. Belmar felt uneasy just being around him.

"We'll need an ambulance for this man, too," Belmar said, turning away and looking at Detective Dierden, who nodded in agreement.

"I am just fine," the old man said curtly. Both detectives were startled by the announcement. Belmar looked back and seized the opportunity to extract more information.

"I'm glad to hear that," Belmar said, again leaning toward the old man but still maintaining a comfortable separation. "Can you tell me your name?"

"I am Dr. Heinrich Borne." The old man lifted his head slightly to stare more directly into Belmar's face. "And that was my son."

The old man didn't move or shed a tear. He remained stoic despite being in the room where his son had just died a violent and gruesome death. Yet he was apparently able and willing to talk, and that was all that concerned Belmar. Perhaps now with the computers in hand and the old man available for questioning, Belmar could get to the bottom of the murders. When he learned later in the day that Vernhausen was in custody in an American hospital, he had all the more reason to be confident. Vernhausen could prove the key to identifying the other players involved in the scheme, for there had to be a web of people at work to carry out an undertaking such as this on a global scale. Belmar knew that while the door was closing on the most immediate chapter of the Emil Weisentrope investigation, deeper secrets had yet to be uncovered.

Epilogue

Three weeks later

IT FELT GOOD to return to the office to finally settle into a routine. Yet Steve's first day back had been anything but routine. Marjorie and Mr. Smythe had a hero's welcome waiting for him when he arrived first thing in the morning. His office was decorated with red, white, and blue crepe paper and balloons, and flowers and cards from clients, family, and friends. Even a few of the merchants from Colonial Williamsburg stopped by to shake his hand. In just a few short weeks, he had been transformed from an unknown newcomer to a local celebrity.

With all the hoopla, Steve found it difficult to get much of anything accomplished. Marjorie was treating him with kid gloves; three or four times he looked up from a document only to see her standing in his doorway smiling at him. Each time he noticed her, she threw out an "Is there anything I can do for you, Mr. Stilwell?" or an "Are you all right, Mr. Stilwell?" Embarrassed by the extra attention and hoping to get some real work done, he'd smile and answer, "Nothing just yet Marjorie, but thanks," and return his attention to the document at hand. But when he reached for his inbox to pull another document from the huge stack that had accumulated in his absence, he felt a tugging pain from the still healing wound in his shoulder shoot down the full length of his left arm. This was not how he'd envisioned making a name for himself in Williamsburg.

Now that it was early afternoon and some of the novelty was starting to wear off, at least among those in his office, Steve was finally able to settle into his work in earnest. Marjorie had scheduled one new client for him at 2:30 p.m. and given him the rest of the day to catch up. He had just started reading the trusts and estates advance sheets when he heard the door to the outer office close more abruptly than usual. He could hear a discourse begin near Marjorie's desk and continue on toward his office.

"I'm here to see Steve Stilwell," the all-too-familiar female voice said, conveying a command presence reminiscent of Steve's days in the Navy.

Steve knew this moment had to come, but he never expected it to come so soon. He knew Marjorie would do her best to head off the impending disaster, but it was no use. He braced himself for the storm.

"Hello, Miss Siegel," Marjorie said with her best fake smile and feigned sincerity. Normally she would have indulged in further trivial chatter to delay the woman's progress, but Michelle was already past her desk and halfway to Steve's office before she got her next words out.

"Excuse me, Miss Siegel, but do you have an appointment to see—?" Marjorie's voice trailed off as she saw her words having no effect. She stood up to chase after Michelle but was too late.

Michelle knocked twice on the doorframe leading into Steve's office but kept on walking to the seats in front of his desk. Knocks were not so much a fleeting attempt at politeness as they were a way of announcing her arrival. Steve looked up and pretended to be surprised.

"Hello, Steve," Michelle said as she made herself comfortable in one of the leather chairs in front of his desk. She crossed her legs and leaned back to make it clear she had an agenda to accomplish before she departed. Marjorie arrived just as Michelle sat down.

"I'm sorry, Mr. Stilwell," Marjorie began. Steve didn't wait for her to say anything else. He knew nothing could have stopped Michelle from getting into his office. The unstoppable force had met the immovable object, and the unstoppable force had carried the day.

"That's okay, Marjorie," Steve said as he looked toward his harried assistant. "I think I've got some time available to see Ms. Siegel." He switched his attention to Michelle. "Ms. Siegel, would you care for a Perrier?"

"Yes, I would, as a matter of fact."

"Marjorie, would you mind bringing Ms. Siegel a Perrier, with a twist of lime if we have it?" Marjorie nodded and left the office to get Michelle's drink.

"So what brings you to Williamsburg, Ms. Siegel?" Steve wanted to get right down to business as pleasantly as he could. What he wanted most of all, though, was to avoid any embarrassing discussion of Michelle's detention in Germany. He hoped his role in catching the man who murdered her father would be enough to overshadow his casting suspicion on her with the German police.

Michelle ignored Steve's question. "I understand you're quite the hero now," she said with enough inflection in her voice to make Steve think she really meant it.

"If getting shot makes you a hero, I guess so. But your father's friend, Mr. Zalinsky, he's the one that captured the man who killed your father."

"I don't find false modesty very becoming," Michelle said sternly. She continued speaking quickly as if in a hurry. "I heard what happened. You and Zalinsky caught the man who murdered my father. For that, I'm grateful."

Steve felt his jaw drop to the floor with a thud. There was absolutely no doubt about it. Michelle Siegel had actually said "thank you." It left him momentarily speechless. Fortunately Marjorie walked back into his office at just that second, giving him a chance to collect himself and figure out what to say.

"Ah, thank you, Marjorie," Steve said as Marjorie handed Michelle her Perrier. Michelle said nothing, and Marjorie quickly turned her attention to Steve so as not to appear overly hospitable.

"Is there anything else *you* need, Mr. Stilwell?"

"No thanks, Marjorie." With that, Marjorie vanished from the office.

Marjorie's interlude was exactly what Steve needed. It took the emphasis off Michelle's "thank you" and allowed her to continue without him having to respond.

"I do have a few questions, if you don't mind." Michelle crossed her hands and set them on her knee, pausing so that Steve could concur.

"Of course," Steve said enthusiastically, hoping now there was a chance she wouldn't mention Germany. "Go ahead." He leaned forward and placed both his elbows on his desk. He felt like he was bracing himself for an onslaught.

"The German press has reported that Hermann Borne's death was a suicide and that the police have nothing on his father. Is that true? Borne has three men murdered and kills himself and that ends it? I can't accept that."

"Detective Belmar doesn't believe Borne killed himself, but if Borne's father knows anything, he isn't saying. On the positive side, Belmar told me he got some leads from Borne's computer and he's running those down. That will take time. He's got a lot of data to sift through."

"So what am I supposed to do, just put my life on hold until Belmar gets around to it? There must be something we can do now."

"We might be able to sue Borne's estate. He was a rich man,

and while a lawsuit won't bring your father back, there's a certain amount of closure to be gained just by going through the process. I'll have to research what the options are and get back to you."

"So what about Vernhausen? He's not dead. What are they going to do with him?"

"He's being held by the Commonwealth of Virginia pending trial. I'm pretty sure Virginia will try him first on attempted murder charges and then they'll look at extraditing him to Germany so he can be tried for murdering Emil Weisentrope."

"What about my father's death?" Michelle demanded. "Who's going to try him for killing my father?"

"I don't know," Steve admitted. "I'm afraid it would have to be Israel, and I don't know if they have enough evidence to consider extraditing him yet."

Michelle's face flushed with anger. "You can't let him get away with killing my father," she said as her voice increased in intensity. Steve could see a storm brewing, but he didn't want to raise false hopes in Michelle that Vernhausen would be prosecuted for her father's death. Michelle leaned forward in her chair to speak more directly to Steve.

"You've got to do something about it, Steve. He's got to pay for what he did." Then she leaned back and softened her voice before tossing the dreaded trump card out onto the table. "You owe me that much after what you did to me in Germany, you know."

Steve winced. He knew she'd play it, he just hadn't known how. He picked up a pen from his desk, leaned way back in his chair and began to rock. He brought the hand with the pen in it up to his chin and held his chin for a moment as he pondered how to respond. Then a possible way out hit him.

"I'll tell you what I can do," he replied. Michelle leaned forward again in anticipation. "I'll make some inquiries with the Commonwealth's attorney to see what's going on with your father's case. I can't promise any action, but I'll see what they've got in mind."

"When can I expect to hear from you on it?" Michelle persisted.

"I'll give you a call with what I know tomorrow. And I'll see if I can have an answer on the lawsuit by then, too."

"All right. Now what's the status of the distributions from my father's estate?"

Steve marveled at Michelle's ability to shift so easily from grieving daughter demanding justice to wealthy heiress demanding cash. There wasn't even an attempt at a transition between the two subjects.

"I'll make the distributions to Mr. Zalinsky and the synagogue next week, and I believe I'll be able to make an interim distribution to you as well."

Michelle wasn't satisfied. "How much can I expect?" she asked, sliding all the way forward in her chair.

"I really haven't worked the numbers yet." Steve knew she wouldn't be satisfied with that so he made an estimate he knew he could easily support given the size of the remainder of the estate. "My guess is it will be somewhere in the neighborhood of five hundred thousand dollars."

Michelle sat back, apparently relieved. Then she suddenly grabbed her purse, opened it, and tossed onto his desk a package wrapped in brown paper.

"This came in the mail for my father while you were in the hospital. It's a package from Emil Weisentrope. He must have mailed it just before he died. I thought you ought to see it."

"What is it?" Steve hesitated to open the package out of concern that he might taint evidence relevant to the murder investigation.

"Just open it," Michelle insisted.

Steve complied and found a tiny gold Star of David and a short handwritten note apparently written by Emil

Weisentrope. Steve couldn't read the note, as it was written entirely in German. "What's it say?"

"Give it to me and I'll read it to you." Michelle took the note and began to translate.

September 30, 1997

My Dearest Friend Felix,

I'm sorry I can't write more but I must get this into the mail as soon as possible. I know you remember back all those years—none of us wants to but we must—the Star of David my father gave me just before they killed him. I knew if they found it they would kill me too, but it was all I had left of my family and I had to hold on to it. It, and you, got me through those dark, terrible days. Take care of it, Dear Friend, and make sure they always remember.

Shalom, Emil

Steve and Michelle each sat in silence, waiting for the other to speak. Anything they said would sound trivial after repeating the words of a man preparing to die.

"Zalinsky should have this, Steve. It's what my father would have wanted."

"That's very kind of you, Ms. Siegel. I'm sure he'll be honored. I'll have to show it to the police, first, though."

"Do what you have to, but just make sure he gets it." Then, as if the note had never happened, Michelle stood up, walked partially around Steve's desk, and extended her hand to close the meeting with a handshake. "Thanks for your time, Steve. You've been very helpful. I'll look forward to hearing from you tomorrow."

Surprised by the apparent end to their conversation, Steve

jumped to his feet a little too quickly and a pain shot down his left arm. He grimaced, but still managed to get his right hand out. The two shook hands. "Thanks for stopping by," he added, not wanting to comment further out of fear it would prolong their meeting.

Michelle turned and walked toward the door. Steve watched her as she walked, intending to rejoice as soon as she cleared his office and disappeared outside. Instead of making a beeline for the door, though, she stopped and turned around in what Steve recognized as a clearly choreographed maneuver.

"Oh, there is one more thing," she added nonchalantly.

"What's that?" he asked, puzzling over what else she could possibly want from him.

"Once you've finished with my father's estate, I'm going to need some estate and tax planning myself."

"Sure. I've got some excellent people I can refer you to."

"You don't understand," she said, smiling a smile that made it impossible for him to dislike her. "I want *you* to do it. Bye."

With that, Michelle turned and whisked by Marjorie's desk and out the front door, leaving a stunned ex-Navy JAG floating in her wake. Just when he had the end of the Siegel dispositions in sight, more appeared on the horizon. The thought of it made sweat bead up on his forehead. So far, retirement hadn't been anything like what he expected.

"Well," he said to himself before he sat back down to work, "at least it can't get any worse than being shot." His musings were interrupted by Marjorie's familiar voice over the intercom.

"Mr. Stilwell, your 2:30 appointment is here."

"Send her in," Steve replied. It was time to move on.

Photo of David E. Grogan by Bob Bradlee

DAVID E. GROGAN was born in Rome, New York, and raised in Cleveland, Ohio. After graduating from the College of William & Mary in Virginia with a BBA in Accounting, he began working for the accounting firm Arthur Andersen & Co., in Houston, Texas, as a Certified Public Accountant. He left Arthur Andersen in 1984 to attend the University of Virginia School of Law in Charlottesville, Virginia, graduating in 1987. He earned his master's in International Law from The George Washington University Law School and is a licensed attorney in the Commonwealth of Virginia.

Grogan served on active duty in the United States Navy for over 26 years as a Navy Judge Advocate. He is now retired, but during the course of his Navy career, he prosecuted and defended court-martial cases, traveled to capitals around the world, lived abroad in Japan, Cuba, and Bahrain, and deployed to the Mediterranean Sea and the Persian Gulf onboard the nuclear-powered aircraft carrier *USS Enterprise*. His experiences abroad and during the course of his career influence every aspect of his writing. *The Siegel Dispositions* is his first novel.

Grogan's current home is in Virginia, where he lives with his wife of 31 years. They have three children.

You can follow Dave on Twitter (@davidegrogan) and Facebook (davidegrogan), and learn more about him at: www.davidegrogan.com.

CPSIA information can be obtained at www.ICGtesting.com
Printed in the USA
LVOW11s1824191214

419646LV00001B/8/P